Oliver J. Dobson is a writer, musician, and keen historian. Born in Norwich in 1984, he spent much of his childhood between England and Southeast Asia, living in Brunei and frequently spending time in Malaysia, Singapore, and other parts of Borneo.

As well as writing books, Oliver writes and records music with UK-based ska/punk/reggae/rap group China Shop Bull, who have to date released music in 75 countries. He met his future wife while on tour in Prague in 2014, and they now live in the Czech Republic countryside with their two daughters, Wendy and Charlotte.

Dedicated to my dear friend, Anthony Roberts (1983–2023), who sadly never got to read the book but on whom the character Francis Fletcher is based.

Oliver J. Dobson

FRANCIS FLETCHER AND THE KNIGHTS OF THE GOLDEN GIFT

AUSTIN MACAULEY PUBLISHERS

LONDON • CAMBRIDGE • NEW YORK • SHARJAH

Copyright © Oliver J. Dobson 2025

The right of Oliver J. Dobson to be identified as author of this work has been asserted by the author in accordance with sections 77 and 78 of the Copyright, Designs and Patents Act 1988.

All rights reserved. No part of this publication may be reproduced, stored in a retrieval system, or transmitted in any form or by any means, electronic, mechanical, photocopying, recording, or otherwise, without the prior permission of the publishers.

Any person who commits any unauthorised act in relation to this publication may be liable to criminal prosecution and civil claims for damages.

This is a work of fiction. Names, characters, businesses, places, events, locales, and incidents are either the products of the author's imagination or used in a fictitious manner. Any resemblance to actual persons, living or dead, or actual events is purely coincidental.

A CIP catalogue record for this title is available from the British Library.

ISBN 9781035867875 (Paperback)
ISBN 9781035867882 (ePub e-book)

www.austinmacauley.com

First Published 2025
Austin Macauley Publishers Ltd®
1 Canada Square
Canary Wharf
London
E14 5AA

Chapter 1

"Hold on, Sholim!"

"Ich kann nicht."

"Hold on!"

"Help; ich kann nicht schwimmen, please!"

"What kind of sailor doesn't know how to swim? Woodland, Kilpatrick, can you reach Sholim?" Captain Fletcher begged of his other struggling crewmen.

"The current is too strong, sir! I dare not let go," Woodland spluttered as salt water splashed into his mouth, almost choking him.

"You must reach out and hold him, or he'll surely drown!"

"I'm trying, sir," Woodland answered his captain.

"Mr Kilpatrick, can you help Woodland?"

"I'll do my best, sir." Kilpatrick took hold of Woodland's shirt and assured him he would not let go.

The white waves crashed onto the splintered wood, submerging what remained of it. Clinging for his life, Captain Francis Fletcher gripped what he could. A wave broke into his face, blinding him and causing him to lose breath as he swallowed a gulp. Still, he held on. Woodland stretched and fought the furious mountains of water that separated them from their drowning companion.

"I've got him, sir!" Woodland shouted as his face took another lash of spray. "Mr Kilpatrick, take his arms!"

"Get him onto the wood. Is he OK?" Captain Fletcher asked.

Woodland and Kilpatrick both nodded as they panted for air. The four men had pushed their muscles to the limit, but a matter of life and death spurred them on. Slowly, they began to drift seemingly in circles, but eventually towards the shore as the four shipwrecked men clung to the shattered wood, a floating part of their broken ship, *Blunderbuss*. Waves threw them this way and that, but despite exhaustion, they held on.

"I can touch the bottom, sir!" Woodland excitedly exclaimed.

"Splendid effort, my boys," Fletcher gasped as he slid from the broken plank onto the seabed where he could wade. The crash of the surf breaking behind them merged with the sound of cannon and shot, which was inexplicably still pounding away into the shredded *Blunderbuss* a mile out at sea.

"Give Sholim to me," Fletcher ordered. "Kilpatrick, take his other shoulder; let's get him to the beach, lay him down."

Upon reaching the beach, Fletcher and Kilpatrick dropped Sholim face-down into the wet sand. They both collapsed beside him, exhausted from their ordeal and watched as Woodland washed up beside them, equally drained of strength. They waited in the heat until their breath had returned. Eventually, Fletcher sat up and watched on the horizon the *Blunderbuss*, his ship, sinking. What was left of her floated in bits and pieces or slipped beneath the waves. As for the rest of the crew, they were either dead or had managed to make it to the island. If there were other survivors, there was no sign of them. As far as Fletcher could tell, only the four of them had escaped the drumming they had received.

Caught unaware in the morning light, they had been pounced upon by a British frigate, which they could not see for the dark sky in the west. They had been silhouetted by the sun rising in the east and given a thwarting so relentless as to finish them off before any shot could answer their enemy.

"Blaggards!" Fletcher muttered under his breath. "How is he?"

"He's breathing, Captain," Woodland assured Fletcher.

"Good. We'll give him some time to recover. Then, we'll go inland and find some water and shelter."

"Do you know this land, sir?" Kilpatrick asked.

"I do not. We chanced upon it yesterday evening. This land did not appear on any map upon which I ever laid my eyes. I studied our charts; I am positive this land is undiscovered."

"Undiscovered in the Mediterranean, sir? Seems unlikely to me," Woodland commented.

"I've been at sea for more than twenty years. I have been through these waters more times than I can remember. Never have I come across this island," Fletcher insisted.

"Can you be certain it is an island, Captain?" Woodland further pressed his captain.

"Yes, Woodland, it has to be. We set eyes upon the east coast of Crete yesterday evening. We tacked north to lose our enemy in the night, but we couldn't have struck the European mainland so quickly; it wasn't possible at our speed. I nearly gave the order to lower the oars and row the rest of the way, as I mistakenly believed we had eluded our pursuer. Check Sholim. Is he still breathing?"

Woodland and Kilpatrick rolled Sholim onto his back. He was semi-conscious and started murmuring something in his language, but no one else was entirely sure what that was. When they heard him speak in English, it was usually very broken and mixed with his language.

"I don't know what he's saying, sir. I think he'll be all right; he's swallowed a lot of seawater, but he'll come around," Kilpatrick informed Captain Fletcher.

"Very well, he's a good man. It would do us well to keep him," the captain replied as he cast his eyes to the horizon and watched the enemy ship. "Blaggards!" he muttered again.

"Well, she's British, sir, that's for sure," Woodland told Fletcher.

"Aye, she is," Fletcher answered. "And she'll put men ashore if they see that there are survivors from the *Blunderbuss*. If their captain, whoever he is, realises that this land is not on any charts, he may be putting men ashore anyway. They'll claim it for the king, no doubt. We must go inland and hope they sail away." Fletcher looked down at Sholim, who was grunting something incomprehensible and coughing up mouthfuls of water. "Wake him up or drag him, you two. We must leave the beach," he ordered Kilpatrick and Woodland.

Once on his feet, the man known only as Sholim came to his senses. He was tall and broad. His arms were strong and muscular and he had the physique of a man who had endured many years of physically demanding work. His face was bearded, his hair short and brown. In his right ear was an earring which shone golden in the sun. On his arm was a tattoo of a howling wolf and something had been inked around his wrist.

"Ich walk," he said in his thick accent. "Ich walk."

They headed into the tall trees lined at the top of the beach like ominous statues glaring at the newcomers. A forest of peculiar trunks and plants thwarted any attempt to move with speed. Fletcher was the only one among them who still had footwear. His long, almost knee-high boots offered some protection from the thorns prickling and scratching at the other's legs.

"Did none of you manage to salvage any more clothing?" Fletcher asked as he could see his crew members struggling.

"Did not have time even to leave my hammock before the first shots hurled me to the deck, Captain," Kilpatrick answered.

"Nor I," Woodland added. Their legs were red with sores, stings and scratches. A deep gash from Kilpatrick's knee down to his ankle was causing him some trouble. He'd picked up the wound during the short battle, but adrenalin had allowed him to continue his escape from the sinking *Blunderbuss* without feeling the pain.

"What about blades? I suppose we're complete without weaponry, too?" Fletcher asked.

No one answered. Fletcher sighed and continued to stride and stomp through the heavy layers of prickles and plants whose natural defences seemed keen to make themselves known. A solemn thought began to weigh upon Fletcher's mind. *Something is not right. These plants do not belong here. It is still winter; how is it so hot?* He thought curiously.

"Mr Kilpatrick, do you notice something strange about this greenery?"

"It is unfamiliar to me, sir," Kilpatrick said as he pulled a branch of sticky thorns away from his torn clothing. "But I am no expert. How about you, Mr Woodland? Your name seems fitting to understand these things."

"No, Mr Kilpatrick, I have little knowledge of forestry. My name may be Woodland, but that was also the jive you gave me about being the ship's carpenter!"

"Do none of you agree that these types of plants do not belong in this climate? No other Mediterranean land carries such strange trees. These trees are more tropical than what is usual in these parts of the world. Something is not quite right with this place," Fletcher told the three men. He was still not sure if Sholim had understood what he was saying. "Let's press on; there must be water here somewhere."

Onwards they went, fighting their way with nature. The feeling of an entity informed them that it did not want them to be there. A soul which displayed its intentions to keep intruders away. A spirit that watched their movements and followed them every step of the way. The sounds of the jungle mimicked the ungodly scenery. Insects buzzed and chirped, adding discomfort, and Fletcher slapped his neck where a mosquito had come to take his blood. Looking up into the tops of the trees, bats hung in their thousands, dangling in their sleep as they waited for dark.

A giant red cockroach violently hissed as Fletcher stepped past the ugly creature, causing a shiver in his spine, which made him feel cold even in the heat.

"I do not like this place!" Fletcher whispered. "There is something in the air that wants us to depart."

"We're lost, sir," Kilpatrick spoke softly. "We have no ship, no means of leaving this land. You said yourself you did not know it was here. Where in God's name are we?"

"Steady yourself, man; keep your head, and we shall find salvation in some form. I have never let you down before, have I?" Captain Fletcher replied, displaying his confidence in his abilities, hoping to reassure his nervous crewman. "Do you remember that day in the Florida Keys, Mr Kilpatrick?"

"That day was more like a week, sir," Kilpatrick answered.

"Yes, it was." Fletcher smiled. "And do you remember afterwards you told me that you did not believe that we had any chance of survival? Surrounded, were we not? Outgunned and trapped, but I got us out of it, didn't I, Mr Kilpatrick?"

"You did, sir."

"So keep your faith, boy, I will see us through." Fletcher patted Kilpatrick on the back and gave the fearful man some hope.

The heat bore down on them directly from above as the day dragged on. Relentless humidity drenched their clothing and unquenchable thirst dizzied their minds. They began to believe that their quest for fresh water may be ill-founded, but they could not possibly turn back to the beach. They had managed to lose their way anyhow. Their best chance was to stick together and keep going.

"Capitan, stop!" Sholim broke their silence.

"What is it, Sholim?" Fletcher asked.

"Wir stop."

"We must keep going. Do you understand me?"

"Wasser!" he said pointing to his ear.

"You hear water?"

"Ich hearing wasser," Sholim said again.

"I hear nothing. Woodland, Kilpatrick, what do you hear?" Fletcher questioned his other two companions.

"Nothing, sir."

"Nothing, sir," they each replied.

They all looked at Sholim, who managed to speak to them by using hand gestures and his poor speech, that he could hear the water.

"We will follow you," Fletcher suggested. "Where's the water, Sholim? Take us to it."

Sholim led the way slowly for several more gruelling minutes through the trees into a clearing where they found a pool of water with a stream flowing away from them. Across the water was a cliff face with rapidly flowing water pouring over the top, falling into the pool below. Two giant rocks straddled the waterfall twenty feet into the air, causing the men to pause and ponder its beauty, highlighted by the sun's rays piercing through the tree's canopy. Thick jungle surrounded the far bank of the water's edge, where a troop of monkeys had stopped what they were doing to glance upon the human visitors. Woodland bent down to scoop some water into his hand, prompting the monkeys to break into a frenzied fit of screaming and jumping.

"That's their water!" Kilpatrick said. The monkeys hurled themselves from tree to tree, howling and hissing, bearing their teeth at the invaders.

"Throw something; get rid of them!" Fletcher ordered. Woodland bent down, grabbed a small stone and lobbed it in the general direction of the angered primates. Some fled away before returning to offer themselves as a likely target. Kilpatrick threw a stone, missing one monkey by only a few inches.

"Come on, let us give it to them!" Fletcher shouted. They each threw several stones and stepped ankle-deep into the cool, inviting water until the last monkeys followed suit and disappeared into the treetops.

"Let us drink," Fletcher said jovially. He knelt into the pool and splashed his sweat-soaked face before sipping lightly from his cupped hands. Sholim stood, stretched out his arms as if he were Jesus Christ upon the cross and allowed his body to fall forward straight into the water.

"Thought you cannot swim?" Woodland laughed. The water was shallow, only just coming to their knees, even in the middle. They drank and played, laughing like children, splashing each other's faces and wrestling in the water. Fletcher sat upright in the centre of the pool and ran water through his long brown hair and over his face. He opened his eyes and looked at the waterfall. The water flowing gently over the edge captured his gaze. He sat and stared.

"What is it, sir?" Woodland asked. The captain did not move. He was mesmerised by the feature that seemed to stare back at him and Fletcher fell into a trance. Woodland approached the captain. He looked up, trying to make out what the captain was staring at and he, too, was trapped in the eyes of the waterfall. Sholim and Kilpatrick looked at each other.

"Captain?" Kilpatrick called out. "Mr Woodland?" He wanted to see what they were staring at, so he paddled into the middle of the pool of water and struck his eyes towards the falling water. All three of them, immersed in the hypnotic trap, were now unable to move. Sholim slowly crept through the water, hearing nothing but the splash of the waterfall. Even the sounds of the jungle and swaying trees had gone. Sholim nudged the captain. He looked up and saw the rocks. From the angle they were now at, the large stones formed a shape like the head of a giant serpent. One could not see it from the water's edge, but here it was unmistakable. Sholim nudged all three of them. He could see what they could see, too, but the mysterious force that had so entranced Fletcher, Kilpatrick and Woodland did not affect Sholim. He dragged all three of them one by one from the water and into the jungle and lay them side by side. After a few minutes, their locked eyes regained focus and their rigid bodies relaxed.

Fletcher stood up and brushed leaves off his shirt, doublet and torn trousers.

"What happened? Did I sleep?" Fletcher asked, rubbing his eyes.

"You no sleep. Du hast looks at snake," Sholim informed him and pointed to the waterfall. The shape of the serpent was not visible from where they stood, and Fletcher was confused.

"What's he talking about, sir?" Woodland asked as he'd also come around.

"I do not understand what he means, sir," Kilpatrick said.

"What do you mean, Sholim? Tell us what you mean, what snake eye?" Fletcher ordered.

"Du nicht sleep. Du looks at snake. Snake eye hast du." Sholim beckoned Fletcher back into the water to show him the snake's eyes from the pool's centre. Fletcher followed slowly and cautiously to where Sholim stood, pointing at the waterfall.

"Good God!" Fletcher whispered as he looked into the eyes of the serpent-shaped rock. His gaze became a stare, and once again, Captain Fletcher was caught, fixated, unable to move or glance his sights elsewhere. He had become immobilised, so Sholim picked up the stricken captain and retook him into the bushes to lay him down.

"Snake eye!" Sholim said to Kilpatrick and Woodland. "No, look at snake."

Fletcher broke from the trance much quicker and with more memory than the first time. He tried to describe what he had seen to the others.

"I cannot explain it. The eyes of the serpent hook you in. There is a force; do not look at the waterfall," he ordered. "What is this place?" he asked. Before anybody could answer, a wind picked up and rustled the canopy of the treetops above them. Simultaneously, they each heard a voice whispering in the wind.

"Who's there?" Fletcher spoke as if someone was in the water.

"Who calls my name?" Woodland cried out, turning to the trees behind them.

"Who calls *your* name?" Kilpatrick asked Woodland.

"I hear my name in the wind!" Woodland answered.

"No, it is my name," Kilpatrick corrected him.

"You are mistaken, Mr Kilpatrick. I can hear my name. A voice speaks my name," Woodland insisted angrily.

"I only hear the voice whispering to *me*. It is calling to *me*," Fletcher interrupted. "What is this place? Who is there? I demand you show yourself! Woodland, what do you hear?" Fletcher questioned him.

"I can hear a voice, sir, in the wind. It is saying 'Tom Woodland.' It repeats, sir, with every gust."

"Mr Kilpatrick, what do you hear?" Fletcher asked.

"The wind speaks. It is saying 'Oliver Kilpatrick.' It knows my name."

"I hear it too. It speaks in a whisper. Upon each gust, my name drifts, 'Francis Fletcher.' Sholim? What can you hear?" Fletcher asked pointing to his ear.

"Wasser. Wasser noise," Sholim said. Fletcher was uneasy. He did not like the sound of the wind speaking his name in the air, and he noticed that Sholim was not trapped in the serpent's eyes and could not hear his name as the others could. What was so different about this man that he could withstand the unnatural happenings around them?

"We should leave this place!" Kilpatrick suggested, eager to run into the jungle and try to find the beach.

"Yes, we must, but I fear British marines will likely await us if we head back the way we came. Let us climb these rocks above the waterfall. We might see something from above the trees. The other side of the island, perhaps?" Fletcher instructed.

They edged around the pool of water to the foot of the cliffs, being careful not to look at the eyes of the snake-shaped rocks. They began to climb, scaling the side of the waterfall. It was pretty easy-going, like jagged steps for most of the way. Fletcher went first and found himself able to see behind where the water fell. On the other side of the falling water, there was a cave. A strange light reflected from the cave walls out of the blackness. He dared not continue alone and waited for his crew to catch him up. The way was narrow enough only for one at a time.

"What is it, Captain?" Woodland asked as he came up next.

"I do not know. Can you see that glow? It seems there is a fire inside the cave."

"I see it, sir. I confess my fears to you now, sir. I do not wish to venture further inside. Let us continue to the summit, sir."

"No. I want to see what it is," Fletcher replied.

"Sir, I must protest. We are unarmed. There may be no escape if the British marines come," Woodland hinted with panic in his voice.

Sholim appeared next to them. Without saying a word, he brushed past and stood behind the water. He turned and faced away from the cave with the yellow glow shining onto his back. Facing the water, he stared into it. Another light appeared on his face. This time, it was orange and red and it flickered.

"What is he doing, sir?" Woodland asked the captain.

"Sholim, step away from there!" Fletcher ordered, but Sholim remained still. "Sholim!" he sternly cried out again. Sholim turned towards Fletcher and displayed a face of sadness with a tear appearing on his cheeks. His eyes were red as if flames were dancing in the whites.

"Sholim? Step away from there. Please understand me. I order you to come away at once!" Fletcher's heart began to beat faster. The eeriness in the air had made goosebumps appear on his arms and another shiver shot through his spine. A gust of wind forced its way from the glowing cave entrance, calling each of the men their names as if it were a personal ghost coming out to haunt them.

Kilpatrick had finally climbed up and joined them to witness what appeared to be fire falling over the crest of the cliffs instead of water.

"For goodness sake, sir, let us leave this place!" Woodland pleaded with Fletcher. "The water has become fire, sir. We must leave; we do not belong here!"

"I agree with Mr Woodland, Captain. Why does the wind call our names? Why does fire fall and not water?" Kilpatrick was sweating terribly from the heat of the flames and a deathly fear had taken over his nerves.

"I cannot stand it, sir. I am leaving."

"I'm leaving too," Woodland said.

Woodland and Kilpatrick steadily edged away from the cave, leaving Captain Fletcher and Sholim inside. Upon reaching the other side of the waterfall, they could instantly see it was water and not fire. They climbed higher and into the thick jungle above the cliff without questioning the mystery behind the rocks.

When they had scrambled and dragged themselves over the crest, Woodland pointed below to see Fletcher and Sholim had left the cave and were climbing up the large rocks to join them. Seldom had he seen fear emanating from Captain Francis Fletcher. It troubled him. They had often been in danger together, but Fletcher had a coolness about him that affected all the crew and it seemed here that Woodland had reason to be afraid if the captain was too, which he undoubtedly was.

Once all four of them had made it to the top, they stood close to each other, almost huddling, still well aware and afraid of the unearthly presence of a surrounding, supernatural entity.

"We should keep going," Fletcher told the three frightened men as he led the way past some trees. They walked silently again, fighting their way through the undergrowth, thorns and peculiar plants. Giant trees that seemed to have eyes that followed them hung huge shadows over them like phantoms cancelling out the friendliness of sunlight.

"Tell me what you saw, Sholim," Fletcher said. Sholim remained silent but continued to battle his way along through the bushes. "Sholim, I command you to tell me what you saw in the falling flames." Again, he pretended not to hear his captain's orders. Fletcher turned around and grabbed hold of Sholim's shirt with both hands. Sholim was much taller and looked down at Fletcher. "I am still the captain here and you will obey me! Tell me what you saw!" Fletcher used his hands to gesture what he was asking Sholim until it appeared that he had finally understood what Fletcher was trying to ask.

"Mutter," Sholim answered angrily.

"Your mother? You saw your mother?"

"Mutter, fire."

"You once told me your mother is dead."

"Mutter tot. Mutter fire."

"What was she doing?" Fletcher put another uneasy question to the giant man still towering over him.

"Mutter, fire."

Sholim grabbed Fletcher's wrists so that he would let go of his shirt and pushed him away.

"She burns?" Fletcher asked.

"Mutter burn."

They continued to walk. The farther from the waterfall, the easier it got, but cuts covered their legs and they each had a variety of thorns and spikes poking into their skin. Soon, the bushes turned to grass and then the grass faded into the sand. Before long, they had rediscovered their beach. They were at a different end of the beach than when they had landed ashore, but they could see it was the same beach. Out at sea was the British frigate. She had lowered her anchor and tied up her sails.

"Look over there, Captain!" Kilpatrick pointed along the beach, which curved away from them, forming a much calmer bay than when they'd arrived. The tide had gone out and the crashing waves had become a gentle, pleasant scenery.

No more violent than a duck pond, Fletcher thought. He sent his eyes to where Kilpatrick was pointing. A rowing boat with a small mast and sail to accompany and about ten marines, dressed in red and carrying long muskets, had landed on the beach. Their officer, a captain, distinct by his shoulder badges, tricorne-cocked hat and sword, examined the footprints left behind by the four marooned men earlier that day.

"What should we do, sir?" Woodland asked again, displaying panic.

"We cannot fight them, sir," Kilpatrick remarked.

"I do not think we need to," Fletcher replied.

Their captain had already thought up a plan.

Chapter 2

"Sergeant Walton, can you track them?" Captain of Marines, Dawson asked.

"Aye, cap'n, they'd have gone straight into the jungle from the beach. They'll likely have left a trail; we shouldn't have trouble finding them. Judging from the footprints, there's only three or four of them," the sergeant answered the captain.

They both sweltered in the heat. Despite sweat and saltwater making his long red coat and tails, waistcoat, stockings and cuffs uncomfortable, Captain of Marines Dawson refused to allow his discipline to drop so much as to remove his cravat or cocked hat. He had neat blond hair, red cheeks and a thin but handsome face. He was tall and slender and took pride in his appearance.

"Have the men load and make ready, Sergeant Walton. We'll catch these pirates dead or alive," Dawson ordered. Walton gave the order and the ten-man search party began to make their way through the jungle, following the trail of Fletcher and his crew.

Dawson swiped with his sword, cutting through the vines and branches, which did their best to prevent them from going further. Thorns and spikes gripped the clothing. Nettles stung their hands and faces and fought them continuously.

"Goodness me, Sergeant Walton, they must have had difficulty coming through here," he grunted over his shoulder as he slashed away at another branch.

"True, sir, true. They can't be far," Sergeant Walton replied. "Reminds me of that time we went looking for them tribesmen in the Singapore River, sir. That was a thick jungle, too. Mosquitos were biting your neck and those big red ants stung like a fury when they attacked your feet. Get a few of them up your breeches and you'll know about it, sir."

"Yes, I remember it well. Strange though. Singapore is known for that kind of environment. I've not seen anything like this in the Med. It is most peculiar."

"Aye, sir, most peculiar it is indeed. I've travelled to all corners of the world, and I'm still surprised by it to this day. Like when I was in Calcutta, I met a man who told me about snow. Can you believe that, sir? Snow, in India, although he said he came from a different part of India, It still surprised me to know that folks like them had experienced snow."

"Yes, I believe further Inland in India, there are mountains where snow does fall. Not likely us being Navy men will ever be sent that far inland, though, is it, Sergeant…" Captain Dawson stopped and searched his surroundings, looking into the trees and raising an ear. He raised a finger to his lips.

"Sir…?" Sergeant Walton questioned the captain, unsure of why he'd stopped.

"Tell the men to stop."

Sergeant Walton gave the order to halt and be silent. Dawson turned to the men and signalled for them to crouch. Several moments passed until Dawson looked at Sergeant Walton and whispered.

"Do you hear that, Sergeant? I can hear water. Can't you?"

"Aye, sounds like running water, sir," Sergeant Walton agreed.

"Yes, it does. And monkeys. Sergeant, I want you to take two men and go forward," Dawson instructed the sergeant.

"Aye, sir." Walton turned and pointed at the two closest red-coated marines behind him, Privates Lockwood and Bairstow. "You two, with me." The two marines nodded and crept cautiously after the sergeant, who had drawn a pistol and a cutlass.

After several minutes of battling further with the undergrowth, the sergeant and two marines reached the pool. The waterfall stood magnificently, a ray of sun piercing through the treetops perfectly shining into the water as it fell, creating a rainbow where the splashes leaped back up again.

"Well, would you look at that, lads! Glorious," Walton said to the smiling marines. On the other side of the bank, the same troop of monkeys frightened away by Fletcher was sitting watching the newcomers. Walton searched the area with his eyes; his military training came to him instinctively, knowing he'd be exposed if he stepped into the water. Once he considered it safe, he stepped forward carefully, only allowing the water to ripple around his black boots. Suddenly, the monkeys let loose a tirade of howls and began jumping from tree to tree again, expressing their desire for the humans to leave. Walton stepped back, wary that their noise could alert the outlawed band they were hunting to their presence. After his foot left the water, the monkeys alleviated almost immediately.

"What strange behaviour!" Walton expressed.

"Shall I fire a warning shot at them, Sergeant?" Lockwood asked.

"No, Lockwood, I don't want those vagabonds knowing we're here. Leave your muskets on the ground and we'll run at them with blades. Un-fix your bayonets."

"Okay, silently now, no shouting, just run and use your blades if you have to," Walton ordered.

They charged at the monkeys, making as little noise as possible, obeying the order not to use their voices. They splashed through the pool, and just as the three men approached their tree-dwelling foes, the monkeys turned and fled, bounding through the jungle out of sight.

Walton smiled and chuckled, pleased with himself for forcing the enemy to flee the battlefield without firing a shot.

"That's how we should do it. Well done. Now, let's get back to Captain Dawson and show them this spectacular place." There was no answer from either of the two marines. They stood still, unmoving. Walton looked at the two men who were statues in the water, gaping with open mouths and fixated stares. Not knowing what they were looking at, Walton spun to send his eyes in the same direction. He became instantly caught in the eyes of the serpent-shaped rock, seduced by its hypnotic gaze, which lured in their black pupils like a magnetic force that could be neither seen nor heard.

"It worked," Fletcher said, watching from some nearby bushes. "Let us go speedily now; do not look at the rocks. Keep your eyes focused only on what is beneath your feet and what is ahead of you. Woodland and Kilpatrick get the two privates. I'll take the sergeant. Onwards now, Sholim, go and get their muskets. Do you understand me? Muskets," Fletcher commanded, speaking slowly and using hand signals for his non-English friend.

They'd been watching Sergeant Walton and the two marines the entire time from further along the pool, where it turned into a stream. Following his own instructions to not look at the rocks and occasionally glancing at his crew to ensure they had obeyed, Fletcher approached the sergeant, who was incapable of movement. The three red coats were dragged along the stream and laid on the jungle floor.

"Bind their hands behind their backs, use their belts. Remove their red coats," Fletcher ordered. Sholim came along a few seconds later with two muskets which they all saw were primed and cocked. Fletcher took the sergeant's pistol and gave the cutlass to Sholim and the two muskets to Woodland and Kilpatrick.

"What do we do now, sir?" Woodland asked.

"Put on their clothes. We'll wait for these three to come out of their daze. First, we will conduct a little experiment. Then, we shall leave them somewhere for the rest of the British party to find. Then after that we'll escape."

"Have you a plan, Captain?" Kilpatrick asked.

"Listen carefully." Fletcher proceeded to explain his plan of action. "While the rest of the British marines are busy looking for these three, we will head to the beach, wait for dark and take their boat. Then we'll row to the other side of the island wearing their coats; if someone sees us, they'll think we're British marines. When we're out of sight of our friends on board that frigate, we will head north. I've lost my lodestone, so I'll navigate by the stars. We may be able to hit the shores of Greece in a day or two, or there are plenty of other Greek islands for us to hide on for some time. The frigate won't leave until these men have returned, so we shall have a large enough head start. They'll need to send a search party to search for the search party." Fletcher smiled.

Woodland and Kilpatrick both grinned. They knew deep down that their captain would come through with a plan. They'd always trusted him and felt glad to have Francis Fletcher as their man to follow at times like these.

"Their hands are bound, sir," Kilpatrick informed Fletcher.

"Good, now gag them and put their clothes on," he ordered. "I'll be the sergeant; you two are the marines."

"What about Sholim, sir?" Kilpatrick asked.

"Sholim can remain in his clothes. When we steal the rowing boat from the beach, we may be seen by those on board the frigate. We will look like three members of their search party and a prisoner. That should see off any suspicions if they see us stealing the boat from a distance. We'll try to signal them that we're going around the island to join the others, but they probably won't see us anyway. It will be dark."

"You are a genius, Captain," Woodland complimented Fletcher.

"I told you we'd find a way, didn't I?" Fletcher smiled and put his hand on Woodland's shoulder. "Now, let's take our prisoners up that waterfall. Remember, do not look into the serpent-shaped rock's eyes."

"What are we going to do with them, sir?" Woodland asked.

"I want to know more about that waterfall."

"I do not think it wise to go there again, sir!" Woodland quickly put to Fletcher.

"Sholim said he saw something in the fire. He said he saw his mother. He also told me a while ago that his mother was dead. There's something about it; curiosity is getting the better of me," Fletcher said.

"Not of me, though, sir. I prefer to wait here," Woodland commented nervously.

"As would I, sir," Kilpatrick added.

"Well, I can't go up there alone; I've got a plan. Let us get going before the rest of the search party discovers they're missing."

The three tied, bound and gagged marines came around once Fletcher had stood them up. They grunted and groaned at each other and tried to wriggle. The four outlaws dragged them by their hands and feet, awkwardly carrying them up the step-like route to the cave behind the waterfall. The wind whistled as it had done earlier that day and each man heard their names in the gusts. The marines were listening to their names too, and they began to squirm, displaying fear in their eyes.

"Alright, you first!" Fletcher pointed at the sergeant.

Sholim grabbed Sergeant Walton by his sweat-soaked white shirt and forced him in front of the waterfall, which sure enough fell in flames now that they were behind it. Walton stared into the fire. His eyebrows raised and his eyes widened. He was trying to scream from behind the torn piece of clothing Kilpatrick had used to gag him.

"What do you see?" Fletcher demanded. Woodland stepped forward to remove the gag, carefully preventing his eyes from meeting the fire.

"Tell me what you see and no harm will come to you!" Fletcher ordered again.

"I…I…I…See me," he stuttered.

"Tell me more!" Fletcher ordered.

"I…I…I…see me! I'm young again."

"How young? A child?"

"N…n…no. I…I'm twenty. I'm running from soldiers. I have stolen the watch!"

"Tell me about the watch."

"I stole it. It belonged to Mr Tewkesbury."

"Who is Mr Tewkesbury?"

"He married my mother. After my father died, Mr Tewkesbury came along. I did not take kindly to him. I stole his watch and joined the Navy soon after to get away from them."

There came a voice from the mouth of the cave, more like a growl than the whispers heard before. It said, "THOU.SHALL.NOT.STEAL." And suddenly, the yellowish glow became as bright as the sun before fading again.

"That's enough. Take that man away from the flame," Fletcher commanded.

Kilpatrick obeyed and pulled the man away from the falling fire.

"You!" Fletcher pointed to one of the terrified marines. "What's your name?"

"Lockwood, sir, Frazer Lockwood!" he answered after Kilpatrick removed his gag.

"Don't, *sir*, this man, Lockwood; he's a pirate!" Walton called out before receiving a back of the hand across his face from Fletcher.

"Look into the fire, Lockwood," Fletcher demanded. "Tell me what you see." Lockwood bravely clenched his fists and looked into the glowing fire.

"I see myself, sir."

"Tell me more."

"I'm a boy. I'm on the docks at Bristol. I was twelve when I started working for the slavers. I can see myself, sir. I saw that one of the dark men had slipped his chain and jumped into the river during the night. I remember looking down at his face. He was watching me. He knew I could see him. My master came along and noticed the iron shackle loose. He asked me if I had seen where the escaped slave-man had run. I told him I did not know! I told him I hadn't seen him, but I knew where he was, only I did not want to say. Later on, they found the dark man and whipped him." The glowing cave lit up again and the same growling voice crept out. "THOU. SHALL. NOT BEAR FALSE WITNESS AGAINST THY NEIGHBOUR!"

Woodland and Kilpatrick were shaking nervously, as were the captured marines.

"We should leave, sir," Woodland advised.

"I agree, sir," Kilpatrick whimpered with terror.

"Very well," Fletcher agreed without trying the third marine, Bairstow. He was beginning to show some nervousness and had no intention of displaying to his crew or enemy that he often feared.

They carefully climbed down the side of the waterfall, where the falling fire turned back into water once they were on the other side. They trod into the pool, each of them still hearing their names calling to them in the wind. They were covered in goosebumps, cold with fright while sweating from the heat and silenced by the mysterious events they had just witnessed.

Various inexplicable thoughts about what they could have discovered were going through their minds. Evidently not intended for their eyes or ears, this supernatural world brought them a new kind of fear.

They slowly plodded to the edge of the water, keen to get away but aware that the rest of the marines were still in the jungle pursuing them, and suddenly, a single shot rang out. The smoke from a pistol emerged from behind some dark bushes. Kilpatrick received the pistol ball through his right side, puncturing his lung, and a patch of blood began to grow through his white shirt. He looked down to where the pistol ball had hit him and lifted his shirt. A small black and red hole oozed thick, sticky red liquid.

"Mr Kilpatrick!" Woodland shouted and ran over to his friend. Kilpatrick dropped to his knees, wheezing furiously and spewing blood that mixed in with the flowing water. The remaining marines from behind their cover simultaneously took one pace forward in line to the water's edge, each aiming their muskets at Fletcher, Woodland and Sholim.

Captain of Marines Dawson stepped forward. He placed his pistol back into his belt and drew his sword.

"Well, well, well," he said. "I believe we have captured the infamous Francis Fletcher! And I believe you have something of mine…"

Fletcher dropped his cutlass and signalled for Sholim to lower his weapon.

"Are you all right, Mr Kilpatrick?" Fletcher asked his wounded friend.

"I don't know, sir," he managed to speak while lying in Woodland's arms, but it was clear from his breathing that he was not in a good way.

"Untie my men and send them over to me, and I shall see to it that your companion receives treatment once we're on board His Britannic Majesty's Ship, Dolphin," Dawson promised Fletcher.

"Doesn't seem like I have many choices, does it?" Fletcher replied.

"That it does not," Dawson answered.

As soon as Sergeant Walton was untied and ungagged, he took his red coat from Fletcher and ensured Lockwood and Bairstow did the same.

"Sergeant Walton, you may do unto this pirate what he has done to you: tie and gag him. Gag them all," Dawson ordered.

"What about the wounded man?" Sergeant Walton asked.

"His friends can carry him, but not before you've tied their hands."

All of them fought their way back through the jungle towards the beach. Fletcher was pushed all the way, gagged and bound, unable to defend his face from thin branches whipping as the person before him let them go.

They reached the sand in dazzling heat with the sun's razor-sharp rays above them. The marines pushed the rowing boat back into the water, and they could all see the anchored frigate gently bobbing on the waves a mile out to sea.

"Sir!" Lockwood called out.

"Yes? What is it?" Dawson answered.

"This man is dead, sir." He pointed to the lifeless body of Kilpatrick, which had been laid on the sand by Woodland and Sholim, who had managed to carry him despite having their hands tied.

"Well, that's a shame. We cannot hang him now! Never mind, leave him here; he can rot and the crabs can eat him."

Woodland and Sholim looked sad and angry as they stared down upon their deceased friend.

Fletcher stepped forward and mumbled into the rag that had been stuffed into his mouth. Sergeant Walton removed it, allowing Fletcher to speak. "I must protest, Captain!"

"I don't take protests from thieves and murderers, Francis Fletcher," Dawson growled back at him.

"I am neither of those things, sir!" Fletcher fired back but remembered to be courteous to the man's rank. "You promised me that this man would receive treatment. That is no longer possible, so at least let us give him a proper Christian burial."

"Alright then, you may give this man a burial, but you must dig the hole yourself. And you may not untie your hands!"

"That is most honourable of you, Captain. For that, I give you my thanks." Fletcher again chose to be as polite as possible. "Help me, please, Mr Woodland. And you, Sholim." However, Fletcher was not sure if Sholim had understood.

They began to dig into the sand with their tied hands. Sholim soon grasped what they were doing and joined them. When they had managed to create an opening in the sand large enough to place the body of Kilpatrick, they rolled him in.

Using his carpentry skills as best he could with bound wrists, Woodland stuck one long sharp stake into the ground and then used a broken vine to tie another to it, creating a wooden cross to act as Kilpatrick's headstone.

"Either of you two got anything to say?" Fletcher asked as they stood above the mound of sand that had covered Kilpatrick. Sholim began to mutter under his breath something that was not in any recognisable language.

"What's he saying?" Dawson demanded.

"We do not know what tongue this man speaks, Captain," Fletcher replied. "His understanding of the English language is limited."

"Something heathen, no doubt. You've buried your man. Now, let us depart this strange island. Captain Talbot would very much like to see you, Francis Fletcher."

"Did you say, Talbot?" Fletcher asked upon recognising the ship's captain's name.

"That's right, Captain Talbot."

"Well, I'll be damned." Fletcher half-smiled. "I must say I am rather keen to see my old friend too!"

Chapter 3

Fletcher, Woodland and Sholim were uncouthly raised from the rowing boat onto the upper deck of His Britannic Majesty's Ship Dolphin. The three-mast, square-rigged frigate had been anchored a mile from the beach where the ship's commander, Captain Percy Talbot, had waited impatiently for the search party of marines to return.

Fletcher stood in anticipation with his hands still tied by a thin rope. Armed marines with bayoneted muskets stood by while other crew members looked on, eager to capture a glimpse of the infamous man. Fletcher counted the guns. There were twelve on a single deck, six pointing to port and six to starboard. There were another twenty-two below on the gun deck and they were all responsible for sinking his ship, *Blunderbuss*, earlier that morning. Not a single piece of her remained afloat. Fletcher had seen many ships succumb to the waves in battle and storms, but never had he witnessed a vessel the size of *Blunderbuss* become untraceable in a matter of hours. Driftwood, masts, sails, barrels, ropes and floating corpses could usually be found at the scene of a wrecked vessel for days or even weeks after she'd sunk, but not here.

A man dressed in the splendid attire of a captain's blue uniform, immaculately presented and well prepared, proudly approached the captive outlaws. He walked upright with a perfectly straight posture and looked down his nose at Fletcher with an arrogant smirk. Fletcher recognised the man's face immediately and chose to speak first.

"Good day to you, Percy," he greeted his captor, thrusting his head backwards to flick his long wet hair out of his face. His own captain's tunic was dirty torn and soaked. The buttons were missing and his rank insignia hung ragged from threads.

"Francis Fletcher," Captain Talbot said with a smile. "It has been a most interesting venture."

Fletcher responded immediately, "I see the admiralty finally gave you a command. How does it feel, Percy? Your first victory, and you managed to attack and sink one of the king's ships. I do say he'll be interested to hear about this," he jested.

"My first command, and I managed to capture the fearless pirate Francis Fletcher, you mean? Your ship, or should I say what used to be your ship, was no longer in the king's service since you stole and renamed her," Talbot buoyantly answered Fletcher. "Mr Ingham, take these men below. Clap them in irons and see that they receive ship's rations."

"Aye, aye, Captain," Mr Ingham, the ship's bosun, obeyed.

"And then, Mr Ingham."

"Yes, sir."

"Have the Dolphin ready to put to sea."

"Aye, Captain." Ingham saluted.

"Master Laine," Talbot called out as he watched Mr Ingham and other armed men guide the prisoners below the deck.

"Yes, Captain Talbot, sir?" Master Laine, the ship's navigator, shouted back.

"We sail west for Gibraltar and then on to Portsmouth. These pirates have a meeting with the gallows."

"Aye, aye, sir," Master Laine answered.

"Captain Dawson and Lieutenant Jenkins, I'll see you both in the great cabin promptly."

"Yes, sir."

"Yes, sir," both, the captain of marines and the second-in-command, Lieutenant Jenkins, answered.

"Would you like to sit?" Captain Talbot offered his two favourite officers chairs in the great cabin and sat himself behind his large oak desk. Red curtains draped behind him, drawn open, allowing light into the room through the tall diamonded windows. A giant globe gently rocked its axis in the corner with the boat's motion on the calm water beneath them. Behind the globe was a large cabinet where Captain Talbot kept his whisky and brandy bottles. There was a large rug in the cabin, emerald green laced with golden silk forming swirling patterns around the edges, and in the centre were three red lions, a symbol of Richard the Lionheart.

"Right, well, Captain Dawson, I must congratulate you for carrying out your task in bringing those ruffians to me from that island. Have you anything else to report?" Talbot inquired.

"Well, sir, yes, I do have something to report. We already thought it strange that the island is here, yet not on our charts, but once on the island, we found it to be most…" Dawson paused momentarily while thinking of the right way to describe the island. "…Odd." That was the only word Dawson could think of.

"Odd, how?" Talbot asked.

"Well, in many ways," Dawson went on. "The greenery itself is not from this part of the world. Sergeant Walton described it as more like the things we found in Singapore. It's more tropical than Mediterranean, sir."

"I see," Talbot said, stroking his freshly shaved chin and removing his cocked hat. "Do continue," he said, gesturing with his hands.

"There is an atmosphere there that seems rather protective of itself. I felt as I walked through the thick jungle, and believe me, sir, it is thick, as though I were particularly unwelcome. One has to fight it to advance through the jungle. Normally, a jungle is very aggressive anyway; one must always chop and cut through it just as in battle, but these plants and trees give the impression that they are fighting back. It is a most awkward feeling, sir. Even the air has a certain unfriendly characteristic. I am finding it very difficult to portray."

Captain Talbot puffed out his cheeks, unsure what Dawson was trying to describe.

"Are you saying these trees had feelings and thoughts? I did not take you for a superstitious man," Lieutenant Jenkins commented to Dawson.

"No, Lieutenant, you are correct in your judgment of me. I have never been one for superstition, nor am I that of a particularly religious man, although I have read through the bible several times; however, this island, whatever we shall name it once we no doubt claim it, has a different character."

"An island with character? What do you mean? I am intrigued to go ashore. If I were not in such a hurry to see Francis Fletcher hang, I would launch an expedition myself to see what this land offers," Talbot added.

"Well, there is something that Sergeant Walton told me on our return to the beach from the jungle, sir. You see, there was a waterfall in there. It flowed onto a stream—the source of the water we never found. We caught up with Fletcher and his criminal subordinates before getting past it. Fletcher is a smart man, sir, and we did not take him with ease. He was able to lure Sergeant Walton and two of my marines and take them for hostages first. They took their weapons and dressed in their clothing. God knows what his plan was, but before we caught him, according to Sergeant Walton, they were forced into the waterfall or a cave behind it where the water which fell was not water, but from behind looked more like fire."

"Mr Dawson, where are you going with this? Has the heat gotten to your head, man?" Captain Talbot interrupted.

"No, sir, I am repeating what was told to me by Sergeant Walton."

"So, Walton was taken hostage by Fletcher?"

"Yes, sir."

"And you rescued him?"

"Yes, sir. I had sent Walton ahead with two marines, Lockwood and Bairstow, to scout the area. Fletcher caught them, took them up the waterfall and forced them to look into the fire. As I just stated, the waterfall from behind is not a waterfall. It is a…Firefall, sir." Dawson realised that he was beginning to sound more and more ridiculous as he went on.

Jenkins began to chuckle. Dawson was not happy with the Lieutenant laughing at him in such a mocking manner.

"Perhaps Lieutenant Jenkins would like to go and see for himself, sir, that what happened on that island is not of this world! Sir, I beg you to interview Sergeant Walton and hear what happened from his mouth. I was not there to see it. We caught up with our marines, who had been captured, undressed and disarmed by Fletcher. I fired a single pistol shot at one of Fletcher's men, Kilpatrick. With Kilpatrick wounded fatally and them all being outgunned and almost surrounded, Fletcher gave up and surrendered almost immediately. We buried Kilpatrick on the beach before we returned to the Dolphin." There was a knock on the door, interrupting the captain of marines.

"Enter," Talbot shouted towards the door. Mr Ingham opened the door and stepped into the great cabin.

"Beg your pardon, sir, but there's something which we believe you should see," Mr Ingham said.

Captain Talbot strolled onto the upper deck past all the crew busy preparing the ship to sail.

"What is it, Mr Ingham?"

"There, sir, on the beach." Mr Ingham handed the captain a telescope. Talbot looked through it and saw on the beach a burning cross. The smoke was visible to the naked eye, but one could only see the cross through the magnifying lens.

"Dawson!" Talbot called out. "Where are you?" he said, looking over his shoulder for the captain of the marines.

"Here, sir."

"What did you leave behind on the beach burning like that?"

"We burnt nothing, sir," Dawson informed the captain.

"Look through that and explain to me why I can see flames rising from a cross on the beach…" Dawson did as ordered and looked through the telescope towards the beach.

"Good God, sir!" Dawson exclaimed as he saw the inexplicable fire. "It's the cross we made for Fletcher's deceased crew member, Kilpatrick! I told you we had buried him on the beach. That other captive, the carpenter with Fletcher, made a wooden cross as a headstone. Now it burns, sir!"

"There must have been more of them to survive the sinking ship," Talbot concluded. "But why would they burn the cross?"

"It makes no sense to me unless it is a signal. They want us to go back for them, sir," Dawson suggested.

"Why would they want that? They know they'll hang once captured."

"I repeat it, sir. The island has a strange atmosphere. It has many things to it which are unseemly," Dawson told the captain once more.

"I'll not return for them yet. I must make haste for England. The ship will be ready to sail soon. Return to the great cabin, both of you. I want to discuss this island further," Talbot told his two officers.

Dawson and Jenkins marched themselves back to the captain's cabin.

"Mr Ingham, please have Sergeant Walton of the marines sent to the great cabin; I wish to speak to him," Talbot ordered the bosun.

"Aye, aye, sir," Mr Ingham replied.

Back inside the great cabin, Sergeant Walton stood to attention.

"You may stand at ease, Sergeant," Captain Talbot instructed. "Now, your captain, Dawson, tells me that there was an incident earlier that involved you being captured by Francis Fletcher, stripped of your clothing and later rescued again."

"Yes, sir. Won't happen again, sir," Sergeant Walton answered the captain and returned himself to attention.

"Well, I sincerely hope not. However, Sergeant, this is not a hearing about your mishaps. I want to know more about the island."

"Tell the captain what you told me, Sergeant. Tell us all that happened before we found you as Fletcher's hostage," Dawson instructed the quivering Sergeant. "Do not hold back now; you are not on trial. We merely want to know what happened."

"Very well, sir," Sergeant Walton continued to tell his version of the day's events. "We first approached a troop of monkeys who were screaming violently."

Jenkins began to laugh. "Monkeys? Don't tell me you had a battle with some monkeys."

"Lieutenant Jenkins, please allow the sergeant to tell his story." Talbot sighed towards the giggling first officer.

"Yes, Lieutenant Jenkins, monkeys," Sergeant Walton repeated, bemused. "We discovered a waterfall where the monkeys were sitting on the far bank. I stepped into the water and that seemed to set them off. I immediately pulled my foot from the water and they calmed down. It was most bizarre behaviour, but the whole forest was giving off an aura of strange manners. So we charged the monkeys with blades. I didn't want any shooting because I didn't want Fletcher and his cronies to know we were there. But they'd already seen us, sir, and were waiting."

"So, how did they manage to disarm and unclothe you?" Jenkins questioned.

"That I am unable to answer. I found myself staring at the waterfall. It had something about it. I stared into the rocks, and they were shaped like a serpent whose eyes were a menace. It managed to hypnotise us somehow and we were unable to move. Fletcher dragged us away, but I noticed he wasn't looking at the serpent. He knew of its powers already, though I am not sure how. Then they picked up our muskets, took from me my sword and undressed us. He told his other men he would pose as us and steal the rowing boat. But first, he dragged us up the waterfall. That's when we heard the wind."

"You heard the wind?" Talbot intervened again.

"Yes, sir. The wind whispered my name. But to my ears only. It called out Marine Lockwood's name to him, and I know to the carpenter Woodland, he could hear his name. Each man only heard their own name. Then, I was forced to go behind the waterfall, where it was no longer water but fire. Fletcher ordered us to stare into the falling flame, where the strangest thing happened. I could see myself as a young man, sir, as if I were watching from afar. I saw a part of my past where I stole a pocket watch. Then I heard the wind come out of the cave behind me, and the cave was glowing, too. The voice said, 'Thou shalt not steal'!"

"The fire was able to show you a picture of your past?" Jenkins queried.

"Yes, Lieutenant, I saw myself but as a younger version of me. I must admit I committed a crime during my younger days, and I was able to see myself stealing a pocket watch. Then the voice called out, 'Thou shalt not steal.' But not only me, sir, Lockwood too. He saw himself as a boy lying to his supervisor at slaver's gate." The sergeant fidgeted nervously with a button on his sleeve as he re-told the story of his earlier encounter. Talbot, fascinated by the tale, turned the captain of marines.

"This is most bizarre, Captain Dawson. Do you insist you have no explanation for this?" Talbot asked.

"I cannot explain what I personally did not see, Captain, but I think if we want to know more about this island, we can call upon another witness."

"Do you mean Marine Lockwood?"

"No, sir, I mean Francis Fletcher."

"Ha!" Jenkins screeched.

"You may find me foolhardy, Lieutenant Jenkins, but I cannot help but question how Francis Fletcher knew about the mysteries behind the waterfall. He must have experienced something himself. I wonder if he can confess what he saw at some time during his final voyage," Dawson pondered, stroking his smooth chin.

"He might. But he does not trust me and I shan't believe a word from his mouth," Talbot went on. "We have, as you know, a history of personal quarrels. He still hasn't gotten over Isabella."

"Your wife, sir?" Jenkins asked.

"Yes, my wife. He loved her once. Still does I expect."

"But you won her fair and square, sir."

"Yes, Lieutenant, I did. I should have killed him there and then."

"It would have been most un-gentlemanly of you, sir. And surely Isabella respects the noble deed of sparing him?"

"Most likely, however, she is aware of the circumstances."

"May I ask you both to explain what you're talking about?" Dawson interrupted.

"Yes, Mr Dawson, but first, Sergeant Walton, you may leave us now. Thank you," Talbot instructed the sergeant and pointed to the door of the great cabin. The sergeant left and Talbot continued to tell his tale of his struggle with Francis Fletcher.

"Francis Fletcher and I were friends once upon a time, Captain Dawson. We've known each other since childhood, our fathers were very close. We grew up together, almost inseparable, like brothers we were. Then, one day, we fell in love with the same girl. Isabella Norris."

"The daughter of the late Admiral Norris?" Dawson asked.

"Yes, the Admiral Lord Norris. However, he's been dead for some fourteen years now. On his deathbed, he wrote to me asking that I take care of his daughter as I had already asked for his blessing in her hand in marriage. She had told me her father was overjoyed at the betrothal; however, she was not. Someone else had taken her fancy." Talbot looked down at his desk as he spoke.

"Francis Fletcher!" Jenkins hissed the name.

"Indeed," Talbot continued. "So I did what any honourable gentleman would have done. I called him out."

"You fought a duel, sir?" Dawson could not believe that Captain Percy Talbot was the sort of man to have fought in a duel.

"I did. But there was one problem. We were both so drunk at the duel that we required our second men to load our pistols, and I remember needing help walking the ten paces. After I turned to shoot, Fletcher was face-down on the ground, fast asleep. He'd collapsed from the drink, unaware of how close to death he was. I could have fired at him as he was a stationary target, but it would not have been a fair fight. Subsequently, I went home after Fletcher's representative agreed that I was the clear winner, as Fletcher could not fire his shot or hold his rapier."

"And so you won Isabella. It sounds like it was fair to me, Captain. If Fletcher wanted her, he could have been willing to sacrifice his life for her, at the very least," Dawson said.

"Both Fletcher and I became laughingstocks at the naval academy. I could barely show my face in Portsmouth Dockyard for weeks after. People laughed at me and said it was the most ridiculous duel ever fought and that we should certainly fight it again to regain our honour, but properly this time. People did not consider my victory sincere."

"So why did you not call him out again, sir?" Dawson asked.

"The war broke out with France and we were ordered not to fight any more duels. Then, Fletcher distinguished himself at Quiberon Bay and became a national hero. He had restored his honour while my reputation lay down in the dirt. Although I, too, served in the war, it was not until the fighting was over last year that I was given the Dolphin as my first command and my promotion to captain."

"But Fletcher turned sir, he's a pirate now. And you've caught him! It's a most justified reversal in fortune, and I dare say you've earned it, Captain," Jenkins added.

"Thank you, Lieutenant. Now, you've heard my story and I have heard yours, Captain Dawson. Now we sail for England, where that nemesis of mine will hang, and I am only too eager to speed up the process." Captain Talbot stood up and walked across the great cabin to a smaller, more hidden cabinet made from dark wood with a small glass window. He took out a bottle of cognac. He poured three glasses and distributed a drink to both of his friends.

"Gentleman, a toast. To the king, to England and the death of Francis Fletcher."

Chapter 4

As the Dolphin sailed west and the peculiar island faded to just a shadow on the horizon, Captain Talbot sat in his cabin pondering about the day's events.

He sat staring at his charts, wondering how it could be that after so many hundreds, even thousands of years, nobody had ever come across this island, or if they had, how it had never appeared on any Royal Navy maps. It just did not seem possible, so he took care to enter the coordinates into his logbook.

His thoughts turned to the stories of Sergeant Walton and Captain Dawson. He told himself that he would appeal to the admiralty to allow an expedition to return to the island as soon as Fletcher was executed. If the tales were not believed, he could use the excuse that there are possibly still pirates on the island that he would bring back for hanging. That should give them sufficient reason to allow such an adventure.

Thinking of England reminded him of his wife, Isabella. He had not seen her for such a long time, nor their children Edward and Estelle. He missed them greatly, but the life of a sailor did not come without its sacrifices, and Talbot had known that before marrying Isabella, and she had known it too. Finally, his thoughts turned to the man who had nearly stolen her from him. The man who had once been a hero of England. The man he'd captured. The man who was now clapped in irons below the decks of the Dolphin. Talbot had spent several hours refusing to speak to Francis Fletcher, but the curiosity of the island had eventually gotten the better of him. At last, he could not wait any longer.

He took himself to the upper deck, where all was as it should be. Master Laine was at the helm and Mr Ingham had the crew working well at their stations. Lieutenant Jenkins stood on the quarterdeck wrapped in a cloak, his face illuminated by a lantern.

"Good evening, Lieutenant," Talbot approached.

"A fine evening it is, sir."

"Anything to report from the upper deck?"

"All is well, sir; if the wind holds, we shall pass through the Strait of Malta in a day or two. Master Laine says we shall reach Gibraltar before the week is out," the lieutenant assured the captain.

"That is good to hear. Now I want your advice."

"I shall advise you the best I can, Captain," Jenkins spoke assuringly.

"Should I speak to Francis Fletcher about this island? I am too intrigued by what I heard from Walton and Dawson. I want to return once we have hung Fletcher, but I want to know more first."

"Well, sir, you did say that you would not believe a word to come from Fletcher's mouth, Captain. However, if he declares a story similar to that of our two marines, you've no reason to doubt him. Have you?"

"I would not have reason to doubt him. What do you think? A waterfall with hypnotic powers? From which behind it appears as a fire? Where does the wind whisper your name and the flame shows you your past? An island that is not on any charts or maps? I want to return," Talbot eagerly expressed his wishes to his second-in-command.

"Then I shall surely request to return with you, Captain."

"In which case, I must speak to Fletcher. I need to know what it is that he saw."

"I don't think it would do any harm, sir," the lieutenant advised.

"Very well. I shall speak with Fletcher promptly. Then, Mr Jenkins, I shall take the rest of your watch."

"That's very kind of you, sir."

"Not at all." The captain paced along the deck until he reached the foremast. "Mr Ingham, please bring the pirate and prisoner Francis Fletcher to the great cabin under your personal escort." Without waiting for a reply, Captain Talbot returned to his quarters and stayed with a fast-pacing heart for his arch-enemy to enter.

Francis Fletcher entered the great cabin, shivering from the cold night after being tightly held in irons with no warm clothing for many hours.

"Thank you, Mr Ingham," Captain Talbot said. "You may leave us now." Once the door was closed, Fletcher paced forward and spoke first as he always did.

"Are you comfortable in here, Percy?" he asked smugly. Talbot stood, turned towards the sizeable mounted globe in the cabin's corner and ignored the ill-humoured question.

"Francis, you're going to hang," he stated as he spun the globe on its axis.

"Will Mrs Talbot be there to watch?" Fletcher asked cockily.

"I wondered how long it would be before you mentioned her, Francis," Talbot commented.

"It would both break my heart and simultaneously fill it with laughter to see her tears as her *true* love dangles before you."

"I did not call you in here so that you could insult me, Francis. We can leave Isabella out of this one. You're going to hang for crimes against the crown and that is that."

"Crimes against the crown?" Fletcher asked with a tone of mocking bewilderment.

"You're a pirate, Francis. Pirates hang." Talbot scowled as he stopped the globe from spinning and faced the guilty man.

"I am a captain in His Majesty's Royal Navy and I will receive a fair trial first. I still have friends in the admiralty, and I have my side of the story. Even Lord John Perceval, The Earl of Egmont, will want to hear what I have to say. I assume he is still Lord of the Admiralty?"

"Yes, he is."

"And Lord Bute was a dear friend of my Grandfather. As prime minister, it is unlikely that he will allow the public execution of a national hero now that we finally have peace and victory," Fletcher remarked arrogantly. Talbot began to smile.

"A national hero? Come down from your dizzy heights, dear fellow. Lord Bute resigned in April last. Lord Grenville is the prime minister now," Talbot informed.

"Even so, the king will not allow it. Of that, I am sure."

"What makes you so sure, Francis? Because of your actions at Quiberon Bay? The country soon forgot about them. The war is over now. We have peace with France, and the victory was ours," Talbot exclaimed.

"Yes, I am aware I contributed to that victory, Percy."

"As did I, Francis. I also saw action against the French; however, we stopped attacking their ships once they signed the Paris Treaty."

"And I would have stopped attacking French vessels had I known about the peace! That is the only reason anybody branded me a pirate! For the entire seven years of the war, I fought against the French, and had I not been at sea, I would have known about the treaty. But I was still sailing the Atlantic, following my orders to disrupt French shipping," Fletcher came back, defending himself.

"So, you will claim to be a privateer, not a pirate? Even after you stole one of the king's ships?"

"I only took the ship after British ships started hunting me down!" Fletcher defended himself staunchly.

"Because you were still attacking the French, and they'd threatened to reopen hostilities if you did not stop." Talbot raised his voice slightly with each word.

"I was not to know of any treaty or orders to stop attacking the French while I was still at sea. In court, they will listen to my case, the admiralty will hear it, and the powers that be will grant me a pardon for my honest mistake," Fletcher insisted.

"For that part, yes, but you still took one of the king's ships and renamed her."

"British ships hunted *me*. I was careful to rename the *Sealion*. A compliment to his majesty, King George."

"A compliment? How?" Talbot asked, surprised by Fletcher's naivety.

"After the battle of Quiberon Bay, I was presented to the king. He gave me a gift and thanked me for my heroic actions. A blunderbuss, a magnificent weapon with a brass plate screwed to the wooden butt. Inscribed, it said, 'For your commitment to the crown and your everlasting loyalty, King George III'."

"So you renamed the *Sealion* to *Blunderbuss* after the king's gift to you. How very sly of you, Francis. Knowing that you'd be found guilty, you decided to compliment the king to seek sympathy even before your trial. How very clever of you."

"Why did you call me in here anyway?" Fletcher asked, changing the subject before the argument became too heated. "I assume it wasn't to give me a pre-trial trial or make fun now that you have caught me, so what do you want?"

"I was hoping you could shed some light on the patch of land we found you on," Talbot answered.

"I believe you may have been too cowardly to come ashore yourself and find me. Or did you want to 'win' another duel?" Fletcher taunted.

"You and I both know that I was not too cowardly. I am the ship's captain, and my place is on deck. I sent Captain Dawson and his marines because that is his job!"

"What a good job he did, too," Fletcher muttered.

"Both Dawson and the sergeant you captured made wild claims about strange happenings on the island. Do you care to give more information?"

Talbot could see that Fletcher had turned slightly pale with the question. There were no words necessary. His face was telling Talbot all that he needed to know. Talbot proceeded to tell Fletcher precisely what he had heard from Dawson and Walton anyway, and when he'd finished, Fletcher silently nodded.

"I confess to you now, Percy, that I regret the sinking of the *Blunderbuss*. I am sad my crew has all but gone, and I regret that Kilpatrick is dead. But I was glad to be on that rowing boat and away from the island."

"Well, that's knocked some wind out of your sails," Talbot remarked.

"There's something not right there. I know I face a trial and I may hang. But I would rather face the hangman's noose than whatever is back on that island. I know I did not show it to my remaining three crewmembers, but I was full of fear after seeing the snake's eyes and hearing my name in the wind," Fletcher admitted.

"Yes, I mean to ask about your crew. Your carpenter, what's his name?"

"Mr Woodland."

"Yes, he heard his name too? And he saw the flames?" Talbot probed.

"He heard his name and the snake's gaze captured him, but he did not look into the fire."

"And the other man? The big fellow with the pointed beard and ghastly ring through his ear, what's his name and rank?"

"That is Sholim."

"Sholim...?"

"We only know him as Sholim. His mother tongue is not English," Fletcher explained.

"Oh? Then what is it?"

"He is from Bohemia, we believe. He speaks some form of Germanic-Slavic gibberish."

"How interesting. Tell me, how did you come to have a Habsburg sailor on your ship?"

"Well, we needed men. We were off the coast of Morocco just before the peace was signed. Of course, I knew nothing of the peace treaty, but he had somehow found himself being sold on the white slave trade. Barbary pirates who may have been Moroccan, I could not tell, they approached us. When they saw how well-armed we were, they told us they would take our cargo but spare our lives if we did not fight. I bargained with them that we would not fight and they could take all our provisions as long as they left us fully armed and spared us some of their slaves. It was agreed. I had no intention of fighting them; they were far too many, but it was clear that they would rather not fight too. So this man Sholim and a few others of all nationalities ended up in my service. He sailed with me across the Atlantic, even as British ships fired upon us and chased us as pirates; Sholim stood by me and swore he would be with me for all eternity for saving him from the slavers."

"How did he communicate this to you?" Talbot asked, fascinated by the story.

"He was not alone when we took him. He had other men who could interpret for him. They are no longer around. That is thanks to you, Percy." Fletcher was now looking more serious than his usual ostentatious self. "There was another man with him, also from Bohemia; he was known only as Proshek. But he spoke English well enough to communicate with me and told me about Sholim. He is a most interesting man."

"Well, we have many days at sea ahead of us, Francis, and I imagine my cabin is more comfortable than your irons down below. I'll bargain with you. You may sit down and have one cognac with me if you tell me all about your Bohemian slave-man," Talbot suggested.

"Very well, for old time's sake," Fletcher agreed as Talbot handed him a glass of cognac. "I shall continue. His interpreting friend, Proshek, told me all about Sholim. He fought against the Prussians during Frederick II's invasion but eventually was on the run from the Habsburgs after lending his support to a protestant uprising in Prague. He is one of those who still believe that Prague should have been the Habsburg capital following the Prussian retreat six years ago. Austrian soldiers came to his house to arrest him, but he escaped from a back window. While the Austrian soldiers were in the house, he locked the entrances so they could not escape and set fire to it."

"He burned down his own home?" Talbot queried, shocked.

"That's how the story goes, but there was a tragedy for him too. As well as now being wanted for the murder of the Austrian soldiers, he hadn't known his mother was still inside, and she did not survive the inferno which he caused."

"Good God!" Talbot exclaimed.

"So, he fled to Trieste, where he boarded a vessel. I do not know where he was headed, but the ship did not reach its destination before Barbary pirates seized them. Not long after, the slave ship crossed my path, and as I have already explained, that's when I took him on." Fletcher downed the cognac in a single gulp after finishing the story of how he had met Sholim.

"So, this man of yours, Sholim, he's had quite the adventure. And how awful that he killed his own mother."

"Yes, and that's another strange thing. I asked Sholim what he saw when he looked into the fire behind the waterfall, and he answered 'Mother'."

"Mother. The crimes of his past. Just like Walton and Dawson," Talbot perceived.

"My thoughts exactly," Fletcher agreed.

A silence drifted between the two captains and it suddenly seemed that the hatred between them had decided to leave the room.

"But the other thing," Fletcher broke the silence, "is that Sholim seemed totally unaffected by the snake's eyes. Woodland, Kilpatrick and myself were unable to move for the hypnosis, but Sholim did not react to it. As if he had some sort of immunity," Fletcher added.

"A most interesting man," Talbot said. "Well, he will face a hearing for serving with a pirate, however, if you were to repeat what you said to me at your trial, his sentence might be reduced to imprisonment. Will you vouch for him when questioned?"

"Of course I will. And for Woodland as well," Fletcher said.

"I fear Woodland may face the gallows. He's an Englishman who decided to fight alongside you. He's an accomplice to your thievery and betrayal."

"You never listen, do you, Percy?" Fletcher said, frustrated.

"Stop calling me by my name. If you insist you are still a member of His Majesty's Royal Navy, you can at least address me by my proper rank!" Talbot finally got fed up with Fletcher's lack of courtesy.

"My apologies, Per… Captain."

"Thank you."

"But if you lend me your ear, you must hear my words," Fletcher continued. "I am not a pirate! I suddenly, one day, found myself and my crew wanted for piracy when all I had done was attack French shipping. I was at sea and unaware of the Treaty of Paris. For that, I will not hang."

"Francis, you refused to turn yourself in and stole the king's ship, renamed her, and now she's been sunk. You have been accused of piracy, and you are going to hang!"

The animosity between the two men returned, and once again, the anger flowed from both sides of the great cabin, clashing in the middle like two tidal waves thrust against each other. The conversation was over. Fletcher was escorted back to his irons and the Dolphin sailed on.

Just as Master Laine had estimated, they had made it through the Strait of Malta and had reached Gibraltar before the week was out. Captain Talbot did not meet again with Francis Fletcher for the rest of the journey, although he wanted to. He decided to act the professional officer he had always considered himself and show his men that he would not stoop so low as to share a glass with a pirate.

They crossed the Bay of Biscay and rounded the French coast near Brest. Then, one morning, Mr Ingham walked from the upper deck to the quarter deck to tell Captain Talbot and his first mate Lieutenant Jenkins that they could see land, and they believed it to be the Isle of Wight. They were correct and the Dolphin sailed into Portsmouth with three captives on board. Captain Talbot thought only of seeing Isabella before anything else. He had something to tell her.

Chapter 5

In the gardens of Enmore Castle, home to Lord John Perceval, Earl of Egmont and First Lord of the admiralty, a young Jamaican housemaid named Molly ran across the grass. The beginning of spring had brought cold rains and the well-trimmed grass was still wet, staining her white socks green in the absence of proper shoes.

"Lord Perceval!" she called out to him as she found the old man strolling around the outer grounds near the small grey chapel. "My lord!" she cried again, this time gaining his attention.

"What is it, Molly?" he asked her as she approached him. "Calm yourself, girl, catch your breath. What is the fuss?"

"My lord, a stagecoach from Portsmouth has arrived."

"A stagecoach from Portsmouth? I am not expecting guests. Who can it be?"

"My lord, it is Captain Percy Talbot," she informed him.

"Ah, he came. That is wonderful news, Molly. Although he could have written beforehand to say he was coming! Prepare a guest bed chamber for him. Is he alone, or did he bring Isabella and their children?"

"No, my lord, he has travelled alone," Molly answered.

"Oh, that is a pity. It would be wonderful to have the full entourage for company. Well, then prepare a room on the eastern wing. That should suffice. Can you inform the kitchen staff that we have a guest and ask if they can cook the ducks tonight?"

"Yes, my lord." Molly curtsied and turned to run back to the castle.

"And Molly..."

"Yes, my lord."

"Can you ask Mr Riddell to carry Captain Talbot's luggage to the chamber and then ask the captain to wait in the solar?"

"Yes, my lord." Molly curtsied and hurried away with cold, wet feet.

Lord Perceval stroked his chin and pondered momentarily why Captain Talbot could have arrived so unexpectedly. It was most intriguing why the captain had chosen to leave his wife and children behind. The old lord concluded that it must be urgent. Using his cane, he hurried back to the castle as fast as his frail old body would allow him.

"My dear Captain Talbot," Lord Perceval announced as he greeted the captain in the solar. "Have you a chill, my good man? I shall have Molly make a fire. Do sit down."

"My lord," Perceval bowed and removed his cocked hat. "Still got Molly working here, I see? You have her working as your footman now, too. My lord, I was surprised to be greeted by her on my arrival. May I ask, where are all your staff?" Talbot asked the aged Admiral.

"Oh, I do not need footmen and butlers these days. Since my wife passed, I am not the host she once was. I like to lead a more simple life now. I need a man to look after the castle, Mr Riddell, who frequently acts as my valet. I never liked valets, though. I am more than capable of dressing myself. The kitchen staff cooks me food and Molly looks after me. We have so few visitors here and I do not see why Molly cannot extend her duties."

"I believe her most capable, My lord," Talbot agreed.

"Yes, she's a good girl. I remember when you were afraid of her." Perceval laughed.

"I was just a boy back then, but I do remember."

"She was just a girl." Perceval smiled.

"Well, that was my mother's doing. She convinced me of her voodoo magic."

"Yes, Molly's parents used to taunt her with it. But Molly was born here and knows nothing of her ancestry, black magic, or witchcraft. As I said, she's a good girl, faithful to my family and me."

"And I do remember your late wife once telling me that if you treat them right, they'll treat you right," Talbot commented.

"Absolutely. After all, Molly is only a human. She's a primitive human but still a child of God. Do tell me, did you see the plantations in Jamaica on your travels? That's where Molly's parents were from. Slaves in the sugar fields, they were. But they were good," Lord Perceval said, pointing his index finger at Talbot. "They never complained and I believe I've told you the story of how I brought them back here?" Perceval asked.

"Many times, my lord. However, I wish to discuss a much more pressing matter with you. That is why I am here." Talbot changed the subject.

"Yes, I wondered what brings you to Somerset and why you came here unannounced and alone. I trust Isabella and the children are well. Would you like some refreshments?" Perceval asked. Before waiting for an answer, he continued to talk, "We've got a room for you in the eastern wing. I assume that will suffice, and we shall dine on duck tonight if you accept my invitation. I do hope we can reminisce about the times I spent with your father."

"No, thank you, my lord. I really have come to discuss a matter of urgency, and I thank you for your concerns regarding my family. They are all well," Talbot replied.

"Oh, do tell, you sound serious, Percy."

"Yes, my lord, it is a grave matter."

"Then you must continue."

The two men sat on solid oak chairs with velvet seats and matching velvet padding on the armrests. Talbot allowed his eyes to wander around the solar while he thought of what to say the old lord.

The solar was an octagonal shape, with every second wall holding a large window, allowing light into the room regardless of the sun's position. Yellow curtains hung, draped in perfect symmetry. The floor was covered by a huge red carpet with emerald green patterns carefully weaved around the edges. A golden chandelier swayed gently above them as a draught blew into the room. A disturbed cobweb broke directly above the young captain's head prompting him to begin speaking.

"I have come to discuss what I feel is the wrong decision to have been made by the admiralty."

"Oh, I see, and what is that?" Lord Perceval asked with a puzzled look on his old, wrinkled face, which looked even older underneath his powdered grey wig.

"That the pirate and traitor, Francis Fletcher, has been pardoned for his crimes!" Talbot answered sternly.

"I see." Perceval nodded. He carefully thought about his following words but then decided to be as direct as possible. As far as Perceval was concerned, the trial and the debacle were over. "He had a fair trial. I see no concern for you in this matter."

"I don't understand, my lord, why no one thought to ask me to speak as a witness," Talbot declared frustratedly.

"Well, I am not certain that you actually witnessed anything. I know you captured the man, and I have learned that you sank his ship without him putting up any fight at all and then sent your men to pick him up from an island in the Mediterranean. I believe, Percy, you displayed some masterly seamanship to give him a full broadside while his ship silhouetted against the rising sun, and you were unseen in the dark western sky. Well done to you, Captain," Perceval complimented the captain.

"Yes, I did, my lord, but I also chased across the Atlantic to capture him."

"And did you witness any acts of piracy during your chase?"

"No, sir, but—"

"—but at the trial, Captain Fletcher gave us a satisfactory version of events, such as how he received orders to attack French shipping crossing the Atlantic during the war and was still at sea when the Treaty of Paris was signed. Therefore, he did not know about the peace. That's nothing unusual. Then a British sloop found him in the Atlantic—"

"...Which he fired upon and fled to the American colonies," Talbot interrupted angrily, stamping his fist onto the chair's arm.

"When questioned about the incident, he informed us that he believed it to be a rouse. The French captured many British ships during the war by lowering their flags and raising a British one. Believing they were French coming in for an attack under false colours, Fletcher fired first. He did significant damage to the sloop, and yes, he fled to the colonies, attacking as many French ships as he could along the way. The sloop also sailed for the Americas, where the governor of Carolina heard the Captain of the Sloop's story and decided to issue an arrest warrant for Fletcher and his crew. When the *Sealion* arrived in several ports, Fletcher left with haste because he realised he was a wanted man. As soon as you got wind that Fletcher had been outlawed, I heard you raised your anchor and joined in the search?"

"Yes, my lord, that is true."

"You left Kingston and discovered him somewhere near Nassau?"

"Yes, the old pirate capital, sir. I feared he was trying to reignite the old republic."

"Well, it was very thoughtful and diligent of you to consider such things. But it has been forty years since we crushed the republic in Nassau. All the old pirates are dead, save Ann Bonny, but no one has heard from her in years. The pirate republic died with Blackbeard and Jack Rackham."

"Yes, my lord." Talbot calmed himself and slumped into his chair.

"I know you have your personal quarrel with Fletcher and that is one reason why we did not call upon you to speak at his trial; his trial had to be fair."

"And what about his crew, my lord?"

"Well, Mr Woodfield, his carpenter—"

"—Woodland," Talbot corrected the aged man.

"Mr Woodland was very sincere. He did not leave his captain's side for fear of unemployment. It happened after the last war we had with the French. Many of our sailors were without work once the war was over, as we did not need them anymore, so they turned to piracy. But not this time. We've hopefully learned that lesson. And then there was the foreign fellow. I did not give him much thought, a Bohemian-Habsburg on the run. Fletcher vouched that he could not be a traitor as he was not one of the king's subjects. However, he helped Fletcher disrupt the French shipping, so we rewarded his loyalty to the British cause by pardoning him from whatever he was actually on trial for."

"So that's that then. Francis Fletcher can steal one of the king's ships and walk away a freeman," Talbot grumbled angrily.

"Absolutely. And as First Lord of the Admiralty, speaking to you, one of my ship's captains, I expect you to obey your orders, as you always do, and drop the matter. It is over." Lord Perceval looked austerely at Captain Talbot.

"Yes, my lord. If those are my orders, I must obey, but I insist in my heart that it is the wrong decision."

"My decision and that of the board is final." The old lord smiled patronisingly.

Talbot huffed and sat in his chair, staring at a painting on the wall. He was no expert, but this was an unmistakable great Renaissance work of art. It had baby cherubs, naked with tiny wings, flying through dark clouds carrying a three-mast ship into the setting sun. A figure of Christ holding out his arms as if he were welcoming the vessel and her crew into heaven stood with a halo. Equally impressive was the large frame, painted gold and decorated with different variants of flowers, all crawling around the masterpiece. Underneath, in black letters on a golden background, read the words *Repent the Verses*.

"Do you like the painting?" Lord Perceval asked, breaking Talbot from his gaze.

"It's wonderful," Talbot smiled as he answered.

"Yes, one can stare at it for too long and still not understand it. Do you know how I came to own this great work of art?"

"I do not, my lord."

"It was Molly's parents. To thank me for freeing them from slavery, they had a vast whip-round from everyone they could think of, from the kitchen staff to my friends with the Navy and in parliament. With my wife's help, some people would never have cooperated with formerly enslaved people, but they deserve the credit for it—a wonderful gesture of thanks."

"I had no idea," Talbot commented. "What does it mean, *Repent the Verses*?" he asked.

"That is something I have no idea about," Lord Perceval laughed. "However, I am famished, and I assume you are too. Will you accept my offer to stay the night?"

"I will, my lord. As you said, we can discuss your travels with my late father."

"Splendid, I already had the kitchen staff prepare the ducks. We'll dine in the small hall, just the two of us." Lord Perceval slapped his knee and raised himself to his feet.

The small hall was well-lit, with lanterns edging around the stone room. Paintings of former sea-faring folk lined the walls. Sir Francis Drake, Sir Walter Raleigh and many others whom Talbot felt slightly ashamed of not knowing who they were. In the corner was the relatively new painting of his father, Adam Talbot.

"I see my father made it onto your wall of famed sailors," Talbot said as he sat down in his place at the table. Lord Perceval sat at the head of the table and sipped a glass of claret.

"His place is well deserved. We had many adventures together in our youths, your father and I."

"Yes, he told me many of them."

"And you're now racking up a good list of your own adventures. I'm so glad to have seen you grow into a man proudly following in your father's footsteps. I hope you, too, shall have a portrait next to his one day. But you must earn it. Tell me, dear boy, if the admiralty keeps you in command of the Dolphin and said you could go anywhere in the world, where would it be?" Lord Perceval asked.

"A most interesting question, my lord, and actually, it coincides with a request I had intended to put to you."

"I am listening intently," Lord Perceval muttered as he took another sip of claret.

"On my last voyage, where I captured Francis Fletcher, we came across something interesting: an uncharted island in the Mediterranean."

"Uncharted in the Med? Impossible!" Lord Perceval showed interest, chewing on duck meat.

"Yes, it was most odd. I believe I have cause to return to it. I departed the island rather hastily, eager to bring Fletcher home as my prisoner, but others from his crew may still be on the island."

"We have British sailors stranded? We must fetch them back, absolutely," Perceval agreed.

"And the other thing is that my captain of marines, Dawson, and one of his sergeants went ashore and reported several strange happenings. It is inexplicable to nature and somewhat intriguing enough for me to want to launch an expedition. Firstly, of course, to rescue our stranded men, and secondly, to find out about the island."

Lord Perceval had a frown grown across his old face. His white eyebrows pointed inwards and his eyes had become dark and severe.

"Tell me about this island," he said, more like an order than a question. Talbot spoke for a full hour, explaining what the marines and Fletcher had reported to him. He told of the waterfall and snake-shaped rocks, which had the power of hypnosis. Reluctantly, he told of how Fletcher had managed to outsmart Sergeant Walton and forced them to stare into the flames, revealing the crimes of their pasts. When the captain had finished, Lord Perceval had nearly polished off the whole bottle of wine, and the duck had already been devoured.

"So, you see," Talbot spoke with food in his mouth, "that is why I want to return." He swallowed his last mouthful of duck, put down his cutlery and waited for a response.

"Well, I must declare that this is a most interesting request, and you seem keen to go. On the morrow, I will make plans to see that your request is received at the admiralty."

"Thank you, my lord."

"However. Now that you have revealed this strange discovery, I wonder if I may press you to lengthen your stay with me in my castle?"

"For what reason, my lord?"

"I would like you to meet someone. A friend of mine, maybe you have heard of him. A scholar by the name of Mr Gale."

"I do not know the name, my lord."

"Mr Gale is a man who has studied many ancient books and has made many discoveries. He even discovered an Inca pyramid once in his younger days. I wonder if he would know anything about your island. If there is one man who would be able to shed some light, I am certain it is he."

"I say, I am most eager to meet with the man," Talbot spoke excitedly.

"I believe he will be just as eager to hear what you have told me. I shall depart first thing in the morning. You may remain here in the castle grounds until my return."

"How long will it take, my lord, I wish to see my wife and children?"

"A day or two. He lives in Wiltshire, so not too far. But it is better to fetch the man myself than to send for him. He is a quiet man who does not like to travel unless necessary and only trusts familiar faces. He is a strange man but a good one. Now, I shall retire to my chamber and be gone before you wake, as I have an early start. I trust you are comfortable in your quarters?"

"I am, my lord."

"Excellent. The castle is emptier than in years gone by, but Molly and Mr Riddell will be here should you need anything, and the kitchen staff are excellent."

"Thank you, my lord. I bid you a safe journey and wait for your return."

They retired to their bedchambers, and as he said he would, Lord Perceval was gone before Captain Talbot had woken the next morning.

Chapter 6

Isabella Talbot Held a candle by its brass holder and squinted as she neared the window. The reflection of the dancing flame spoiled her view of the dark outdoors. She had closed the front gate, locked the stables and barred the front door as she did every night. Living alone while her husband, Captain Percy Talbot, sailed the seas had made her diligent with the security of their family home in Hampshire. Upstairs, their children Edward and Estelle slept soundly.

"Just the wind," she sighed as she returned to finish cleaning the kitchen.

The house was an old thatched cottage with white walls and wooden beams. It was crooked but cosy and appeared warm from the outside, where the light of the candle shone brightly in the night. One could see white plumes rising from the chimney.

Francis Fletcher stood holding the reins of his newly purchased Welsh cob, which he'd named Kingston. She had proven to be a fine horse in the few days since he'd bought her, but she whinnied loudly, with which Fletcher was displeased. The candle he had just seen approached the window again, and then, Isabella's face leaned towards the diamond-leaded glass panes, causing them to steam as she breathed.

She left the candle in the holder, and a few seconds passed before Fletcher heard the door's bolts and then the sound of a key turning. The heavy wooden door swung open.

"Who is there?" she called into the darkness. "I'm armed!" she warned. Fletcher remembered her voice, which sent a warm feeling through his body as fond memories of the girl he'd once loved quickly reemerged. He watched her standing on her toes, trying to peer over the head-height hedge as she scoured the surroundings. She looked older than he remembered. She'd aged with the years, and the burden of motherhood had not been kind to her looks, but she still was worth something to Fletcher's eyes. He paced forward slowly.

"Who is it?" Isabella asked again. Fletcher continued to the wooden gate, leaned over and lifted the hook which kept the entrance secure. He urged Kingston forward by gently tugging on the reigns and then stopped as he came to a shadow cast by the house against the bright crescent moon. He left Kingston to stand alone, stepped into the hallway's light, raised his head and removed his hat, revealing his face.

"Good evening, ma'am!" he said. He was unsure if she recognised him at first, but suddenly her eyebrows raised from a suspicious frown to a look of shock and surprise. Her mouth gaped open and she stood speechless in the doorway. Fletcher looked into her eyes, also lost for words.

"What are you doing here?" she finally spoke.

"Are you surprised to see me?" He smiled, hoping to force her to smile, too, but it hadn't worked. She was certainly surprised; however, she did not appear pleased to see him.

"Francis, why are you here?"

"Well, I thought I'd take a chance to see if an old friend was home," he said with an arrogant grin.

"In the middle of the night? The children are asleep and Percy—"

"—has gone to see Lord Perceval so that he can complain about my pardoning," he finished the sentence for her.

"How do you know that?"

"Oh, Isabella, you should know me better than that. I can read his face like a page of the bible. May I come in?"

Fletcher and Isabella sat at the kitchen table, lit by the glow of several more candles and the roaring fire, which compensated for the cold outside. She still did not know what to say to her former lover and could not understand why he had come.

"So you knew Percy was not here?" she questioned him as he continued to smile at her.

Fletcher puffed out his cheeks and released air, slowly leaning back, creaking the wooden chair.

"He was so eager to see me hang. Did you see his face when they pardoned me at the trial, declaring I was not guilty of piracy? It was priceless." Fletcher smiled. Isabella did not smile. Instead, she stared angrily, raising the right side of her lips as she did not take kindly to Fletcher mocking her husband.

"That is my husband you are making fun of, Francis," she said and folded her arms.

"I beg your pardon, but he was so desperate to see my neck snap that I could only laugh when he heard that I was a free man. You know he did not even capture me, though he takes the credit."

"Well, you know how it goes. The ship's captain is the one to whom the victory can be attributed," Isabella answered, confronting him.

"No. Percy only sunk my ship. I admit it was masterly how he crept up on me in the dark like that. It was my mistake, though. I thought we'd lost him in the night, but I underestimated him."

"So he's beaten you twice?" Isabella took her turn to mock and refer to the duel the two captains had fought in their younger days.

"Ha. This time, I was not drunk, and until I was finally captured, I did not even know that it was Percy as my pursuer. Right across the Atlantic, he chased me. I thought I'd lose them in the Med, but they kept coming. Then, one morning, I was taken by surprise. The *Sealion*, or *Blunderbuss* as I'd renamed her, sank with only myself and three crew surviving. We managed to get to a nearby island where your husband sent his marines to fetch me. Bloody coward did not even come for me himself. Yet he wants to take the glory, typical Percy."

"And so he should take the glory. He's beaten you," Isabella remarked. Fletcher chose to ignore her stubborn defence of her husband's victory.

"And here I am, no ship, no crew, nowhere to go," Fletcher stated.

"I see you kept your commission. You still wear a captain's uniform," Isabella observed.

"Yes, but I doubt they'll give me a command anytime soon. I'm still on full captain's pay, though." Francis ran his fingers through his long black hair and slouched. "But the war is over. What shall we sailors do with ourselves now that we've no French ships to sink?"

"You can always go home, Francis!" Isabella bluntly put to him as she folded her arms again.

"Lancashire is a world away. I have no love of farms and the surrounding poverty."

"You've never loved anything other than the waves, Francis."

"I loved you once!" he threw back at her, hinting that he still held his grudge.

"And my feelings for you were deeper than all of your oceans, but you belong at sea. It's the reason I chose Percy over you. You know that, don't you?"

Isabella asked, desperately trying to hide the uncomfortableness she found this conversation becoming.

"Oh, I thought he won a duel?" Fletcher scoffed sarcastically.

"I can't possibly have married you, Francis. Even if you had both fought the duel properly and you had won. You're married to the sea, your boats and every whore in every land you've ever been. You've undoubtedly got a hundred illegitimate children swimming up the Nile, down the Amazon and every port in between! Percy Talbot was never like that. He does not crave the adventure that you do. The war is over and he swears his time at sea is finished. We shall spend the rest of our days together, happily raising our children."

"Are you sure they're his?" Fletcher remarked. Isabella stood up and walked around to the other side of the table. She stopped and stared at the man who had insulted her unforgivingly, raised her right arm and slapped his cheek hard enough to turn his face and leave a red imprint. She sat back down and scorned him with her fiery eyes.

"I'll never make that mistake again!" she spoke with venom. "And neither will you!"

"Yes, I forgive you for turning my cheeks red." Fletcher managed to find humour in the incident.

"Not the slap, Francis. You deserve that. I shall never commit adultery again, especially not with you!" She raised her voice.

Fletcher sat back on his wooden chair and puffed his cheeks again before deciding to change the subject. "Your husband is so desperate to make a name for himself. I suppose being the man to capture me, Francis Fletcher would have achieved that for him. But I have escaped death again and his name remains below deck, unheard. He's gone to see Lord Perceval to convince him to reverse the decision, but it won't happen…"

There was a rustle outside, and before Fletcher could finish his sentence, they could hear Kingston's hooves on the cobbles.

"Who's outside?" Isabella asked.

"Oh, that's probably Sholim," Fletcher answered.

"Who is Sholim?" Isabella worriedly raised the pitch in her tone.

"He's my companion. I rescued him from Barbary pirates. He's sworn to stand by me indefinitely. At least, that's what I think he said. He's not so good at English."

"Is he from the Barbary states?" Isabella asked.

"No, he's a Bohemian-Habsburg on the run for supporting a protestant rebellion in Prague." Fletcher was speaking far too casually for Isabella's liking.

"Well, honestly, Francis, you never fail to surprise me. Truthfully, it is good to see you well, and I am sincerely glad they did not hang you, but you must leave. I cannot have you here sitting at my table while Percy's children sleep upstairs. And this, bo-humanian-barbarian or whatever he is skulking outside!"

"Bohemian-Habsburg," Fletcher corrected the frustrated woman.

"Yes, that," she sighed.

"Well, I had to see you. I knew I could clear my bad name with the admiralty and the public, but I had to clear it with you. And…"

"And what?" Isabella rolled her eyes.

"We've got nowhere else to go!"

"Go home!"

"Lancashire is many days ride away."

"Do you not have officer's quarters somewhere?"

"Yes, but even so, Sholim does not."

"Where have you been staying all this time?" Isabella asked, showing her exasperation.

"Until the end of the trial, we were in cells!" Fletcher answered.

"And since the trial?"

"Anywhere, really. Inns mainly," Fletcher answered with a glum tone.

"You mean whore-houses!"

"Well, I had to show Sholim a good time. I'm an ambassador for our country!" Fletcher again managed to find an amusing comeback.

"Then, out of the kindness of my good heart, you may sleep in the bloody barn!" Isabella's voice had grown angrier, but allowing him to sleep on the premises was considered a victory for Fletcher.

"The barn, you say? That sounds wonderful!" he smirked.

"And your friend, he can sleep there too but be gone in the morning, for goodness sake!"

"What about Sholim?"

"I just said he could sleep in the barn too."

"Oh, I thought you meant Kingston, my horse!" Fletcher continued to joke.

"Francis!" Isabella grew impatient with him, but she knew what Fletcher was like and could not bring herself to cast him away, and Fletcher could see that she was hiding a smile behind the frown.

"Fine, the barn it is. For breakfast, I'd like some roasted tomatoes with cheese and—"

"—for breakfast, you'll be bloody gone!" she said and pointed to the front door, knowing that he already knew where the barn was.

Chapter 7

Two nights went by quickly for Captain Talbot, as he enjoyed the comforts of Enmore Castle almost all to himself. Only Mr Riddell, the porter and garden caretaker, occasionally wandered the long corridors and dark passageways. Molly kept to herself apart from when she came to find the captain to ask what he would like for his meals.

He tried to speak to her, but she seemed distant and uninterested in conversing with her childhood friend than he had hoped.

They had spent many years as children running through the gardens and playing amongst the orchard's apple trees. Molly had been born in the castle, but her Jamaican parents had been rescued from slave plantations by Lord Perceval. He had been in Jamaica when news from England came to inform him that his father had passed away, and he was recalled to England to take up his father's title. He took the two slaves with him after they had saved his wife from falling to certain death from cliff tops that overlooked the Caribbean Sea.

One windy afternoon, while taking a stroll along the top of the cliff tops, Lady Cecilia Perceval had tripped on her skirt. A heavy gust had blown by miraculous misfortune, and Cecilia stumbled, tripped and eventually rolled over the cliff's edge. If her hat had not fallen and blown up into the air, then a slave named Sebastien, who was working in a nearby plantation, would not have found her. As luck would have it, Sebastien had seen the hat floating through the sky; realising from its pink ribbon that it was a lady's hat, he became uncharacteristically concerned for the whereabouts of its owner, as it was so close to the cliffs. As the kite-like headwear swooped below the cliff's edge, he dropped his tools and ran the fifty metres to where the hat had disappeared. Several of his guards began to shout for the man to return to his post, but Sebastien continued running. Fearing he was trying to make an escape attempt, they opened fire with their muskets. Accuracy notwithstanding, the guards were left with little choice other than to give chase, only catching up with him once he had reached the cliff's edge and was pointing to something below and shouting in his broken English.

Meanwhile, a woman from the adjacent field, Lucinda, had seen her husband, Sebastien, being chased by guards and was afraid they would kill him if they caught him. She had also decided to drop her tools and sprint after them, prompting her own guards to give chase. They were also too slow for the slave girl and could not catch her before she reached her husband. Eventually, Sebastien and his wife held each other tightly at the edge of the cliff with four guards pointing bayoneted muskets at them. They shouted obscenities accompanied by instructions to return to their posts or take more lashes than they would already receive.

Sebastien, clasping his wife Lucinda tightly, tried to explain that a woman behind them was clinging for her life on little more than a clump of grass and a stone that could fall at any second. One of the guards edged closer to take a look and witnessed Lady Cecilia Perceval was only a few seconds away from certain death. The guard, fearing that she was already beyond the reach of his help, lest he should plummet too, ordered Sebastian to help her.

With little choice, Sebastien lay flat on his stomach and reached his long arms down towards Lady Cecilia, who was in fits of tears. Sebastien edged closer and closer until he couldn't go any further, or he, too, would fall. Lucinda decided to sit on her husband to weigh him down, but her acting without permission awarded her a musket butt in her face from a guard. Sebastien spoke encouragingly to Lady Cecilia, convincing her to let go of the grass with one hand and make a reach for his hand. She did and Sebastien could drag her back to safety. As soon as Sebastien pulled her over the cliff, a guard gave him an enormous wallop with a musket.

To the guard's surprise, Lady Cecilia came to Sebastien's defence and demanded the guard issue her rescuer an immediate apology. She then took the names of all four guards and later protested to their company commander that they receive punishment for cowardice in not rescuing her themselves. She insisted that further punishment be given to the guards for treating both Lucinda and Sebastien cruelly and unfairly while they were merely trying to save her life. All four guards received six weeks of half rations and no pay.

Upon hearing how the two slaves had shown courage and disregard for their own safety, Lord Perceval wished to thank the married couple and visited them the next day on their plantation. Appalled by seeing that Lucinda had a broken nose, Lord Perceval invited the pair to accompany him for breakfast in his private quarters. During the meal, he was so pleased with them for their good nature and heroic deeds that he felt they deserved more of a reward. He subsequently invited them to accept lodgings in the castle at Enmore and told them that they would no longer be enslaved but instead, they were to be staff.

Within a year of arriving in England, Lucinda was pregnant and gave birth to a baby girl who they named Molly. Sebastien and Lucinda were forever grateful to Lord Perceval until their deaths shortly before the war with France had broken out, leaving a teenage Molly to reside in the castle as an orphan.

Captain Adam Talbot, a close friend of the new Lord Perceval, had visited on many occasions, bringing his son Percy. That is how Percy came to know Molly, and he had been fond of her friendship, even though she was Jamaican and her parents had been slaves and had strange practices and customs of their own, which had at first frightened him. They were now both grown adults and it bothered Percy that she acted as if she were trying to keep her distance.

Maybe it is I who has changed, Percy thought to himself as he watched her bow her head and walk away after taking his breakfast order in the small hall.

After the captain finished eating his breakfast of eggs, bread and cheese, the highly anticipated Lord Perceval returned with his aged friend, Mr Gale.

"Lord Perceval will see you in the solar now, sir." Molly came to the breakfast table of the small hall to inform him.

"Thank you, Molly. I will surely inform Lord Perceval that you have been an excellent host in his absence." He attempted to start a conversation again, but Molly curtsied and walked away, showing no interest.

Lord Perceval and Mr Gale spoke too quietly for Captain Talbot to hear their conversation when he entered the solar. He studied Mr Gale as he approached the two elderly men. He was wearing a cloak, a blend of white and grey reaching to his ankles. His shoulders were hunched and his face was round with squinted eyes. His jaw was slightly to the side, probably due to the man's age, and he breathed heavily with a wide-open mouth as if he were out of breath, displaying several gaps where his teeth had fallen out.

"Aah, my good man, Captain Percy Talbot, I have the privilege to introduce you to a most welcome friend, Mr Gale," Lord Perceval spoke as Captain Talbot crossed the red carpet of the solar.

"It is an honour, Mr Gale." Talbot bowed as he met the short and funny-looking man. Mr Gale did not answer or change his facial expression. He looked

Talbot up and down, muttered something inaudible under his breath and took something from beneath his cloak. He slammed down a heavy package tied with string on the table, causing dust to fly up in all directions.

"Do you know your ten commandments?" Mr Gale asked Talbot in a voice that was more like a husky growl than an ordinary tone.

"You'll find I have sound knowledge of bible studies, Mr Gale," Talbot responded quickly, somewhat taken aback by the question.

"And have you prayed this morning?" the old man grumbled at him. The captain was unsure where this was going, and a confused look grew.

"What is this, a witch trial?" Talbot laughed. Lord Perceval was bemused.

"Answer Mr Gale, Percy," Lord Perceval ordered.

"I must admit that I have not prayed this morning, but I shall," Talbot confessed.

"What do you know of the New Testament, Captain?" Mr Gale put his third question out for Talbot to answer.

"I know the four gospels, the story of the nativity, I know of Jesus Christ the saviour and many of his miracles. I can recite the crucifixion story almost by heart. What is all this about?"

"Four gospels, you say?" His chest rattled with phlegm.

"Yes, the four gospels of Christ. Matthew, Mark, Luke and John" Talbot answered confidently.

"Then you already know too little."

"I have a bible at my home in Hampshire and I have one I take to sea with me, always in my cabin," Talbot added.

"You have not heard of the fifth gospel, though, have you, Captain Talbot?" Mr Gale husked.

"A fifth gospel?" Captain Talbot asked, surprised.

Lord Perceval leaned on his cane. "I told you, Percy, that Mr Gale is a scholar. He has studied many books of old and he knows many things that much of the world is yet to discover. It would do you well to listen to this man."

"Yes, sir. A fifth gospel, now I am listening. Please continue, Mr Gale," Talbot said.

"A fifth gospel, long removed from the bible, exists." Mr Gale untied the package, untying the string and the dusty brown paper wrapping. Three books, clearly older than anything Captain Talbot had ever seen, sat before him with a strange smell rising from the crinkly brown pages. Mr Gale opened the top book and began to run his fingers down the page. "I assume you do not read Aramaic?" he asked Talbot.

"You are correct, although I remember some Latin from my school days."

"Latin is no use here. For this, you must speak the language of Christ. The language of God himself. The language that was spoken to Mary by the angel Gabriel and of Judas Iscariot."

Talbot's spine tingled. The tone in which Mr Gale spoke sent an uneasy feeling right through him.

"Some called them wise men. Some called them kings. Whatever they may have been, they were Balthasar, Melchior and Gaspar. They each brought with them a gift for the newborn Messiah in Bethlehem. Can you recall to me what those gifts were, Captain Talbot?" Mr Gale asked as he pointed a finger in the air.

"Gold, frankincense and myrrh?" Talbot answered as if he was no longer sure of himself. He had become afraid to say the wrong thing and his heart was beating heavily.

"Good," Mr Gale said, causing Talbot to breathe a sigh of relief. "The frankincense and myrrh, both oils representing deity and death, may have been used by Mary and Joseph. It might be that they just tossed them into the sand. They could have used them for bargaining as payment for lodgings in Egypt once Mary and Joseph had fled King Herod; no one knows. But what of the gold, Captain Talbot?"

"I have not given it much thought; it never crossed my mind," the young captain admitted, looking towards Lord Perceval to see if he agreed.

"Exactly. It seems to have evaded most people's minds, Captain Talbot, and do you know why?"

"No, I do not."

"It is because only the fifth gospel speaks of it, and until a few moments ago, you were still in the belief that there were only four gospels!"

Talbot's jaw began to drop in disbelief at what Mr Gale was telling him. "Then Mr Gale," he asked, "what happened to the fifth gospel and indeed, what happened to Christ's gifts?"

"That is what I am about to tell you, but before I begin, I must hear from your lips that you will never speak of this day again. It will be as if it never happened. To know about the gold is almost a sin itself."

"You have my word, on my absolute honour Mr Gale. I shall not speak of this day or the things I learn," Captain Talbot promised, again looking to Lord Perceval for reassurance.

"Good, then I shall begin." Mr Gale turned another crooked page of the old brown book and blew away more dust. The pages looked as if they would crumble at any moment. They were stained, yellowish and brown. Their lettering was unrecognisable, Talbot assumed it was Aramaic.

"After the young saviour was born in Bethlehem, you will know that King Herod ordered all infants below the age of two to be murdered. Some escaped through hiding and some were sent away. It would be thoroughly impossible for Herod to catch them all. Not much is known about the messiah once Mary and Joseph fled Bethlehem. However, it is believed that they fled to Egypt. With them travelled a man who swore to protect the three fugitives, and his name was Amos, the bearer of burden. One night, before Joseph and Mary, with their newborn child wrapped and hidden in cloth, crossed the desert into the land of the Pharaohs, they were caught up with by four of Herod's men. Amos fulfilled his promise to serve the lord by protecting his son and held off the four men long enough for Mary and Joseph to run out of sight into a mild sandstorm. Amos was killed and the four soldiers of Herod never found Mary and Joseph. They searched the body of Amos and discovered that he was carrying gold."

"The gold was the gift from the wise men and Amos had offered to carry it for Mary and Joseph?" Talbot rightly guessed.

"That is correct. Next, the four soldiers made a pact. They would keep the gold and take it back to Joppa, a city some now call it Jaffa, where they would buy passage to the Roman lands and live the rest of their days as wealthy men. However, one soldier named Jagur slit the throats of his companions in their sleep and took all the gold for himself. He journeyed to Joppa alone and managed to find himself a ship that would take him across the sea. God was angry with Jagur and cast a strong storm in the sea that destroyed the boat and sent Jagur below the waves. He tried to swim, but the gold weighed him down and he refused to let go of it; he was so attached to it. Then, something happened that even God had not anticipated. Under the sea, Satan himself appeared before the drowning Jagur and decided to bargain with him. For Satan was pleased to see that Man had betrayed God, so he made an offer to Jagur: Surrender the gold to him and he would save his life."

"Why did Satan not just take the gold from Jagur?" Talbot asked.

"It is thought that the gold was not useful to the fallen angel, but to see a man so easily make a deal with the devil pleased Satan as he knew it would anger God further. That was Satan's prize, to see God betrayed by one of his own creations. And so, Jagur was spared as he was washed up on an island which Satan had created. Even the devil sometimes keeps his promises. The gold was stored on the island, and a gateway to Satan's lair was forged."

"You mean Hell, Mr Gale?" Talbot whispered.

"If you dare to speak the name of his dwellings, yes, that is what I mean. Behind a wall of fire and a rock shaped like a serpent's head lies the entrance to Hell, and just beyond the entrance lies What is known to the Knights of the Golden Gift as Jagur's gold. If you have sinned, you will pass the entrance through the flame. You will hear your sin whispered in the wind and you shall see it for yourself if you look into the fire."

Talbot turned white. Everything that had been described to him on the island where he had captured Francis Fletcher was now becoming more real. All that Dawson, Fletcher and Walton had told him now made sense.

"Who are these Knights of the Golden Gift?" Talbot asked.

"Jagur soon grew lonely on the island and pleaded with Satan for a woman. Satan granted his wish to him on one condition: that they multiply and their descendants would grow up to become future protectors of the gold and even the secret of its very existence. They call themselves the Knights of the Golden Gift. They are loyal to God's enemy and If anyone ever discovered the gold, the knights will hunt them down and slay them."

"God have mercy!" Talbot exclaimed.

"The Knights of The Golden Gift are the keepers of the secret and assassins to those who know," Mr Gale added.

"And are they many in number?"

"After one thousand seven hundred and sixty-four years, they have managed to reproduce in large enough numbers to have seen off many discoverers of the gold. The crusades, Viking exploration and even Mongol hordes saw many men silenced by death for chancing upon the island or hearing a whisper of its existence."

"Well, please forgive my rudeness in asking, but how have you managed to stay alive, Mr Gale? Unless these are just tales to frighten people away from something else?"

"I have never spoken of it to anyone. In my younger days, I travelled the known world many times. I was a missionary in North Africa until the Ottomans came and banished me. Then, I explored all of The Southern Levant disguised as a wandering Jew. I learned how to survive as a street rat on the streets of Jerusalem. Years later, a cardinal in Rome offered these books to me. He was interested in hearing about my travels. He told me never to speak of the things I discover in my readings, for these are the last surviving holy scriptures that keep the fifth gospel. For centuries, the Knights of the Golden Gift have searched for them. They destroyed the gospel to prevent people from searching for the gold. They destroyed them all except these three."

The three men intently stared at the open book before Talbot posed another question.

"And the Knights of the Golden Gift still search for it, even now?"

"They do. But I do not wish to become a victim of the knights and I suggest that if you don't want to be on their death list, you shall not speak of it either. But you have been to the island. Lord Perceval tells me that you discovered the island for yourself. That is most unusual, for the island only appears when it wants to be found. That is why you will not find it drawn on any naval chart."

"Yes, well, sort of. I sailed to the island but did not set foot on the island myself. I was chasing a pirate, a man named Francis Fletcher. He washed up on the island, so I sent my captain of marines to go and fetch him."

"And this man, Francis Fletcher, found the gold?" Mr Gale queried.

"He discovered the waterfall, as did my captain of marines and some of the other men. It is as you have described: A rock shaped like a serpent and a wall of fire that falls, crimes that can be seen in the past when the flame is looked upon. A voice that speaks your name and tells you of the commandment you have broken. However, about the gold, I am not entirely sure," Captain Talbot told Mr Gale.

"Then they might be safe," Mr Gale said as he waved his index finger at Captain Talbot. "And you will be if you keep your mouth shut."

"But, Mr Gale, Lord Perceval, why have you informed me of this information if I might be slain just for knowing it? I'd rather not have known!"

"You cannot guess the purpose of this knowledge being passed to you?" Mr Gale asked the frightened captain. Lord Perceval stepped forward, resting on his cane, seeing the question asked by Mr Gale as his cue to intervene.

"You have heard Mr Gale speak, Captain Talbot and you now know the truth behind the mysteries discovered by your own ship. And you already told me you wish to return to the island."

"But, I do not need to return to the island now. I wanted to make a discovery and claim the island for the throne of Great Britain and pick up any lost British sailors, but now I see there is no need!" Talbot suddenly became a quivering child, looking for an excuse to avoid what he knew he was about to be tasked with.

"You want to make a name for yourself, do you not?" Lord Perceval sternly asked.

"Yes, of course."

"And you know of something that you should not!"

"And that too, but…"

"Then I will grant you permission to return to the island and bring back Jagur's gold!"

"But my lord!" Talbot protested to no avail as Lord Perceval continued.

"As far as we know, not a single living soul other than we three know of our little discovery. Fletcher and Dawson may have been there, but they know not of the gold or what were the strange happenings. That means as long as you speak to no one and keep the mission in utmost secrecy, you shall be able to go to the island and retrieve the gold, and the Knights of the Golden Gift will remain unaware. When you return with gold meant for Jesus and present it to the king, who again will ever doubt his legitimacy to the throne? No Jacobite will dare rise again and never will we fear an enemy such as France or Spain. This will be the making of a Great British Empire and your name will forever shine in glory, not just here, but in the eyes of the almighty! God himself will surely reward you greatly for taking back from Satan that which was stolen from his son so many hundreds of years ago!"

"Then I must make preparations at once!" Talbot suddenly became excited, forgetting his fears.

"Tomorrow, we shall take my carriage to Portsmouth. You may summon your officers to return to the Dolphin and we shall create a false expedition to challenge Barbary pirates, causing some problems to our garrison in Malta or something along those lines, just to deceive anyone who might be suspicious. From there, you may begin possibly the greatest quest of all time. Greater than the search for the holy grail. Greater than the conquest of Jerusalem. The greatest event in history since the resurrection of Christ!" Lord Perceval said, holding his cane above his head triumphantly.

Chapter 8

Molly's screams could be heard all around the castle and the grounds. Piercing shrieks echoed through the walls of the eastern wing where the shrill awakened Captain Talbot. In only his pantaloons and a loose white shirt, he ran along the long stone-floored corridor and into the chamber of Mr Gale, where he found Molly standing over his bed, hysterically panting and crying out for help.

"He's dead!" she called out to Captain Talbot as he swiftly ran to the four-poster bed where Mr Gale lay. His throat was sliced open from ear to ear. Blood had formed a sea over his white bed sheets and black patches started to appear where the blood had begun to dry. It spilled everywhere, creating a puddle nearly covering the whole floor. Talbot looked down at his bare feet. They were smothered with sticky red liquid.

"Good God!" Talbot winced away and held his hand over his mouth. Molly ran to him and held onto his body as he wrapped his arms around the crying woman. He had nothing to say, so he just stood there staring at the body of Mr Gale and holding onto his childhood friend. Lord Perceval appeared at the door entrance. The sound of his cane on the stone floor alerted Talbot and Molly, who both turned in panic.

"What is all this noise?" the frail old man demanded. His eyes lit up and his face dropped wide open as he saw the corpse of his scholarly guest before him. "Out of there! Both of you!" the aging lord ordered. Molly ran out of the room, leaving red toe prints on the floor. She hid behind Lord Perceval and wiped her tears onto his sleeve as Talbot walked away, also leaving red marks on the stone.

"Who has done this?" Talbot whispered to the lord.

"Quickly, everyone into the solar. We must find Mr Riddell," Lord Perceval replied.

In the solar they sat around the same small table, stunned by what had happened. Molly continued to sob into a handkerchief. Many minutes of silence passed until Molly managed to calm herself enough to look Lord Perceval and

Talbot in the eye. All three of them took turns looking at each other. Obvious suspicion drifted between them all.

"Well, don't look at me!" Talbot broke the eery quiet air of the solar.

"I only found him, my lord. You must believe me," Molly whimpered with a terrified look.

"He appears to have been dead for quite some time. The blood on the sheets is almost dry and his body is stiff and cold." Lord Perceval stroked his chin.

"Where is Mr Riddell?" Talbot asked.

"I do not know. He often hides away in his quarters, in the gardens, or the kitchens," Lord Perceval answered. "And as for the kitchen staff, I have heard nothing today."

"Begging your pardon, my lord, the kitchen staff have yet to arrive," Molly informed her master.

"You mean they do not reside on the premises?" Talbot queried.

"No, Captain. I let them in every day," Molly responded quickly.

"So they have no keys to any of the castle buildings?"

"Only I and Mr Riddell keep the keys," Lord Perceval informed the captain. "Molly gets the key from Mr Riddell daily and opens the rear entrance to the kitchens every morning. But it is still early. They will not yet have arrived. We must send them away for the day when they come, but where is Mr Riddell?" Lord Perceval slammed his fist on the table angrily.

"The murdering swine!" Talbot exclaimed. "Why would he have done such a thing? I'll see the man hanged for this!"

"What makes you think he is a guilty man, Captain Talbot?" Perceval leaned forward and stared at the captain.

"Because...because he isn't here!" Talbot retorted, not understanding how Lord Perceval did not perceive it obvious.

"Mr Riddell is a man I have trusted with my life since you were just a babe in blankets, Captain Talbot. I do not suspect him of murdering one of my guests quite randomly."

"Is it random, though, my lord?"

"What do you mean?"

"I mean...I mean...well, isn't it odd? Coincidental?"

"Coincidental, how?"

"That Mr Gale arrives and tells us these stories of knights and assassins, keepers of a secret that somehow only he knows about and has never told anybody. He spills his clandestine knowledge to us, and the next day, he's dead, not only dead but clearly murdered?"

"You cannot for one second believe that Mr Riddell is one of these knights?" Lord Perceval asked in shock.

"No, but he may have taken payment or let them in during the night," Talbot responded.

Molly sat shivering with fright, showing her awareness that if Lord Perceval did not believe it to be Mr Riddell who had committed the murder, she was undoubtedly the number one suspect. Lord Perceval put his hand on hers to calm her.

"Fear not, Molly, I do not have you down as a cold-blooded assassin," Perceval said, forcing her to nod her reassurance to him.

"Then who has been here? Surely you do not suspect that I have done this?" Captain Talbot asked.

"No, Captain Talbot, I do not. I believe that if these knights have survived unknown for this many centuries, and as Mr Gale told us last night, they managed to keep out crusaders, Mongols, Vikings and everybody else since the birth of Christ, then they would not have trouble with my small castle walls. Somebody knew that Mr Gale had this knowledge of the fifth gospel of Christ and must have followed him here and heard him talking to us."

Molly suddenly sat upright. Talbot caught her eye. It dawned on him that she had not known about the fifth gospel because she was not in the solar the previous evening to discuss it with Mr Gale; however, by pure accident, he and Lord Perceval had let slip to her the motive of the killer's actions. Now she knew, too!

"A fifth gospel?" she whispered to the two men, who now realised their mistake. Lord Perceval and Captain Talbot reluctantly revealed the rest of the story to her. They decided she already knew enough to be a likely next victim should the assassins return. She looked terrified beyond words.

"And where are Mr Gale's books now?" she quivered her next question.

"Oh my goodness, the books!" Talbot stood straight up and rushed for the door. He ran up the spiral stairs of the castle into the room where Mr Gale lay dead. Talbot scoured the room, even squirmingly pulling up the blood-soaked bedsheets to see if the books were there. He reached his arms underneath the mattress but could feel nothing. The wardrobes, curtains, chest of drawers, every nook and cranny offered by the simple square room. Talbot wiped the sweat from his brow, staining his forehead with some of Mr Gale's blood. Molly and Lord Perceval appeared in the doorway.

"The books are gone!" Talbot told them. "They're not here. I've searched everywhere!"

"What are we to do?" Molly asked as another tear rolled down her cheek.

"We must leave here at once," Talbot announced.

"I am not leaving my family home!" Lord Perceval spoke, almost gasping as he began to pant at the preposterous idea.

"If you stay here, my lord, I fear you shall be next."

"I cannot just depart my family home with a dead body in one of the guest bedrooms. It would appear to whoever found Mr Gale that I had murdered him and fled the scene! Mr Riddell or the kitchen staff are bound to come looking for me sooner or later once they notice my apparent absence and they'll search the castle first! They'll find Mr Gale and I shall be branded a murderer!" Lord Perceval sounded almost as if he were breaking into a panic.

"Then we have to bury Mr Gale first. We'll dig a hole—"

"—you mean *you* will dig a hole!" Lord Perceval corrected, implying he had no intention of putting his back into any hard work.

"Molly and myself will dig a hole. We'll bury him with the sheets and Molly can scrub the floors while we prepare your carriage. I will ready the horses from the stables and we must flee. We'll travel with no banners or symbols, Lord Perceval. No one must know who we are."

"And just where are we fleeing to, Captain Talbot?"

"To Portsmouth. We'll stay in our naval quarters until we've readied the Dolphin. Then we will set sail. The Knights of the Golden Gift won't be able to catch us at sea, sir. Once we've set sail, nothing can stop us."

"And what am I to do with Molly? I cannot take a Jamaican woman into my quarters or onboard a ship! It is most absurd, Captain Talbot!"

"Then I can take her to my family home, where she can stay with my wife as my guest until we return."

"That sounds logical," Lord Perceval agreed. "Very well. We dispose of Mr Gale, clean this mess and travel to Portsmouth, leaving Molly at your home on the way."

"It is a small detour to my home in Hampshire, my lord, but it will only cost us a delay of one night, and my wife will be happy to accommodate us."

"Then we must make haste!" Lord Perceval said, rubbing his old wrinkled hands nervously.

By the time Captain Talbot and Molly had dug a grave hidden at the back of the apple orchard, Mr Gale's body had stiffened completely. He was incredibly cumbersome to carry and they had to stop and put him down awkwardly several times as they held him by his arms and legs through the castle. Occasionally, a splatter of blood dripped onto the floor, which Molly knew she would have to clean once he was underground.

They took the corpse, dropped him and the red-stained sheets unceremoniously into the hole and began covering him up. Once the mud was piled back on top of the hidden grave, they stamped on it in vain to make it look less like they had just buried a body there. It was almost laughable. It was too apparent to even the most dull-witted simpleton that this was a grave. Thinking quickly, Captain Talbot took a pile of cut grass and hay from the stables and covered the mound. The grass and hay still looked out of place, randomly piled in an orchard, but at least it no longer looked like a place where a secret dead body was buried.

"That'll do," Talbot told Molly. They were both exhausted, but they still had plenty to do. Molly wasted no time gathering hot water, mops and rags and cleaned the mess left behind in Mr Gale's room. She knew the kitchen staff would arrive promptly and was desperate to get the job done and be away before they came.

Captain Talbot and Lord Perceval readied two Cleveland Bay horses and a carriage. Talbot packed his cases and Lord Perceval loaded a trunk with his admiralty uniforms and any personal belongings he knew he'd miss, aware that he would be away for quite some time. When Molly had mopped as much blood as she could, allowing the room and corridors to look as close to what they had looked before Mr Gale's arrival, she gathered her few belongings.

They were ready to depart. Lord Perceval glanced at the castle, missing his lifelong home already. "Goodbye," he whispered as if it were for the last time. Indeed, he didn't know that it would not be. Captain Talbot took up the reins with Lord Perceval and Molly inside, and the carriage rolled away.

Chapter 9

Isabella and her two children, Edward and Estelle, ate warm and sweet porridge at the kitchen table. Just as Edward, the last to finish his breakfast, put his spoon into his bowl, the sounds of hooves on the cobbled country lane drifted into the open window.

"I wonder who that could be?" Isabella looked at the two children questioningly.

"It's Father!" Edward guessed excitedly.

"No, it won't be your father. He has gone to Enmore, he surely won't have returned so soon."

Edward and Estelle's faces were saddened as their mother dismissed their hopes.

"Come on, let us go and see for ourselves who comes on such a morning," Isabella instructed. Upon opening the front door and tiptoeing her eyes above the hedge, she saw two horses and a black unmarked carriage. She squinted her eyes, inched her neck forward and tried to make out who it could be.

"My goodness, children! It *is* your father!"

"Father!" Edward called out and ran to the gate.

"Papa!" Estelle shouted and followed her older brother to meet their father. After the carriage finally stopped, Captain Percy Talbot jumped and hugged his two children. He picked them up and spun them around, and they laughed joyfully at his return. Isabella walked towards them with a smile until her eyes met Percy's.

"You're early," she said radiantly, clearly pleased, with her hands on her hips.

"That I am," he answered. Before he could say another word, Isabella stepped forward and the four Talbots happily embraced each other.

"Have some water boiled, dear; we have some guests," Percy said after the family let go of each other.

"Guests?" she asked. Percy reached out his arm and opened the carriage door, waking the two sleeping passengers. They were both looking rather uncomfortable, tired and worn.

"My goodness, Lord Perceval, it is my pleasure," Isabella gasped. "And Molly… Why, sweet girl, I haven't seen you in many years, You must both come in at once."

They all sat inside the house, again around the kitchen table. Isabella boiled water, presented them with their finest cups and saucers and made tea. She could sense that something was not quite right. Molly had not managed to change her frown since arriving and there was something sheepish about her husband's mannerisms. Isabella did not like the atmosphere and decided to approach the situation directly.

"Right, there we are," she said as she poured herself the last cup of tea. "Now, Lord Perceval, It is always an honour to have such pleasurable company, especially in our own home. And Molly, a family friend for many years, knowing Percy when he was just a young boy, and Percy, my brave captain, I am more than happy to see you returned safely, as are our children, but who is going to be the brave soul to tell me what is going on? This does not appear to be some friendly visit."

On their journey from Somerset, Captain Talbot and Lord Perceval had stopped for a night at an inn. Conspicuously leaving Molly to spend the night in the carriage, they had discussed their plan over an evening meal. They had agreed on the yarn that they should spin for Isabella, and now the time had come for them to spin it, and they knew they had to spin it well.

"Isabella, my love." Percy volunteered himself to be the breaker of bad news to her. "It is with regret that I am here today with Lord Perceval, the Lord of the Admiralty, to inform you that even though the last time we spoke, I promised my time at sea had come to an end, that I must set sail one more time." He had never had to lie to his wife before and he felt guilty for doing so.

"But why?" Isabella put the question to Lord Perceval. "Why, my lord, must it be Percy?" She turned to Edward and Estelle, who had both stopped playing and had lent their ears to the conversation. Even as small children, they knew what their father was telling their mother. "Children, go and play outside. Molly, would you please take them?" Isabella politely asked Molly.

"Of course," Molly answered and took the children to play. When they were out of earshot, Lord Perceval began to speak.

"Mrs Talbot, I see in your eyes that you are despondent, but the admiralty faces a minor crisis. We have decided that Captain Talbot is the most qualified man and, given his recent exploits, the most well-suited of our captains to take on the mission. We must embark before the situation grows completely out of hand." Lord Perceval spoke with absolute conviction and supped at his teacup. Percy was impressed and suddenly wondered how often this lord had lied to other families about their men going to sea.

"A minor crisis?" Isabella repeated the words.

"Yes, Mrs Talbot, a minor crisis. But to prevent it from becoming a larger crisis, we must put to sea at once and crush the wrongdoers before it is too late."

"Then please, my lord, I beg you to tell me, who are these wrongdoers, and what is it that they have been doing so wrong that my husband, who promised never to sail again, is now leaving us to do just that!" Isabella almost began to cry, partly from sadness but also anger.

"A situation in the Mediterranean Sea. One of our armed cargo vessels, returning with goods from Corsica, has been seized by Barbary pirates and held for ransom. Now, Mrs Talbot, you know the Royal Navy never bargains with pirates, so we are despatching an armed frigate to take back the captured merchant ship by force. Your husband has just returned from the Med; he knows the seas well, so we have chosen him. He has a ship and a well-trained crew, and that is our decision."

Isabella's heart raced. "Did you say Barbary pirates?" she said, suddenly remembering that there was a man who had been rescued by Barbary pirates sleeping in her barn, along with her husband's arch-enemy, Francis Fletcher.

"Yes. Brutal people, they often capture European ships, steal the cargo and sell the crew into slavery in North Africa."

"But this time, they're holding the ship to ransom?" Isabella said, showing a sign that she may yet not fully believe what Lord Perceval was telling her.

"Yes…But this time, they'll get quite a shock when Captain Talbot arrives with HBMS Dolphin to settle the score!" Lord Perceval slapped his knee and gulped down more tea. "Isn't that right, Captain? You'll show them not to play games with the Royal Navy once and for all."

Percy was not as good at misleading his wife as Lord Perceval, so he nodded and sipped his tea.

"There we are then. He'll be back with you in two months, a hero, and then we will offer him a position at the training academy in Portsmouth. You'll never have to worry about him going to sea again!"

Talbot was surprised, for he had not rehearsed this part of the yarn. Isabella could see with her own eyes that something was not quite right, but she had no real choice other than to accept what they were saying. She would soon have to come clean about her own little secrets, and she knew her husband was not likely to take kindly the fact that Francis Fletcher had slept on the property.

"Very well," she said.

"Splendid!" Lord Perceval slapped his knee again. "Haha, how I would love to be young again and thrive on an exciting adventure. But I'm too old now, Mrs Talbot. My bones can't hack the waves anymore."

"I should think not," Isabella agreed, much to his disapproval. "My Lord Perceval, how long do you intend to stay with us?"

"We shall depart on the morrow, my good lady," he replied.

"Good, so may I show you to our guest bedroom where you may keep yourself? Humbly, our house is your house, so you may do as you please. No doubt you will need to speak to my husband in great detail over the next day, but you must also be tired from your journey, and I must plead with you to give me some time with my husband before he too departs."

"Absolutely, dear girl, of course." The old lord brought himself to his feet and followed Isabella up the crooked stairs and into a small guest bedroom with a single bed and window allowing only a partial ray of sunshine.

Percy stood waiting in the kitchen with an uneasy feeling of guilt hanging over him. He hated lying to Isabella like that, but he knew he had to do it to protect her. He was still baffled that Mr Gale had been murdered and nobody could explain who had killed him. If an assassin had managed to silence the man so easily in a castle, it would not be difficult for one of them to do the same here in his small cottage. He only hoped that his silence might protect Isabella, and misleading her into thinking he was on a different mission may lead the Knights of the Golden Gift away from her. That was all, of course, if the knights knew of their whereabouts. They may have managed to escape the castle and travelled to Hampshire unseen. It was the not-knowing that was causing suspense around Percy.

The kitchen door opened and there stood an unhappy-looking Isabella. "Come on, walk with me, you!" she ordered her husband. Walking down the garden path, she stopped and looked him in the eye. "What's going on?" She abruptly began an inquisition. "Who are these Barbarys? Why do you have to sail again, and what are you not telling me?"

"Isabella, I…"

"Out with it!" she scorned.

"I speak the truth. It is just that, well, it is a secret mission. I begged Lord Perceval to allow me to pass up the mission, but he would not allow it and said I should see it as a final attempt to make a name for myself, and I hate the fact that I have to break my promise to you, and I hate the fact that I lied, and I hate the fact that…"

"Shhh." She put a finger to his lips. He looked like he was the one who would break into tears and that had been enough to convince her finally. Although she was more than disappointed at hearing that he would still rather make his name than keep his promise to his family, she was now more certain he was telling the truth. No wonder he was upset with himself. He'd been forced to lie to his wife. Now, it was her turn.

"Look, Percy, if you wanted to go on another mission, you should have told me first instead of allowing me to believe you would stay on dry land forever. It means a lot to you, so I will let you go if this is the last time."

"I did not want the mission. I have been given orders. It is definitely the last time!" Percy said, not needing to lie to his wife about that and thinking it would not be her decision anyway; it would be the admiralty's.

"Then there is something I must tell you." She fidgeted nervously with her cuffs.

"Please speak freely."

"While you were away at Enmore…" She gulped as a lump began to appear in her throat.

"What is it?"

"*HE* is here."

"Who is *HE*?"

"*HE*!"

Percy was not sure who she meant. Was it a Knight of the Golden Gift? Was it Mr Riddell? What could she mean by *HE*?

Isabella opened the barn door, and there, fast asleep, lay the *HE* she referred to.

Percy's face became a dark cloud. His fists had clenched and his shoulders raised.

"What Is *HE* doing here?" His face turned red with rage and his nose began to curl like a snarling dog.

"Please, I only allowed him to sleep one night, but he stayed for two…"

"You allowed him? Isabella!" Talbot stamped his foot.

"Please listen—"

"You allowed that man, that pirate…that criminal to stay here?"

"You have to listen to me." Isabella put her hands together as if to pray.

"While my children slept and played, *HE* was here, with this pet gorilla he keeps by his side?" Percy growled, referring to Sholim, snoring away, grasping a liquor bottle and drooling in his sleep.

"Percy, please listen to me. I did not want him to come here, but he arrived two nights ago. I wouldn't let him in the house. I told him to sleep in the barn."

"Why? Why would you even give him that?"

"Because I am a Christian and this man needed shelter."

"Oh, don't give me that nonsense. He has his own home. He has plenty of places to be."

"Yes, but he arrived in the dead of night. I couldn't refuse a man a simple barn to sleep in at such a late hour."

The furious captain had heard enough. He strode vehemently to where Francis Fletcher was sleeping and kicked him in the buttocks. Fletcher woke suddenly and, in a mild panic, reached for his sword. The sword was not there, but Fletcher was still feeling for it. Hay dangled from his long, matted hair and mud had smothered across one of his cheeks. Stubble had been allowed to grow, giving Fletcher an uncouth appearance that would not have one guess that this was a captain in His Majesty's Royal Navy. His eyes searched the barn interior. It was clear to anyone watching that he was still drunk and unsure of his whereabouts. Talbot kicked him again, grabbed his loose, flapping shirt and raised him to his feet.

"You have exactly five seconds to get off my land, or I'll have you executed for trespassing!" he shrieked. He stepped towards Sholim and gave him an equally hard kick in the buttocks, waking him immediately. Sholim cried out something in his tongue, utterly incomprehensible to everyone else, and rubbed his eyes. His breath was foul and drool was still slimming down his chin. Isabella grimaced at the sight of the Bohemian drunkard.

"Good morning, Percy!" Fletcher said. "Though I've experienced less rude awakenings."

"Get off my land!" Talbot shouted.

"Now, come on, there's no need for that," Fletcher pleaded audaciously. Talbot swung a punch that cracked Fletcher straight in the jaw, forcing him to fall back into the hay like a plank of wood. Sholim immediately jumped to his feet and knocked Talbot to the floor by ramming his shoulder into Talbot's waist. They began to wrestle and roll over one another until Sholim gained the upper hand and pinned the captain to the floor.

"Take your hands off him!" Isabella screamed and ran over to Sholim, holding onto her skirt as she dashed across the barn. Fletcher realised that Talbot stood no chance against the giant foreigner and ordered Sholim to stop.

The three men sat on the barn floor, out of breath from the minor skirmish they'd had with each other. Isabella came to her husband's aid and asked if he was alright. He nodded before sending his eyes towards Fletcher.

"Why, in the name of God almighty, are you here, Francis?" he asked. Fletcher held onto his jaw. It would soon bruise where he'd taken the punch and he wiggled it to see if it still moved as it should.

"Had nowhere else to go," Fletcher uttered quietly.

"You've got a home; go there. For goodness sake, I shall not hide my utter dismay at the decision the admiralty made upon your release but then to find you here, alone with Isabella!"

"Have no fear, Percy. Your wife is ever faithful to you. That is why I resided in the barn these past two nights," Fletcher said. Isabella looked at Fletcher, grateful for his honesty and the compliment he had given her about her fidelity.

"Come on, all of you. Let's get you cleaned up. Then you can leave, Francis," Isabella said. "You will allow me the short time I have left with my husband before he departs to be spent actually with my husband!"

Talbot did not like Isabella inadvertently informing Fletcher that he would soon go away again. Fletcher appeared to pay no attention to the comment, so Talbot hoped she would not bring it up again.

They all walked away from the barn and towards the house. Seconds before reaching the front door, it opened from within. Lord Perceval stepped into the entrance and stretched out his arms.

"Captain Fletcher, it is a surprise. What brings you to this neck of the woods?" He smiled, which displeased Talbot even more. No one should be happy to see Francis Fletcher in Talbot's eyes.

"My goodness, Lord Perceval, what a pleasure to see you, sir!" Fletcher saluted and stood to attention.

"Come in, dear fellow, let's have a word or two," Perceval invited him in. This made Talbot even angrier, but he could not do much. Fletcher brushed past Talbot and Isabella into their home as if it were his own.

"You wait here, Sholim," Fletcher instructed his ever-faithful companion. He gestured with his hands and repeated slowly, ensuring he had understood, "Wait…here."

"Oh, would you please give Captain Fletcher and me a moment? Please forgive my lack of manners," Lord Perceval said to Talbot and Isabella, who were both standing in the doorway to their own home, now unable to go inside as Lord Perceval closed the door.

"Do something!" Isabella ordered Percy.

"Like what?"

"I don't know, be a man!"

"I can't argue against a superior officer and a lord!"

"This is our home, not his!" She folded her arms crossly.

Sholim, whose stench was unbearable, looked at the couple. Isabella looked back at him, uneasily wondering what that *thing* was doing here anyway.

Lord Perceval looked Fletcher up and down. "Got into a ruffle, have we, Captain?"

"Yes, sir," Fletcher answered.

"You do not have the appearance of a captain, yet I know you to be a good one. I still have not forgotten your heroic display at Quiberon Bay."

"For that, I give you my thanks, my lord." Fletcher smiled.

"The nation once thanked you; now, We almost had you hung as a pirate!"

"I am forever indebted to you for voting against seeing me hang at the end of the trial, My lord."

"Nonsense, Mr Fletcher, we could not hang a national hero. What will you do with yourself now? You've retained your status and rank, but it is hard for the Navy to find a use for you with no war and no ship."

"My intention, sir, was to get myself to Portsmouth and be given command of a ship."

"Oh, and where would you be taking this ship if given a command?"

"Well, my lord, it is yet of the utmost secrecy, but may I tell you about a discovery I made in the Mediterranean before my capture?"

Fletcher began to tell the story of his time on the island but was interrupted by the old lord, who informed Fletcher that he already knew. Lord Perceval told the story of the fifth gospel, the Knights of the Golden Gift, and Mr Gale's death. He explained precisely why they had travelled to Hampshire and told Fletcher everything, sparing no details. He spoke quietly and occasionally looked towards the window, afraid someone might be listening.

Percy and Isabella had become frustrated by the time the door opened again. Lord Perceval came out of the house first with a serious face. Fletcher stood above him, tall and grinning smugly.

"Have you quite finished in our home?" Isabella asked sarcastically.

"My dear, please accept my humble apologies. I know you wish to spend time with your husband before he leaves," Lord Perceval answered.

"Right, well, you can be on your way now, Francis," Talbot sternly told Fletcher. "And take this beast with you." He nodded towards Sholim.

"Well, actually, Percy, I am not sure if I can," Fletcher continued with his cocky smile.

"What do you mean?" Talbot asked.

"I mean, well, you're setting sail soon."

Talbot rolled his eyes, unhappy with Fletcher being within that knowledge. "Yes, what of it?"

"I am your new first mate!" Fletcher grinned.

Talbot immediately looked at Lord Perceval. "My lord, surely you jest. You cannot possibly expect me to sail with this man!"

"And why not? He has also just returned from the Mediterranean and knows the waters just as well as you," Perceval replied.

"May I remind you, my lord, that he came back on *my* ship because he'd lost his own!" Talbot spoke angrily.

"No, Captain Talbot, he came back on your ship because you sank his ship! He has been found not guilty of any crimes, kept his rank and expressed his wish to return to sea. Now, with no war and indeed no ship, it is difficult to find placement for him, so he came up with the idea of me allowing him to return to sea as your first mate!"

"But I have a first mate; Lieutenant Jenkins is my first mate," Captain Talbot protested.

"Lieutenant Jenkins will also be going with you. However, he will have to be your second mate. Won't you come inside, Captain Talbot, so that we can discuss this further?" Lord Perceval impudently invited Captain Talbot back into his home, leaving Isabella to stand outside with folded arms and a face full of anger.

"Do make yourself at home, Lord Perceval!" Talbot announced acrimoniously as they re-entered the kitchen.

"You have my gratitude for your kindness, Captain," Lord Perceval remarked.

They sat down at the table and began to discuss their plans. Lord Perceval started to speak, "Captain Talbot, I know you have strong feelings against this decision. However, it would be best if you allowed me to explain. All of our lives are in danger. Yours, your wife's, Molly's and even your children's lives are at risk. We are all under the watchful eyes and a genuine threat of the Knights of the Golden Gift. Just two days past, Captain Talbot, you will remember Mr Gale. You buried him in my apple orchard!"

"Yes, my lord, I understand," Talbot sighed, knowing the old lord to be correct in what he was doing.

"Captain Fletcher has been to the island. He has seen the fires and the serpent. He surely does not want to fall victim to the Devil's assassins." Fletcher stayed silent but shook his head. "Therefore, it is imperative that he goes with you to get this job done." Fletcher began to nod his head. His arrogance and his mannerisms were irritating Talbot. Lord Perceval continued. "We must order your entire crew and the marines who sailed with you last. It must be the same crew. You can only inform your officers of the real mission once you are at sea. Otherwise, the danger still lingers over us all."

Talbot began to think. With himself being away at sea, he would feel uneasy leaving Isabella alone with Fletcher on the prowl. Taking Fletcher with him would mean that he could no longer harass Isabella.

"Lord Perceval, I am willing to take Fletcher with me," he said.

"You are?"

"Yes. Now that he knows I am going away, I would rather have him with me. Then, at least, I know he is not here bothering my wife!" Talbot looked at Fletcher. "There can be only one captain on the ship. That will be me. I propose

Francis Fletcher shall be a Lieutenant for the mission, and I will refer to him as lieutenant Fletcher."

"I do not see that as necessary, Percy." Fletcher sat up.

"You will, from now on, refer to me by my rank. Is that clear, Lieutenant?" Talbot spoke down to his adversary.

"Clear. However, I am not a lieutenant. I am a captain," Fletcher spoke sternly.

"Not on board my ship!" Talbot insisted.

"Gentlemen, please," Perceval intervened before the two started at each other's throats again. "I must press onto both of you now the importance of this mission. It shall be victory or death, for this is not the French. This is not a Jacobite uprising or a Spanish fleet. We are going to the gates of Hell to steal back gold that was taken from our lord and saviour Jesus Christ, seventeen hundred and sixty-four years ago!"

"We, sir?" Talbot asked.

"No, I mean you!" Perceval replied. "And you two must be able to cooperate! I know you have history, but this means more. You are both captains. You shall both remain captains. Talbot, it is your ship and you will lead the mission, and Captain Francis Fletcher will obey your orders. Is that clear, Captain Fletcher?"

"Clear as day, my lord." Fletcher grinned.

"Good, now I am tired and I will rest. On the morrow, we ride for Portsmouth. We will summon your crew, Captain Talbot, and you will depart as soon as the Dolphin is ready to sail."

Chapter 10

"Good Morning, Molly," Isabella greeted her guest the next day. "The sailors have departed already. I am sorry they said they did not have time to say goodbye."

"And good morning to you, ma'am," Molly curtsied before stepping into the kitchen, where Edward and Estelle ate a breakfast of cheese and bread.

"You may dispose of the courtesies in my house, Molly. You may call me Isabella. You are our guest here while the men are away playing sailors."

"Thank you, ma'am. I mean Isabella." Molly giggled childlike as she felt she'd been given a new societal status.

"Honestly Molly, what is it with men? Can they not just simply live in peace? Percy promises me one thing, then does the opposite," she complained about her husband and offered bread and cheese to Molly, who graciously accepted but stood up to eat.

"I don't know. I never had the luxury of a man," Molly sighed.

"Oh, I do apologise. How thoughtless of me wittering on while others have suffered much worse."

"It is all right, ma'am. I have a good life thanks to Lord Perceval. You know he took my parents out of the plantations in Jamaica?"

"Yes, I know the story well. And you have rewarded him in kind with your service and dedication. You were born here, though, were you not?"

"I was born in Enmore Castle, ma'am. As a child, I often played with your husband when he came with his father to visit a younger Lord Perceval. And Fletcher, too. I always remember them being great friends, and then they both went off to join the naval academy together."

"Yes, that's when I met them both. Well, it took me, a woman, to come between them. Another reason for men to fight." Isabella rolled her eyes.

"And now they sail together once more. Let's hope they can bring back the gold." Molly took a bite of bread, oblivious to the implications of what she had just said.

"Gold?" Isabella put her hands on her hips. "What gold?"

"Jagur's gold, ma'am?" Molly said.

"Who is Jagur?" Isabella took a step closer towards Molly, and Edward and Estelle also stopped eating to listen to the imminent conversation that their mother was about to have.

"The man who stole the gold from the baby Jesus, ma'am," Molly said with a face of innocence as she had, now spilled information that had bypassed Isabella deliberately.

"Molly."

"Yes, ma'am."

"My husband and his first mate, Francis Fletcher, have been sent to the Mediterranean Sea to rescue a British ship and her crew that Barbary pirates have taken hostage. At least, that's what I have been told. I now feel that I have been lied to, and you knew the truth of their deployment." She picked up a knife and pointed it at Molly, jostling it up and down between her finger and thumb. "You had better tell me what is going on if you wish to remain a guest in this house!"

"Yes, ma'am," Molly agreed.

Molly stood the entire time as she explained the whole story to Isabella. Isabella chose to sit and put her head in her hands with her elbows on the kitchen table as she listened to the story getting wilder and wilder. Isabella, Edward and Estelle sat dumbfounded and silent when the story finished.

It was many silent minutes before Isabella chose to speak again.

"And now, Molly, there are assassins, killers, murderers, many in number, all going about cutting the throats of anyone who knows about this Jagur's gold?"

"Yes, ma'am. Just like Lord Perceval's friend Mr Gale."

"And that is why you've fled here in an unmarked carriage?"

"Yes, ma'am."

"So, you're not a guest. You're in hiding."

"Yes, ma'am." Molly began to play nervously with the tassels holding up her skirt.

"And my husband and Francis Fletcher have been sent to recover the gold, lying to me and everyone else about a British ship being held by Barbary pirates?"

"Yes, ma'am."

"And now my children are in danger?"

"And you too, ma'am," Molly told her. Isabella ran her hands over her eyes despairingly.

"MEN!" she quickly burst out. "What is it with men? They can't even set off on some insane adventure without lying to their wives first!"

A rustle outside forced Isabella, Molly and the two children to turn their heads towards the window. Instinctively, Isabella rose to her feet, rushed to the front door and put the heavy bar across it. It was undoubtedly just the wind blowing through the front hedge, but it had startled them all nonetheless.

"Molly, is your bedroom window shut?" she asked.

"It is, ma'am."

"Good. Estelle, Edward, did you open your bedroom window?"

"No, Mother, I left it closed," Edward replied. "Mother, I am frightened," he whimpered. "Will the Knights of the Golden Gift kill me?"

Isabella walked to her children and embraced them both. "No harm will come to us, do you hear me?"

"Yes, Mother," Edward answered, clearly not convinced. He was shaking.

"Estelle? Do you hear me?"

"Yes, Mummy," she said.

"Good. We are going to stay at Aunt Martina's." Isabella turned to Molly. "We have to leave. We will stay with my sister, who lives not far from here. If my children are in danger, then we must flee. You have no idea if these Knights of the Golden Gift have followed you here or if they are listening at the windows?"

"No, ma'am. I only know that the day after Mr Gale told your husband and Lord Perceval of the gold, he was dead the next morning and I found him. Lord knows who will be next!"

"Then we must leave and hope we are not followed." Isabella began to panic.

While Isabella sent the children to gather their belongings, Molly turned to her. "Ma'am, we can take your children to your sisters. I am quite certain that they shall remain out of harm's way. But you and I, we will not be safe. I have come from Enmore Castle. I may have been followed here and I fear there is only one safe place for us now."

"Where is that, Molly?" Isabella asked blankly.

"All those who have this knowledge of the gold will sail to the island. Fletcher, your husband and all of his crew. I wouldn't put it past Lord Perceval that even he intends to sail."

"Molly, if you suggest we join them, you are absurd. They won't allow women on ships. They certainly won't allow a former black slave girl on board. There'd be mutiny before they raised anchor!"

"What if they did not know of our presence?" Molly suggested.

"Stowaways?"

"What can they do if they find us on board and we're already at sea? They will not return to England without the gold for fear of the assassins, and your husband, the captain, will not exactly throw you overboard. No doubt he will be horrified, but what could he do?"

"And what about you?" Isabella asked.

"He won't harm me. Lord Perceval values my lifelong service to him; your husband knows this. They'll give us a cabin, tell us to be quiet and stay out of everybody's way until we reach the island. At least we'll be safe from the Knights of the Golden Gift."

"I cannot leave my children, Molly."

"Then they will likely find your body one morning before they, too, have their throats slit. Staying away from them might be the only way to keep them out of danger, ma'am."

The unwelcome comment frightened Isabella. She thought for a while before concluding that Molly was probably correct.

"You're right. We would be safe on the ship. And the further I am from the children, the less likely harm will come their way." Isabella felt a thrill. The prospect of a great adventure rose through her body. It was farcical that two women should stowaway onboard a Royal Navy frigate. The thought of joining a crew and embarking on a secret operation to locate and steal lost biblical gold excited Isabella.

"We've no time to lose Molly. Let's pack our things," Isabella instructed. In an utmost hurry, Isabella and Molly packed all their belongings into small brown portmanteaus, only enough for them and the two small children to carry.

The walk to Isabella's sister Martina's home was only three miles across several country lanes and one meadow. Isabella was constantly looking over her shoulder and stopping to search the horizon for people who might be following them. They'd come across one or two other people she knew and politely said "good morning" to them, hoping she was not giving away that she was more afraid than ever.

Upon arriving at her sister's house, Isabella was greeted warmly, but she declined to enter and told Martina that Percy had been summoned to London. She explained that her husband had told her he would be there for some time and wished his wife to be by his side. As the journey was too long and troublesome, she asked if it would be possible to have the children for some time until she returned. It was no problem for her sister, who was thankful for the company.

Isabella crouched down and whispered to Estelle and Edward that if anybody asked, they must tell them that their mother and their father were both in London. Never under any circumstances were they to mention the gold, the Knights of the Golden Gift, or the island in the Mediterranean.

With tears in their eyes, they said their goodbyes, and swiftly, Isabella and Molly departed, secretly for Portsmouth.

Chapter 11

It had taken a week for the summoned crew of the Dolphin to prepare the vessel for sea. The preparations had gone smoothly enough; Captains Fletcher and Talbot chose to stay out of each other's way, and as soon as it was announced that the ship was seaworthy, they cast themselves off.

Captain Percy Talbot balanced on the quarterdeck, inspecting his crew's fine work as the Dolphin raised her bow and slammed down again into the rough waves of the English Channel. He had to hold onto a line of rigging to keep himself steady. Behind them, England's coast had faded to a grey outline, which would soon not be visible because of the poor weather. Spray soaked the crew who gripped sheets and rigging, some eighty feet above the decks at the top of the masts. Cries were inaudible over the howling wind and the constant patter of heavy rain pouring down on them mercilessly.

"Stay true, Mr Laine!" Talbot shouted towards the wheel, which had three other crew members aiding the navigator in his struggle with the helm.

"Hold fast!" Fletcher cried out as he appeared over Talbot's shoulder from nowhere.

"Hold…Fast!" Talbot repeated along the upper deck to the crew, desperately clinging to what they could. He was not entirely sure why Fletcher had come to the upper decks, but he was particularly vexed by him giving out orders.

"I'll give the orders here, Francis," he yelled over his shoulder as saltwater and rain whipped into his face. Fletcher ignored him and called out again.

"Mr Ingham, heave-to on a close reach, trim the jib to windwards!"

"Francis, I give the orders here!" Talbot shouted at him again. Fletcher shook his head and he could barely open his eyes.

"Percy!" He almost broke his voice, shouting so much through the noise of the storm. "We need to push the bow down, or we'll lose steerageway!"

"We should have taken in sail, Francis!" Talbot called back.

"It's too late for that now, heave-to!"

Talbot knew Fletcher was right but could not bring himself to admit it to his face. He edged forwards along the upper deck until he was able to communicate with Mr Ingham more clearly to re-deliver Fletcher's order to heave-to.

The sky had turned dark grey, with frequent blue flashes of lightning illuminating the sunless sky above them. Up and down they went over the waves, occasionally rolling enough that the gunwales were beneath the surface of the angry sea for a few seconds until they were bowled over the other way. Unabating, they continued through the unyielding squall like a corkscrewing pendulum, which raised the hull out of the sea over mountainous waves before plunging back into valleys of water beneath them.

Down below on the mess deck, Lieutenant Jenkins was in charge. One of the cast-iron guns had slipped loose on the gun deck. He was able to hear and feel it above him. He climbed up to the gun deck to check it for himself. Instantly, it slithered towards him. He managed to slide himself out of its way before it smashed into another gun. Someone would have to secure it again; otherwise, it would create carnage. The cannon slid back across the entire deck as the ship heeled over. Jenkins ordered eight men of the gun crews to take control of the cannon before it did considerable damage. The able men did precisely as Lieutenant Jenkins instructed, ensuring they did the job quickly and efficiently, aware that this could be their death if they did not.

Holding onto each other as well as the fixed tables in the mess deck, Sholim and Woodland struggled to keep their stomachs in order. Pots, pans, cups, plates and other objects, including crew members' personal belongings, were flung around the deck aimlessly. The crew struggled to hold balance dodging random items flying about the place dangerously.

First, Sholim vomited yellow and red liquid stinking of bile and alcohol. At the sight of the spew combined with the stomach-churning motion of the ship, Woodland fetched up his last meal. Then Sholim took another turn before Woodland threw up his next offering. It went on for some time, each of them spewing whatever was left in their empty insides.

Fletcher and Talbot both enjoyed a storm. They knew that with an experienced crew and a strong ship, they would overcome the tyranny of the sea. The Dolphin and her well-trained workforce did just that and before long, the raging howls became a tender wind and the mighty billows turned to friendly waves that allowed them to sail at ease.

Talbot ordered the cooks to prepare a hot meal for all crew members and summoned the commissioned officers to the wardroom. He'd deliberately placed Fletcher at the far end of the rectangular table, hoping that the symbolism of the distance between them would not be lost on the other officers. Equally symbolic, Talbot had on his right Lieutenant Jenkins and his left Captain of Marines Dawson. Then came the ship's surgeon, Dr Brennan, and the ship's chaplain, Reverend Cunningham.

The cooks brought a fine meal of boiled salted meat, onions and pepper stewed with the ship's biscuits.

"Lobscouse, Delicious!" Fletcher excitedly exclaimed before diving into his meal without waiting for Reverend Cunningham to say grace. Fletcher's action prompted the other officers around the table to do the same, which annoyed Talbot greatly, although he said nothing and began to eat.

"Lieutenant Jenkins, who has this watch?" Talbot asked.

"Mr Ingham has the watch," Fletcher replied.

"Thank you, Mr Fletcher. However, I was speaking to Lieutenant Jenkins!" Talbot glared towards Fletcher.

"Yes, I assumed you had made a simple mistake. It should be a question for your first mate. Normally, this is Lieutenant Jenkins; therefore, I forgive your error, but you have your answer from me."

Talbot was furious.

"Francis Fletcher, in the presence of all these witnesses, I hereby relieve you of your duties as first mate. My new first mate will be Lieutenant Jenkins. You shall be a passenger if I am forced to take you on this journey. If you become a troublesome passenger, then I shall take you to Gibraltar and turn you over to be imprisoned in the fortress there."

"Captain Talbot," Fletcher calmly interrupted. "You have no authority to relieve me of my rank's duties. You do not outrank me, for I am a captain and have been given a special place as your first mate for this mission! Due to the nature of the mission and the fragility of its secrecy, I suggest you follow your orders to the letter as given to both of us by Lord Perceval."

Again, Talbot knew Fletcher was right but could not help but cringe at the thought. He had no choice but to accept Fletcher's words.

"Very well, the secrecy of this mission will now be revealed, but if I feel that you are in any way to jeopardise what we intend to achieve, then I will not hesitate to throw you over the side of the ship. I will happily explain to our admiralty that you became too much of a liability for me to allow you to remain on board!"

The room was silent. As far as the other officers in the room were concerned, they were on a mission to rescue a British ship held for ransom from Barbary pirates. Captain of Marines Dawson spoke first.

"What do you mean the secrecy of this mission? We have all been briefed, have we not?"

"I'm afraid not, Mr Dawson," Talbot replied. "Sadly, this time, the admiralty saw fit to deceive you from the truth until we were at sea."

"Do you mean to say we're sailing under pretences?" Reverend Cunningham questioned the captains, looking from left to right, not knowing which of the captains he should have asked the question to.

"Gentlemen, the matter at hand is somewhat more serious than a skirmish with some North African thieves," Talbot went on. "You see, there is no rescue mission."

"We can't let these scoundrels steal one of our ships. We must rescue her!" Dawson slammed his fist on the table.

"No, Mr Dawson, there shall be no rescue attempt. There is not even a ship for us to rescue. As I said, the admiralty deliberately misled you. The real mission is much more dangerous than anyone in this room could possibly imagine."

The atmosphere in the wardroom changed as if a dark cloud had entered, dimming the candlelit lanterns.

"Then may we press you for the truth, Captain Talbot?" Reverend Cunningham asked, mimicking the impatience of the other officers sitting around the table. Captain Talbot could see the keenness in their eyes. He glanced at Fletcher, who was staring at the table and stroking his chin. He knew the real reason they'd been sent to sea and was the only man at ease.

"Very well." Talbot lifted his glass and sipped wine before beginning his briefing, "Gentlemen, friends, officers of His Britannic Majesty's Navy. We are now at sea on a mission of the utmost importance. You will remember the last time we voyaged together when we sunk *his* ship and captured this man here, Francis Fletcher." Talbot gestured his hand in Fletcher's direction. Fletcher continued to stare at the wooden table but could feel the other officer's eyes looking at him. Knowing these men were enemies who had captured him and intended to see him hang just a few weeks earlier was uncomfortable.

"For sinking my ship and killing my crew, you have my forgiveness," he said through gritted teeth, still avoiding the awkwardness of eye contact. "Please, Captain Talbot, carry on. We must focus on *this* mission, not our previous encounters," he said, finally lifting his head to look at Talbot with sincere sadness in his eyes after the faces of his lost crew and his beloved ship appeared in his mind.

Talbot nodded and began to speak. "Dawson and some of his marines landed on an island to which Fletcher and other survivors managed to escape. I'm sure you know that the other two crew members also sail with us now amongst our crew. On the island, they experienced some strange phenomena inexplicable to us. So, we have been sent back to the island to discover it further. I assume that at least some of you will have heard obscure, non-believable tales and rumours from the men on the island. Therefore, we will go there again and see what this land offers. That is our real mission, gentlemen."

"So we're explorers now?" Reverend Cunningham commented, removing his spectacles and placing them on the table. "Forgive me, Captain Talbot, but I must ask why it is necessary to bring along two captains, one serving as your first mate, and why something so trivial as exploring a new-found island is to be kept such a secret. Something does not add up here. Is there something else, I wonder, that you're not revealing?"

Talbot felt uneasy and turned to Fletcher, hoping he would take over. Sweat appeared upon his brow and his inability to continue misleading the men before him was all too apparent. Fletcher suddenly saw an opportunity to gain favour with the officers serving under him. He stood up and took a sip of wine. "Sir, if I may?" He looked at Talbot, who was relieved by Fetcher's interruption. Talbot nodded and sat down, finishing his wine.

"As you may know," Fletcher began, "the island, as Captain Talbot has tried to explain, has what would appear as some supernatural force. That is not exactly the case, but it is a portal. A door. A gateway."

"And where does this gateway lead?" Reverend Cunningham asked with raised eyebrows.

"The island has a waterfall that does not fall like water from the rear but falls as fire. I have seen it for myself, Reverend. The rock from which the fire falls is shaped like a serpent's head and it has a hypnotic power that paralyses one's body and mind. In fact, as a certain legend would have it, it is the gateway to the underworld…Hell," Fletcher added.

Reverend Cunningham threw down a napkin on the table and stood up with a red face full of anger.

"You mean to tell me we're sailing into Satan's lair?" He spoke with a raised voice. "I'll not have this pirate blaspheming on board this ship, Captain Talbot! This man or his devilish companions, that carpenter whose name I can't remember, and that Germanic chimp who follows him everywhere!"

"My carpenter is Mr Woodland, a respected man; the other is a Bohemian in exile!" Fletcher protested.

"Whatever they are, they're filth! Mr Woodland should have been hanged next to you, Fletcher, and do you know what we do with Bohemians?" the irritated reverend questioned.

"No, Reverend Cunningham, I do not know what we do with Bohemians, but *my* Bohemian is a good, loyal man. He will and indeed already has followed me to the gates of Hell and back!" Fletcher stood up to meet with the reverend's stance. The two men came to a silent standoff with their eyes, each pouring fury towards the other. Cunningham looked away first, which Fletcher was pleased with, but then the reverend began to speak.

"In the year 1346, while England was again at war with France, King Edward III fought at the Battle of Crecy and routed a much larger French force. He'd chosen his position wisely, so the French were forced to charge uphill. The advantage of holding the higher ground also meant that the English and Welsh longbows had a farther range than the French, and the casualties inflicted on our greatest enemy were horrific. Also on that day, in support of the French, was King John the Blind. While being the Count of Luxembourg, he was also the King of Bohemia. Despite having no eyes to see, he led his mounted army up the hill towards the English lines and was cut down by the arrows that fell like snow.

"Edward III's eldest son, also called Edward and known as the Black Prince, rode his horse into the enemy lines and came across King John the Blind, easily recognisable from his ostrich-feathered plume. The Black Prince swiped his sword and cut the Bohemian king's head from his shoulders. The Black Prince then carried the head, still inside its helmet with ostrich feathers attached, and presented it to King Edward III. On one knee, he said, 'Ich Dien.' Latin for 'I serve.' That, Captain Fletcher, is what we do to Bohemians!"

"Reverend, I thank you for the history lesson, but you are a man of faith, and if you listen carefully, I will reveal something about the bible that even a distinguished servant of the lord such as yourself will be shocked to hear."

Francis Fletcher spoke for a full hour, explaining the entire story of everything he'd seen with his own eyes on the island and then into the legend of the hidden fifth gospel, Jagur's gold, the Knights of the Golden Gift and the death of Mr Gale. When he'd finished re-telling everything with expert precision to the tiniest detail, the other officers in the room were rendered speechless. It seemed too unreal.

"I had heard the tales from the island, Captain Fletcher, for I was on board when you were captured, but I must declare this is not what I expected," Lieutenant Jenkins announced with a hint of fear. "I suppose it is an honour to be granted such an expedition. The king must think highly of us!"

"Lieutenant Jenkins, the king, has no idea about any of this," Fletcher replied. "For his own protection, he must not know. The Knights of the Golden Gift do what they can to protect the secret of the fifth gospel and the gold. We cannot put his majesty in danger. We must take the gold and bring it back safely to England, only then can we tell the king, and after that I do not know what will happen. The knights might try to steal it back again for all I know. For the best part of eighteen centuries, they have murdered on such a scale that the secret remains a secret. By pure misfortune, we chanced upon the island, and by pure luck, Lord Perceval knew a man who could shed some light on its mystery. That man is now dead and I assure you all that if the knights become aware that you hold this knowledge, they will come for you, too. That is why we have no choice other than to fulfil the mission and put an end to the descendants of Jagur. This time," Fletcher raised his glass, "it is death or glory!"

There was a knock at the door, which startled them all. No one answered until the knock came a second time.

"Enter," Talbot ordered.

The door creaked open and standing in the entrance to the wardroom with a face only visible by the dim light of a lantern was the carpenter Tom Woodland with a look of terror staining his face.

"Beg pardon, sirs," his voice quivered and his chin shook. Naturally, he looked towards Captain Fletcher, seeing him as his leader. "But there has been a murder!"

Chapter 12

"Good God!" Fletcher remarked, putting a handkerchief to his mouth as he looked upon the body of Mr Ingham.

"I beg you to cease using the Lord's name in vain, Captain Fletcher!" Reverend Cunningham complained. Fletcher ignored the comment and looked down at Mr Ingham's corpse, which still had warm blood seeping from his cut throat.

Captain Talbot decided to take action. "Lieutenant Jenkins, escort Mr Woodland below. Find out what he was doing on the deck and how he discovered the body. Treat him as a suspect, please, Lieutenant."

"Excellent, sir," Jenkins obeyed, saluted and took Woodland below by the scruff of his neck for questioning.

"Mr Dawson," Talbot called out, "have your marines secure the deck. Arrest anyone who should not be here, search for a weapon, a bloodied knife perhaps, and have the crew empty their belongings to see what we can find. When you've finished with the crew, have your most trusted men search your marines; it may be one of them!"

"Aye, sir." Dawson disappeared below, calling his men to arms.

"Reverend Cunningham and Mr Brennan, prepare Mr Ingham for burial at sea."

"Aye, Captain," they both replied.

"And Francis Fletcher, Join me in the great cabin," Talbot ordered his first mate. Fletcher nodded and made his way down to Captain Talbot's quarters.

"Close the door if you would," Talbot said as Fletcher entered the dark room.

He lit the cabin with two lanterns hanging above the rear windows. Then he reached into his cabinet next to his giant globe and poured two glasses of whisky, handing one to Fletcher.

"What are we to do now?" Talbot asked as he drank.

"Was he a good boatswain?"

"One of the best, I'd say."

"Then we must first drink to the life of Mr Ingham." Fletcher raised his glass. "I did not know him well, but he seemed to be on point."

"That he certainly was. But…" Talbot stuttered.

"But, what? You need a new boatswain?"

"But…why has he been murdered?"

"There are many reasons why one man might slay another. However, we both know what we're thinking. We've been at sea for one day. There's no way anybody on board knew of the real purpose of our mission other than those in the officer's wardroom just now, so how can it be that someone among us is trying to jeopardise what we set out to achieve?" Fletcher asked.

"You know whom it is that I suspect, Fletcher."

"My Bohemian? Sholim?"

"Well, him and your carpenter," Talbot added.

"It can't be. I told them both that the laws of England had pardoned them, and they shall sail with me wherever I go to retain their service in his majesty's Navy. Although they know of the island, I spoke nothing about the truth of our deployment to them. They have no idea about the gold or the Knight's."

"They've both seen the waterfall! Are they simpletons, Francis?" Talbot asked.

"No, they're not, but they're loyal sailors. The Knights of the Golden Gift are many and they are always secret. How many souls have we onboard, two hundred?"

"Aye, near enough, two hundred." Talbot nodded.

"So, it could be any one of them. Sholim and Woodland know not of the fifth gospel or Mr Gale. Only you and I and the officers know about that."

"That's not true, Francis. Lord Perceval and our servant girl Molly know. They could all be in danger! Fortunately, my wife and children are not aware otherwise, they may even be hunted by the knights!"

"Well, we've no choice other than to continue. There's no turning back," Fletcher said firmly, pointing at Talbot and staring sincerely.

"I know that. We must go on but with a murderer on board? Our first priority must be to outwit our enemy's next move as we sail on. Why would they take out Mr Ingham and who might they target next?" Talbot thought hard.

"They took out Mr Ingham because he was the highest-ranking man on deck at the time, and so they took their opportunity. All other officers were present at our meeting. We must be vigilant, Percy. Anyone could be next. Mr Laine he's our navigator. They have every reason to kill him next, have they not?" Fletcher put another problematic question to Talbot.

"Yes, Mr Laine is in danger. More so than gun crews, for example," Talbot agreed, sipping on his whisky.

"May I say something, Percy?" Fletcher asked.

"Go on."

"I think it best that you and I leave our rivalry behind. We need to stay together. We cannot become divided in this mission, Percy."

"Then you must accept two things, Francis," Talbot immediately answered.

"And what might they be?"

"First and foremost, I am the number one captain on this ship."

"Agreed. As long as you recognise me equal in rank and accept that Lord Perceval has made me your first mate and not Lieutenant Jenkins," Fletcher insisted.

"Then you and I have an accord, Francis. We will run this ship together. However, I carry the weight of the captaincy."

"Very well." Fletcher nodded.

The two old friends who had become enemies chinked their glasses, shook hands and drank to the agreement of their ranks given to them by the highest authority within the admiralty, Lord Perceval.

"What's the second thing?" Fletcher asked after he'd cleared his throat from the burning liquid.

"Forget about Isabella. She is not yours. She is the mother of my children and has exchanged her vows with me, not you! There are plenty of other women in the world. Why must you have mine?"

Fletcher smiled wryly but nodded slowly, indicating that he knew Talbot was right. The duel had been a shambles, and even Isabella herself had told him he was not for her. He thought about the nights he had slept in the barn, how she had shown him kindness but only in friendship.

"She is a lost cause to me," Fletcher spoke sadly.

"So, have we agreed?" Talbot asked.

"With regret, Percy, we are agreed. I shall cease my wooing of Isabella. I surrender her to you."

"You're an arrogant man, Fletcher. You don't '*surrender*' her to me. She was already mine. She chose me over you, and I hope this is finally the end of it.

If you keep your promise, you and I can return to friendship. A mere mishap, a small fallout. Shall we drink one more whisky to the restoration of our friendship?" Talbot put to Fletcher.

"It's a strange scenario that a few weeks ago, you were so keen to see me hang, Percy." Fletcher grinned.

"It is strange that times move so quickly. Both of our lives are in danger. We sail together for his majesty. If I am to forgive you for your interference in mine and Isabella's lives, I shall ask for your forgiveness in wishing you tried and executed as a pirate. Fate has placed us side by side and we must cooperate."

"You have my forgiveness, Percy." Fletched stood tall and looked at Captain Talbot with a raised glass.

"And you have mine!" Talbot stood equally tall to Fletcher. They raised their glasses and drank once more.

"Now," Talbot said, "let's find that killer!"

Before either of the two captains moved, there was a knock at the door and the voice of Lieutenant Jenkins requesting permission to enter. Talbot permitted him and he walked in with urgency in his stride.

"Sirs, I have questioned the carpenter, Woodland."

"And? Do tell," Talbot answered him. "Take your time, Lieutenant, catch your breath." He saw some nervousness in his lieutenant's body language and insisted on keeping calm while telling them of his inquisition with Tom Woodland.

"Mr Woodland informed me that Mr Beatty, *our* carpenter, had asked him to inspect the masts for any damage that may have been incurred during the storm. He found only a cleat had broken on the foremast, easily replaced."

"And during this inspection of the masts, he found Mr Ingham?" Fletcher asked.

"Aye, sir. He said he checked the foremast first, returned and found Mr Ingham kneeling but still alive, clutching his throat next to the mizzen. He said he did not see anybody else trying to make a getaway. Nobody was there at all. He said he assumed the killer to be hiding nearby and was startled. Mr Ingham dropped to the ground and was clearly in his last breath, so Mr Woodland ran to the wardroom to search for officers. That's when he interrupted our meeting. Sir, I've spoken with Mr Beatty and the story is true. Mr Beatty had asked Woodland to make a damage report on the masts."

"Excellent, Jenkins, thank you. Where is Mr Woodland now?" Fletcher asked.

"Swinging in his hammock, he's rather shaken, sir. I don't think he'll be sleeping or leaving his hammock tonight."

"Very well, we shall leave him there for the time being," Talbot instructed. "Can you please leave us and go and check on the reverend and the surgeon, see that they're preparing Mr Ingham for burial at sea and ask if they need anything, then return to us after with a report on how Mr Dawson's crew inspection is going."

"Yes, sir." Jenkins saluted and departed the great cabin.

A half-hour passed in the great cabin, but Captains Talbot and Fletcher barely spoke. They each had another whisky, and Talbot sat behind his desk with Fletcher looking distantly into the dark, cloudy night sky through the tall diamonded windows. The wooden frame creaked and some faraway voices passed through the ship, but they were too quiet and inaudible. The sounds of the waves splashing and lapping away at the wooden hull beneath them as the Dolphin sailed smoothly stole their concentration.

Jenkins returned with a dishevelled expression on his face.

"What is the news, Lieutenant?" Talbot asked.

"A rather strange report, sir," he replied before glancing towards Fletcher.

"Proceed, Lieutenant. Let us waste no time," Talbot instructed.

"There has been a brawl in the mess deck, sir."

"A brawl? A common sailor's brawl or something more serious, spare us no details," Captain Talbot ordered.

"Two of our gunners, sir. They've been badly beaten."

"Which gunners?"

"Glynn Forrester and Dafydd Jones, sir. Both Welshmen."

"Were they beaten for their Welshness?" Talbot queried with concern.

"Not to my knowledge, sir. Sergeant Walton was the witness; however, I heard it from Captain Dawson. Apparently, someone saw them sitting opposite each other during their dinner and they chinked their glasses and said, 'Cheers.' I know there's nothing out of the ordinary except there was a bowl of water between them."

"A bowl of water between them?" Fletcher was confused.

"Yes, Captain Fletcher, a bowl of water," Jenkins repeated.

"Am I missing something here, Percy?" Fletcher turned towards Talbot, who had one hand slapped across his forehead and the other firmly pressing into his desk.

"Jacobites!" Talbot exclaimed. He ran his fingers through his hair and clutched to a large clump. His face went red. "Bloody Jacobites!" he growled.

Fletcher was still somewhat perplexed by the meaning of Jenkins' report.

"Could one of you please enlighten me on what this is about?" Fletcher asked.

"A bowl of water, Fletcher. Are you so unlearned that you do not know the symbolism?" Talbot returned a question.

"It's what Jacobites do," Jenkins went on. "When King James II was exiled to France in 1688, he became known as the king over the water. The Jacobites who supported him used to chink their drinks over a bowl of water to symbolise their support for the restoration of James II. After he died, the Jacobite rebellion remained at large despite being defeated several times in support of his children being put on the throne. The line of the House of Stuarts continues."

"But they were finished off, what is it, eighteen years ago, were they not? On the field of Culloden!" Fletcher commented.

"That they were, Captain, but that fat drunk who still claims the throne lives on," Jenkins informed him.

"You mean James II's Grandson? The one they call Bonnie Prince Charlie?"

"Yes, the Italian. The illegitimate bastard, the young pretender who raised a Jacobite army in Scotland and invaded England. Fortunately, the English Jacobites failed to support him, so he returned to Scotland and was defeated, as you say, at Culloden. I hear he spends most of his time in France making love to his cousins. Either there or in Italy," Jenkins explained.

"Well, that's two history lessons I have been taught this evening. Thank you for that, Lieutenant Jenkins." Fletcher nodded his thanks to the lieutenant.

"Jenkins, we must have those Jacobites arrested. They'll be Catholics and I'll not have them on board. They'll stir up trouble, and now we might suspect that it be them who have murdered Boatswain Ingham and not these Knights of the Golden Gift," Talbot ordered. "Have Dawson cuff them and bring them to me here as soon as he has finished the inspection of his marines."

"Oh, his inspection is complete, sir. He found nothing of suspicion among the crew or the marines, sir. The beaten Welshmen is the only thing we have to report," Jenkins said.

"Then that is the lead we shall follow. Bring me these Jacobites if you please, Lieutenant!"

The two gunners were escorted into the great cabin, cuffed at the hands with Captain Dawson and Sergeant Walton escorting them. They stood deadly still, their faces dressed in fear.

"Heads up, gentlemen!" Captain Dawson ordered. "You look an officer in the eye when he speaks to you!"

The pair obeyed their orders and made eye contact with Captain Talbot, who chose an imposing stance to begin his questioning. He was taller than them and glared down, his hands firmly behind his back.

"What is this I hear of you drinking to the health of the lineage of the Stuart dynasty?"

There was no answer, only a glum look of idiocy in their eyes. On Talbot's left stood gunner Glynn Forrester staring back at the captain, unable to bring so much as a mutter through his lips.

"What is wrong with your eyes, Forrester?" Talbot asked. "Why do I see one green eye and one eye that is brown?"

"It…it…it's the w…way I was born, sir," he stuttered with nervousness.

"I see. And now they're both black from a pulverising from others within the crew?"

"Y…y…yes, sir," he answered, fidgeting with his fingertips.

"And why were you delivered such a cruel blow from fellow Englishmen such as yourselves? Is it because you're not true Englishmen? You are, in fact, both Welsh?"

"N…n…no sir."

"I should hope not. Welsh, you might be, but British, you still are. Subjects of his Majesty King George of Hannover, are you not?" Before waiting for the two terrified Welshmen to answer, Talbot answered for them. "Or do you give your allegiance to house Stuart? Supporters of the Bonnie Prince, whose claim to the throne of England, Scotland and Ireland perseveres through those loyal to him?… Jacobites!"

Dafydd Jones tilted his head forward to look at the floor.

"Eyes up, Jones!" Talbot ordered sternly. "Your silence deafens my eardrums! I take that as an admission of your guilt! I go by the assumption that you are both Catholics?" More silence followed, answering Talbot's question for him. "I see. So guilty that you remain both dumb as the day you were born! Take them below, Captain Dawson!"

"Aye, sir!" Dawson answered and carried out his order.

Captain Talbot ordered that all crew members remain below deck in their bunks or quarters unless they had duties. The remainder of the night passed silently. Fletcher withdrew to his cabin and lay in his bunk with the door firmly locked. He kept a knife, a dagger and a loaded pistol on a small table next to his bunk. Before closing his eyes, he replayed in his mind his promise to Talbot to discontinue his pursuit of Isabella. He was still unsure of whether it was a promise he intended to keep. However, he knew he had more immediate concerns to think about. Who amongst the crew could have killed Mr Ingham and why? Indeed, the Knights of the Golden Gift cannot have placed one of themselves within the crew, and surely simply being a Jacobite was not sufficient reason to commit random murder.

Tiredness eventually consumed Fletcher and he drifted to sleep.

When morning came, Fletcher realised he had overslept. Quickly dressing into his full captain's uniform and being sure to keep his loaded pistol with him, he left his quarters and made his way to the upper deck. On the quarterdeck stood Captain Talbot, alone and watching the crew working. The wind was strong and many hands clambered busily, keeping the ship going well.

"Good morning, Francis. Did you sleep at all?" Talbot asked as he saw Fletcher walking up the steps to join him.

"A little too well, sir," Fletcher replied.

"Well, that is good. I slept sufficiently. Not well, but enough."

"Where is Lieutenant Jenkins, sir?" Fletcher asked.

"He's asleep. I secretly gave him the night watch. I didn't want anyone other than those who needed to know, who would be on duty through the night," Talbot explained. "He's not feeling too well. He does this quite often, you know."

"Oh, does what?"

"Gets sea-sick. Every time we set sail, about two or three days into the voyage, the boat's motion catches up with him and he spends half a day lying down. I've never had seasickness myself, but it is not uncommon."

"I am familiar with the condition but have not suffered with it for many years. I suppose I have managed just to get used to it."

"Yes, but not Jenkins. The poor soul has to get used to it every time we sail. Anyway, enough about Jenkins." Talbot sharply changed the subject. "At noon, we will hold a ceremony for Mr Ingham and commit his body to the deep. We should be well into the Bay of Biscay by then. Keep your eyes peeled, Mr Fletcher. We have a murderer among us. Are you armed?"

Fletcher patted his side, indicating he had a loaded pistol tucked away. "I am armed, sir. And may I ask what you intend to do with our Jacobites, sir?"

"It is a good question. I can't hang them without a trial and a guilty verdict. Have you any other suggestion, Francis?"

"Well, you're right. They must be found guilty before hanging and an open trial on board the ship must take place. It's time-consuming, and what if they're to be found innocent? No doubt they have their alibis and no doubt there will be someone on board who can bear witness to their presence during Mr Ingham's killing," Fletcher commented. The waves had started to get bigger and a lash of spray whipped them both in the face. "If this were my ship and the burden of command upon my shoulders, I'd sail them as close to the coast of Spain as you can and send them adrift."

"Why Spain? Why not France or Portugal?" Talbot asked.

"Their Englishness will probably see them imprisoned as spies in France and they'll be executed. Portugal, well, all right, why not Portugal? But I believe their Catholicism will see them safe in Spain. They'll probably be treated well if they admit to whichever authority captures them that they support house Stuart. I don't know what you should tell the rest of the crew. They didn't seem too popular anyway. They've already been beaten for chinking their drinks over a bowl of water."

"Maybe I should ask if any other Catholics on board or non-Catholic supporters of the Stuarts wish to join them, then they may do so. I doubt anyone will go."

"I think that a wise plan. Leniency will make sure we have the support of the crew," Fletcher added.

"Then it is settled when noon arrives and the sea has calmed, we shall bury Mr Ingham. Then, when we have Spain's coast in sight, we will cast off the traitors."

At noon, the sea had calmed sufficiently for the ceremony to take place. Sails were raised and the ship was brought to a halt. Four crewmen brought Mr Ingham's body onto the deck on a wooden board, wrapped in sail and weighted with cannonballs. Talbot had ordered the ceremony to be brief and instructed Reverand Cunningham to say only a few words. The reverend began to speak the Lord's Prayer when the whole crew was visible. Talbot and Fletcher both stood on the quarterdeck, looking for anybody in the crew they might suspect of the murder. Even Forrester and Jones were present, guarded by Sergeant Walton and two other armed marines. They were still cuffed and looked haggard as they had not slept.

"We, therefore, commit his body to the deep, to be turned into corruption…" The reverend continued following on from the Lord's Prayer, "…looking for the resurrection of the body, when the sea shall give up her dead and the life of the world to come through our Lord Jesus Christ. Who at his coming shall change our vile body, that it may be like his glorious body, according to the mighty working, whereby he is able to subdue all things to himself."

When the reverend finished speaking and closed his prayer book, Talbot nodded to the burial crew, who lifted one end of the board over the ship's side, sliding Mr Ingham's plump body into the sea. After the sound of the splash faded, Talbot gave Lieutenant Jenkins a nod and the whole crew seemingly already knew what to do. Men climbed the rigging, lowered sails and pulled on ropes and sheets. Fletcher was impressed at how well-trained Talbot had his crew. Like clockwork, they had the Dolphin well underway again in minutes.

"Now then, Francis, when Mr Laine brings me the coast of Spain, we shall lose two more of our crew," Talbot said. "You can have this watch, Mr Fletcher."

"As you wish, Captain," Fletcher obeyed. Still with a loaded pistol and ever vigilant, he remained on the quarterdeck and took command of the ship.

Three more days passed until Mr Laine, the ship's navigator, informed Captain Talbot that the coast of Spain was in sight. The two captains and Lieutenant Jenkins watched the quarterdeck for eight hours each during those three days. It was exhausting work, but they agreed that they would trust no one else except the officers present during their meeting on the night of Ingham's murder.

Captain Dawson and his marines were on constant guard. There were to be two musket-men in the crow's nest, guarding each mast and the steps to the quarterdeck at all times. The gun and mess decks were similarly protected, with orders to apprehend anybody behaving strangely or arousing suspicion in any way.

Since Ingham's burial at sea, there had been nothing to report. The two suspected Jacobites had been clapped in irons on the gun deck the whole time, eating thrice daily and frequently brought water. With Spain now in sight, they would soon be cast off.

"We'll do it tonight," Talbot told Fletcher, who accompanied him in the great cabin. "We'll untie them, put them in a rowing boat with a single oar and point them to Spain. I doubt we'll ever see them again. I'm not entirely sure this is the right thing to do, Francis."

Fletcher sat down on a wooden chair with a velvet covering. "I don't believe we can do anything else. Where we're going, we can't take them with us."

"We could have had a trial at sea?" Talbot suggested.

"We could have. But what use would it have done? If they're guilty, you can hang them. If they're not, then what? There's still a killer on the loose. Your situation does not change. They'll only cause trouble among the rest of the crew. This is not a normal mission, Percy; remember that."

"Yes, I suppose you're right. Then tonight it is. We only have a few more hours of light left anyway. We'll send them off in a few hours. Then they're somebody else's problem," Talbot replied.

The Dolphin sailed on as evening brought cooler air. As Spain's coast faded into the darkness, some lights from shore lanterns made themselves visible. A small village and a few larger houses dotted the black horizon. Talbot and Fletcher could hear men singing below in the mess deck from the great cabin. It seemed as good a time as any to get the two Jacobites off the ship. Lieutenant Jenkins had already received the order to have a rowing boat placed in the water for their departure and raise sail to bring the boat to a standstill. Talbot left the great cabin and entered the wardroom to find Captain Dawson.

"I need you and two men at arms, please, Dawson. You are to bring the prisoners from the gun deck onto the upper deck. Thank you."

Slightly aggravated as he was just about to eat, Captain Dawson grumbled, "Aye, Captain," and followed his order.

Talbot returned to the great cabin where Fletcher was still waiting. "Shall we have a nightcap before we see our friends off?" Fletcher asked.

Talbot smiled. "Any excuse for a nightcap, hey Captain Fletcher? Let's see, we've got whisky, rum, port and I believe some red wine is hidden in my cabinet. Which would you prefer?" Talbot asked as he paced the cabin towards the drinks cabinet.

"It is getting brisk out tonight. I rather fancy a bottle of red wine, Percy," Fletcher answered.

"Red wine it is. We shall drink to the end of Jacobitism on board this ship!" Talbot said.

Dawson and two of his marines, Lockwood and Sergeant Walton, marched the gun deck length to where gunners Glynn Forrester and Dafydd Jones were restrained in irons. Walton held a lantern over Captain Dawson's shoulder enabling him to see the chains. The two Welshmen had sores on their hands and feet where the heavy iron had rubbed away their skin.

"Good evening, Jacobites!" Dawson said to them. "Your time has come. The captain has a special gift for you two!"

"Are we going to hang, sir?" Forrester asked.

"No, no, lad, you're not going to hang. The captain can't order execution without a trial, and in case you haven't noticed, there has been no trial!" Dawson answered. He turned to Sergeant Walton and beckoned him closer. "Bring that lantern forward if you please, sergeant. I can hardly see the chains with this dim light." The sergeant leaned closer, and suddenly, two metres on the other side of where the prisoners were sitting, peering over a cannon, a face became visible. It quickly disappeared behind a hood, and Captain Dawson saw a figure slipping into the shadows.

"Who's there?" Captain Dawson called out. "Show yourself!" He pulled a pistol from a holster and ordered Lockwood to make ready. Dawson could see that Sergeant Walton needed no orders as he'd drawn a cutlass on his own initiative.

"I order you again; show yourself!" Dawson called into the darkness. "Walton, the lantern, hold it up!"

Walton held the lantern above his head and the light attacked the shadows. Dawson saw the figure again for a split second, but it slipped away into an even darker corner of the ship.

"You have my permission to fire at will, Lockwood!" Dawson told him. Lockwood was poised with the butt of his musket pressing hard against his shoulder. The two prisoners were helpless and sat there breathing heavily, unsure what to do. Below them, in the mess deck, they could hear the singing crew, which was loud enough to cover the sound of creeping footsteps.

Walton lunged forward with his cutlass and the lantern, illuminating the dark corner from where the hooded figure had hidden. There was no one there. Walton swung around again, lighting another dark patch, but nothing could be seen. Seconds later the sound of something being knocked over startled them.

Lockwood spun around and fired a musket ball down the gun deck to where he could see the figure bounding over a cannon and then onto another, hurdling the rows and rows of heavy guns. The musket ball missed its target, but the muzzle flash lit up the deck enough for them to see the person dressed in a brown hooded robe, a white rope around the waist acting as a belt. The phantom-like figure leaped over one more cannon and dashed to the doorway. Before anyone could take any more action, the mysterious person had gone.

"Who the hell was that? Did either of you two catch the face?" Dawson asked.

"No, sir."

"No, sir," both Walton and Lockwood replied.

"Neither did I. What about you two?" Dawson questioned the frightened Welshmen who were still chained up.

"I just saw a face, sir. A black face stared at me for only an instant. It vanished as soon as you brought the light. I think we've seen a ghost, sir!" Forrester answered the captain of marines.

"Nonsense, we've not seen a ghost, you fool. We've spotted the man who killed Ingham. And I wonder what he was doing down here, so close to you two?" Dawson replied, stroking his chin.

"Please believe us, sir. We know not who that man was!" Forrester pleaded. "He was so close to us! Please, sir!"

Dawson thought for a second. "Walton, Lockwood, stay here. Guard these two with your lives; I will get the captain," Dawson ordered.

The captain of marines hastily made his way from the gun deck to the great cabin, bursting in without knocking. The two captains, Talbot and Fletcher, were already preparing to leave the room, having drunk their wine and armed themselves, loading their pistols as Dawson entered.

"What's going on, Dawson? We heard a gunshot!" Talbot asked.

"There was a man, sir, a ghost-like person hiding on the gun deck. I was just about to un-chain the Welshmen when this person's face appeared. I asked, 'Who's there?' but the person hid in the darkness and escaped to the door. Lockwood fired at him, but it was too dark. He missed."

"And you've no idea who might have been there or what he was doing?" Talbot questioned the panting captain of marines.

"Only that he was not supposed to be there, sir, and did not want to be seen!" Dawson answered. Talbot glanced at Fletcher, who understood the seriousness of the situation perfectly.

"Was he helping the Welsh Jacobites?" Fletcher asked.

"I think not. They both denied knowing who it was and appeared as startled as we were. This figure had a black face and was dressed in a brown robe with a hood. They absolutely did not want to be seen, sir," Dawson continued.

"Call all of your marines to arms, Captain Dawson, light every lantern, search every—"

Before Talbot had finished his order, there was a mighty crash behind them. The windows of the great cabin shattered, sending shards all over the room, some of them hitting the three unsuspecting officers in the face. A piece of broken glass sliced Talbot's eyebrow, and Fletcher took a piece to the hand, which stung but did not pierce the skin. Instinctively, they all got down on the floor, covering their eyes and faces. When the dust had cleared, they gazed in shock and horror. What had come through the window was Mr Laine swinging from a rope around his neck.

"Good God!" Fletcher cried out. He pulled a knife from a sheath in his belt and stood on the desk, trying to cut away at the rope. Mr Laine was dead. His tongue was firmly writhing down his chin, his eyes closed, his neck snapped and his body lifeless.

"Search the entire ship, Mr Dawson!" As he brushed away some dust and broken glass, Talbot ordered angrily, "I want every man accounted for, I want every barrel overturned, every storage space searched thoroughly!"

"Aye, Captain!" Dawson answered, still shaking with adrenalin.

Fletcher cut the rope and Mr Laine dropped to the floor in a heap. Fletcher jumped down and grabbed Talbot by the arm. "Captain!" Even though Talbot was beside him, he shouted, "Where's Lieutenant Jenkins? How can Mr Laine have been hung from the quarterdeck without him knowing?"

"To the quarterdeck, Fletcher, arm yourself!" Talbot ordered.

The two captains raced out of the great cabin to the upper deck and the quarterdeck. The rope with Mr Laine attached to the other end was tied to a bollard. On the floor next to the ship's wheel lay the body of Lieutenant Jenkins. Blood seeped from his head and it seemed clear he'd been struck with a blunt object.

Fletcher crouched next to Jenkins and felt his neck. "He lives, sir," he assured Talbot.

"Are you certain?"

"Yes, sir, I am quite sure. He still has a pulse and he is breathing. He's been hit with quite a force on his head, and then, whoever it was got a sheet around Mr Laine's neck and lobed him over the stern. I am no master detective, sir, but it was planned. Lifting a man over the edge must have taken quite some strength," Fletcher observed.

"Yes, that looks apparent, Francis. I'm now down a boatswain and a navigator. Plenty of men can fulfil the roles, but these two were my best! I'll need to find another qualified pilot-quartermaster to take the wheel, as Jenkins is now out of action. Let's get him to the surgeon," Talbot ordered.

They grabbed the unconscious Lieutenant Jenkins by the arms and feet and carried him slowly down two flights of stairs to Dr Brennan, Where they laid him on a table. Dr Brennan examined the head and was confident he would wake up soon. He recommended they leave him in the surgery until he came around.

"Very well, Dr Brennan, you're the expert here. I must insist we have two marines guard him, though. It will be for your benefit, too, Dr Brennan. You're also a target for the Knights of the Golden Gift," Talbot informed the ship's surgeon.

"If you insist, Captain, send them to me. I'll appreciate the company," Dr Brennan replied.

"Good man, send word to me immediately when he wakes up. Thank you."

Talbot and Fletcher departed the surgery and returned to the great cabin where Mr Laine still lay. When they next saw him, he had turned blue and his body had stiffened.

"Poor Mr Laine," Fletcher remarked, looking at the body. "Those bloody bastards!"

"David," Talbot muttered.

"I'm sorry, sir?" Fletcher asked.

"His name, his name was David. David Laine." Talbot had red eyes. Fletcher could see the sadness on Talbot's face. He knew how he felt. He'd not so long ago lost his entire crew and although his skin was thick enough to hide his feelings, he was deeply saddened by the loss.

Noises started coming from the decks below. Captain Dawson continued his search, tipping over barrels and crates, causing thuds to reverberate through the vessel.

Talbot was pleased to rely on his captain of marines to do a thorough job. He was a man who did not need his orders spelled out for him, a man who could use his initiative.

When the shouting grew louder, it became apparent that something was afoot. Suddenly, the door burst open and the room filled with several red-coated marines struggling to contain two wriggling bodies of people with hoods over their heads.

"Excuse me, Captain Talbot, Captain Fletcher, sir! We've found them!" Captain Dawson announced. "Hiding in the food stores, they're both soaked in grog. They thought they'd hide in a barrel and chose the wrong one. The sound of liquid splashing over the floor alerted me to their whereabouts, and there they were, both sat in a barrel apiece, soaking from head to foot!"

"Stand them up!" Talbot gave a stern order before speaking to the two captives whose faces he had yet to see. "Stand straight, both of you, or you'll hang before dawn!"

"This one's a vicious bitch, sir; bit my arm!" Sergeant Walton interrupted.

"Remove their hoods, dammit. I want to see who or what we've got!" Talbot commanded. Sergeant Walton removed the hood of one of the figures. The dark-skinned figure spat at Sergeant Talbot, who smacked them around the back of their head as the hood came off. Both Talbot and Fletcher stood with mouths gaping wide open.

"Molly?" Fletcher spoke, shocked. Molly stared back at both captains; her heart raced. Fletcher removed the hood from the second figure, which almost caused Captain Talbot to faint. He breathed heavily and sat down on his chair, ignoring that Mr Laine was still lying on the floor, stone-cold dead.

"Hello, Percy!" Isabella said.

Chapter 13

Mr Laine had been taken away to Dr Brennan so that he could be prepared for burial at sea just as Mr Ingham had, and the broken glass had been swept from the floor. Captain Talbot had Mr Beatty create a temporary draught barrier in the form of a huge heavy curtain, which he hammered into the space where the broken window had been. Then he issued orders for the Welshmen to remain in irons and for Fletcher to take and interrogate Molly.

Talbot had no idea of the hour; a message had come from Dr Brennan that Lieutenant Jenkins was awake but in pain. The surgeon had fed him and given him water. Talbot would visit him shortly, he'd told Dr Brennan, but the guards should remain with him. Although they'd caught the suspects who had been seen hiding in the gun deck and captured in the food stores, Talbot and Fletcher remained unconvinced that the two stowaways could be the murderers. Mr Laine was far too heavy for either of the women to strangle and lift, even if they'd worked together. Fletcher had examined the knot at the standing end of the rope with Mr Laine hanging from it and could see that it was a professional sailor's knot, convincing him even more that this could not have been the work of either Molly or Isabella.

Thoughts of despair and disbelief raced through Captain Talbot's mind. So many questions bounced around his head that he had to pinch the bridge of his nose and squint his eyes tightly. How had his wife and Lord Perceval's servant girl got on board the ship? Why were they here? Where were his children? Was there still a murderer on the loose? What should he do now with the Jacobites?

Isabella had still not spoken. Her long brown hair was matted and her manly clothes were still sodden from trying to hide in a barrel of grog. The smell was particularly unpleasant. She looked at her husband with a grave look on her face.

"I don't know where to begin!" Talbot exclaimed, throwing his arms forward. He turned to look at his wife, whom he had never seen wearing a man's clothes. She appeared slightly less appealing when he saw her in such masculine attire.

"You can begin by going back to when Lord Perceval and yourself came into our home and told me you were on your way to rescue a British ship from Barbary pirates, but this time, tell me the bloody truth, Percy!" Isabella scoffed.

"Isabella! This is a secret mission. We misled you from the truth to protect those who should not know the truth. You do not understand that you are in serious danger!" Talbot defended himself.

"I understand perfectly well! You left our children and me to be slain by a descendant of some biblical myth!"

"How is it you know the truth about our deployment?" Talbot asked, disturbed that she knew. "The state has secrets which no one knows! I am sworn to secrecy…"

"So much that you lie to your wife?" She stood with her hands on her hips.

"For your own protection!"

"What protection can you give when you set off on a deployment while assassins are out there eager to cut mine, Estelle's and Edward's throats?"

"Your lack of knowledge was your shield and armour!" Talbot threw back at her viciously.

"But you left Molly with me and she knew all about it! She knew of the fifth gospel and the Knights of the Golden Gift. You knew she had this knowledge; she helped you bury Lord Perceval's friend. What was his name, Mr Gale?" Isabella shouted.

"Mr Gale, yes, that is correct. Molly found him in his bed at Enmore Castle with his throat slit from ear to ear, and the last copy, as far as we know, of the fifth gospel was gone! But she had no right to tell you!"

"She did what you couldn't!" Isabella lashed out, pointing her index finger at her husband. "She told me the truth! And she and I travelled from our home to Portsmouth, a considerable distance, to climb on board this ship so that we could be safe with you!"

"Where are our children, Isabella? Are they safe?"

"Maybe, maybe not. I took them to my sisters. They'd heard Molly telling me about this Jagur person, so I now have no idea if they're safe!" Isabella admitted.

"We must turn back if our children are in danger!" Talbot almost sobbed in grief at his situation. "They might already be dead!" Isabella burst into tears, fearful for her children's lives.

"Does anybody know they're there?" Talbot asked her.

"No. Molly and I were careful not to be followed. I told Martina I'd been called to London to accompany you on business there. I told the children the same," Isabella explained with tears in her eyes.

"Ah, so you lied to our children to protect them, understanding that if they knew the truth, that could see them in danger?" Isabella had been outwitted. She sighed heavily and turned around, unhappy to meet eyes with her husband.

"Yes!" she finally accepted.

"You see, we did the exact same thing! We misled our loved ones. But now that I can be absolved from blame on the fact that I may have been untruthful, I need to address another more urgent situation," Talbot explained to her.

"What can possibly be more urgent, Percy?"

"I do not believe you to be a murderer, Isabella, but someone has cut down two of our crew since we set sail. My first mate Francis Fletcher and I know that one of the Knights of the Golden Gift is on board. At least one; there may be more. It will be difficult to convince the remainder of the crew and the officers that you did not commit these crimes. Do you know it is a bad omen among sailors to have a woman onboard the ship? And Molly, although you and I are able to see beyond the colour of her skin, much of the crew will be disheartened to sail alongside a black woman. If not you who killed Mr Ingham, my boatswain, and Mr Laine, our navigator, then who can it be? There are two suspected Jacobites chained on the gun deck. We thought it was them until the killer struck again while they were incarcerated. So, I had our captain of marines, Dawson, search the entire ship, and we found you and Molly hiding in the food stores! Was it you that was fired upon in the gun deck earlier? Or Molly?"

"It was Molly," Isabella answered. "She'd gone to see if she could steal a blade to cut some of our food supplies, which we had already stolen, but then heard shouting and a lot of commotion, so she hid in the long room filled with cannons."

"The gun deck," Talbot corrected his wife.

"Yes, the gun deck, but someone saw her and fired at her. Fortunately, she escaped and returned to the food stores below."

"How did you get on the ship in the name of God in the first place?" Talbot continued his questioning.

"It was so easy, Percy. We travelled to Portsmouth on foot for much of the way but caught a ride on a merchant wagon. We walked along the dockside searching for the Dolphin and discovered she had not yet sailed. She was still being loaded with supplies. So many people were walking the gangways that all we had to do was blend in. So, we went to the town and bought some robes from a tailor's shop and these hoods to hide our hair and mask the darkness of Molly's face. As long as we did not look out of place, we could walk right onto the gangway and pretend we were carrying supplies on board. When you return to England, you should have a word with the admiralty about the security because even the armed soldiers didn't so much as glance at us twice. As I said, all we had to do was blend in."

"My goodness, as easy as that?" Talbot was surprised at the low-level security.

"As easy as that, Percy."

"You know we can't turn back," Talbot almost whimpered to her. "We'll never be out of danger, nor will our children if we do not complete this quest."

"I know," Isabella agreed. "Molly and I must come with you. We're not safe anywhere else."

"Yes, it is true." Talbot nodded. "Then I suppose we'll just have to take you with us, won't we?" He smiled.

"I am in a mess now, Isabella. I am truly glad to see you and I believe the children are safe, but my God, what a mess I'm in. You and Molly must not walk the ship alone. You may both use my quarters and my cabin, but the crew will not take kindly to you being here, and if there's still a murderer among us, you are also now a likely target. We will continue as before. We shall rid ourselves of the Jacobites and then we'll continue into the Med and bring back the gold!"

Fletcher had taken Molly to the wardroom, where they sat at the table and drank a glass of red wine each. Molly was not used to red wine and grimaced at the taste.

"I'm sorry, sir, I haven't ever tasted such quality. I'm just a servant girl."

"Relax, Molly, I know you. I've known you since we were children. You'll get used to the taste. And you may stop referring to me as 'sir' if you wish. To you, I am Francis."

"Thank you, Francis," she said.

"Now, Molly, tell me what you're doing here?" He got to the point quickly.

"I made a mistake, Francis." She began to cry. "I wasn't to know of her lack of knowledge, her innocence in all this. I thought she knew!"

"Thought she knew what, Molly?"

"Why you and Mr Talbot have sailed again. A slip of the tongue, I did not know that Percy had lied to Isabella about why you had been sent to sea, so I just mentioned that I hoped you bring back the gold, and then she asked me, 'What gold?' and then she demanded that I tell her the truth, and so I did. So she realised that we were in danger and we fled. We took her children to her sisters'. Then we came to Portsmouth, bought some robes and hoods, pretended to be loading the ship with supplies, and just walked on…"

"Woah, slow down, Molly. You were able to walk onto the ship as easily as that? Because you were wearing these ridiculous clothes?" Fletcher said, pointing at the clothing that Molly was wearing.

"Uh-huh." She nodded.

"Good God! Were there no guards?"

"Yes, but we managed to make ourselves look like we were supposed to be there," Molly answered him.

Fletcher scratched his head. He was not sure whether to believe what she was saying. He thought for a few more seconds, struggling to find words that could match what his mind wanted to say. Ultimately, he gave up and tried to spell out to her the seriousness of the mission.

"You know where we're heading, don't you, Molly?"

"Uh-huh." She nodded again.

"And you know that two of our crew are now dead and we are looking for a murderer?"

Molly displayed a facial expression which told Fletcher that she was unaware of this news.

"I did not know that! We have been hiding below for days and knew nothing of what was happening above us," she informed him, praying he'd believe her.

Fletcher wiped his forehead and brushed back his hair. He had started to slump, which was helping to calm Molly down as it was evident that she was incredibly nervous.

"Well, Molly, we must find some quarters and clothes and see what the captain wants to do with you." Fletcher had heard enough. His brief interview with Molly was kept very short, and he felt he had no reason not to believe her.

It would not change their immediate situation even if she were not telling the truth.

"Come on, let's go and see Percy."

When all four of them assembled in the great cabin again, Fletcher felt incredibly uneasy. He looked at Isabella, and although she seemed rather peculiar, dressed in men's clothing and soaked in grog, he still felt something of an attraction. He thought about his promise to cease his pursuit of Isabella. It seemed an easy promise to make in her absence, but now she was here on board. They would likely see each other daily for the foreseeable future, making things complicated. Suddenly, the promise had become a much more complex reality.

"Well, it seems both of your stories align with one another. It is safe on our part," Talbot looked at Fletcher, "to say that you have not murdered our crew members. But now that we also believe it not to be the Welsh Jacobites, we know that someone is still on board, eager to see us all dead. So, I'm giving all three of you a clear order regardless of rank or gender. Not one of you will ever walk the ship alone. Is that clear?"

"Yes, sir," Fletcher immediately answered in a manner of second nature to a seasoned military man.

"Ladies?"

"Yes, sir," Molly answered.

"Isabella?" Talbot raised his voice, somewhat irritated by his wife's lack of cooperation.

"Aye, aye, Captain!" she answered with a giggle.

"This is no time for fun and games, Isabella. Remember that," Captain Talbot informed her sternly, not for a second allowing his rank to be taken lightly, even by his wife. They may be married, but he was the ship's captain and she was his subordinate.

At dawn, before most of the crew had risen from their hammocks and with the sea as calm as it had been since their journey began, Talbot ordered a rowing boat lowered. He sent the two Welsh Jacobites into the boat with a single oar and a day's food rations. Spain's coast was still visible on the horizon, with a few coastal lanterns still glowing dimly in the morning light.

"Goodbye, Captain," Forrester said as he cast the rowing boat away. Dafydd Jones still said nothing. He looked into Talbot's eyes with hatred firing in his direction like a full broadside of cannon.

"Good luck," Talbot said before turning away to ascend the steps to the quarterdeck.

Before long the small rowing boat was no longer in sight. Talbot thought deeply about what he'd done. It was too late now. He would have to live with guilt or the consequences if it turned out to be a mistake. He was not likely to ever see them again, however, the responsibility would be a burden on his mind for the indefinite future.

"A captain must do what a captain must do," he muttered. "Good morning, Mr Campbell. I trust you know where we're headed?" Talbot asked the new man at the helm.

"By way of Gibraltar. She's already on the horizon, sir," Mr Campbell answered confidently.

"Very good, Mr Campbell…"

"Black sail ahoy!" came a cry from the crow's nest. Talbot instantly ran down to the mizzen and demanded that the sailor on the lookout so far above them repeat what he'd said.

"Black sail ahoy!" came the reply. Talbot decided to see for himself and began climbing the rigging. It was tiring work, struggling up the netting eighty feet, but he was still physically fit and managed to get there hastily enough. The wind was more potent and much cooler at the top of the mast than below on deck.

"Let me see!" He prompted the lookout to hand him his telescope. He balanced on the netting, leaning towards the bucket-like crow's nest, extended the telescope and peered through. Sure enough, there was a ship with more guns than the Dolphin and a black flag hoisted above them.

"Pirates!" Talbot hissed.

He returned the telescope and put his hands to his mouth to enhance his voice before shouting, "BEAT TO QUARTERS!"

Chapter 14

"Cross that 'T' Mr Campbell," Talbot bellowed through the wind. "The weather favours our position!"

The upper deck had become a calamitous mass of confusion. The drummer boy hammered away, drowning out the sound of men and officers shouting at each other about where they needed to be. Talbot knew his crew were trained and was a captain who knew he could trust his delegates to be where they should be, but from where he was in the crow's nest, it looked like a hive of chaos below him.

He dropped from the rigging at a height which he would have reprimanded any other crew member for having done so. Still, given the exceptional circumstances, the adrenaline-fuelled captain allowed his panic-stricken body the freedom to break his own rules just this once. He landed with a pain in his ankle and immediately cursed himself for jumping down from so high up.

"Blast you, Percy, you fool!" he thumped himself on the thigh.

He hobbled up the steps to the quarterdeck, where he joined Fletcher, standing on the stern, peering out to sea through his telescope. The wind rushed his long black hair, blew his coattails behind him and displayed the appearance of a frightfully brave sailor. For a second, Talbot felt inspired that his old friend, looking as bold as could be, was going into battle alongside him.

"What do you see, Francis?" Talbot called up to him.

"I see a pirate ship armed to the teeth, Percy." Fletcher grinned down to Talbot, making him feel somewhat uneasy. "Three masts. They've got more guns than we have, probably twenty-four-pounder long guns, but they've also got a pair of long nines. We'll be in their range soon. We must take advantage of the wind. If we give them a broadside or two from our starboard batteries and swing her into the wind, we can have the port side ready with grapeshot by the time these bastards pull alongside us. What do you think?" Fletcher offered his advice.

"She's heavier than we are. Perhaps we can harness the wind, full sail, and outrun her?" Talbot replied.

"Did you not hear me, Percy? She has a pair of long nines; we can't outrun her. She'll blast our magazine to pieces," Fletcher insisted.

"Then I think our only option is to do what you said. Let's put our gun crews to work!" Talbot agreed. "Let's try and get three broadsides. We can fire accurately with a bar shot from one thousand yards, then give them two volleys of round shots before we ready about. Understood, Francis?"

"Aye, sir," Fletcher saluted, still striking his pose upon the stern.

"And Francis…" Talbot added.

"Yes, sir."

"You have the upper deck."

"Me, sir?"

"Yes, you. Ingham is no longer with us; we need someone to take control of the upper deck. It's yours!"

"Very well, Percy, but I'll haunt you forever if I should die!" Fletcher smiled.

Before he could jump down to take up his position on the upper deck, the vessel with black sails emitted two yellow flashes followed by white puffs of smoke from her bow. A second later came the sound of the guns firing. Like thunder, they roared. They next heard the air tearing apart as the shots from the long nines hurtled towards them. Two plumes of water sprayed upwards from the sea, well short of their target.

"They're still testing their range. It won't be long until they find it, Francis. Let's prepare our first volley!"

Talbot ordered.

Below on the gun deck, Woodland and Sholim watched as the twenty-two guns were expertly attended. The crews prepped the massive weaponry like well-oiled machinery, following the procedure they'd trained for and practiced repeatedly. The parchment cartridges were placed in the gun barrels, followed by cloth wads. The rammers rammed in perfect timing with each other. Sholim stared, impressed at how each team worked in great synchronicity as bar shots were loaded and forced into the heavy iron barrels.

"Run out the guns!" Came a voice shouting above all. Lieutenant Jenkins had managed to escape from the surgery upon hearing the drums beating to quarters. He had smothered his head with a white rag with blotches of red where blood had seeped through.

Men heaved in crews of twelve, displaying their strength on the gun tackles until the front of the gun carriage was firmly pressed against the ship's bulwark. Powder monkeys with fear drawn across heavy faces managed to hold their young teenage nerves together. Only courage would win them the day and they knew it. Protruding out of the gun ports, gleaming brilliantly in black, was the sight of a loaded battery, which was most fearsome.

"Come on, Sholim, help me with these," Woodland told his giant bearded friend. There was little response. The big Bohemian looked blank as if he had not understood a word and continued to watch the gun crews at work.

"For Christ's sake, Sholim, learn some bloody English!" Woodland said, aggravated. "Here, take these!" He handed Sholim a bucket full of tools and continued to explain what he had to do. "When we start taking fire, we patch up the holes. That's our job, got it?" Still, nothing but a blank expression came Woodland's way. "When there is fire, we put it out…when there are holes, we patch them up!"

He gestured for Sholim to stay close to him, knowing that Sholim had probably not understood, but there was little that Woodland could do about it other than see the funny side. He let out a small chuckle of despair to himself.

Two more booms raced through the air towards the Dolphin, sending two more plumes of spray out of the water. This time, they were closer. Another shot and they might well be in the range of the pirate's long nines.

Isabella and Molly were in the great cabin, sweating their fear through their new, dry men's clothing, far too large for them both.

"Take this!" Isabella gave a loaded pistol to Molly. She took it and looked at it, not knowing how to use it. "On second thoughts, give it back," Isabella instructed. She grabbed the pistol and proceeded to show Molly how to work it. "Make sure you hold it with two hands; the kick will be strong and you must keep it steady. You've never fired one before?" Isabella asked. Molly shook her head.

"I can hold a sword easily enough," Molly informed Isabella. "Get me a sword and a dagger. I can use them. My father told me that on the plantations, many of the slaves used to steal daggers and practice throwing them when they were unguarded. Many of them, I heard, killed their guards in their attempts to escape, so they all learned how to cut a throat and throw a dagger."

"Is that so, Molly?" Isabella answered, showing genuine interest while strapping on a holster for her pistols. "And your father taught you how to use one?"

"He did, ma'am. At Enmore, we used to kill the pigs for dinner. He said the veins on a pig's neck were similar to that of a human, and if I were ever to end up a slave, I best know how to cut a throat. When I was a girl, I used to practice throwing a knife or a dagger into the belly of a slaughtered boar that would dangle in Lord Percival's kitchens. I'll never forget the day I first made it stick. My father was so proud of me," Molly explained.

"Well, Molly, I am glad to have you in this cabin. I'll shoot the first two with my pistols if these blaggards enter. Then you get the next one with the dagger. Then, we fight with swords. Show no mercy, Molly, for you shall receive none in return. As soon as they realise that we're women, well…" Isabella hesitated at the thought. "Well, Molly, they'll take full advantage of us. You understand?"

"There'll be no taking of my advantage, ma'am. I'll die before they breach these britches!"

"Good. I shall die with you. But, Molly, please stop calling me ma'am."

The two women armed themselves as best they could with swords, daggers, knives and Isabella's two pistols. All around them, through the creaks of the great cabin, they could hear men shouting. Suddenly, the door to the great cabin opened, prompting Isabella and Molly to act. Isabella raised her two pistols and Molly drew back her arm to throw the deadly blade at whoever had entered.

"Do not shoot!" Reverend Cunningham cried out. "It is I, the reverend."

"Lower the blade, Molly. It's Reverand Cunningham."

"Our enemy is still a way off. The fighting has not yet begun!" Reverend Cunningham said with his arms forward, indicating the women to lower their weapons. "Captain Talbot ordered me to come and join you in here. He said that the presence of a man of God might prevent any man forcing themselves upon you should we lose this battle."

"Well, at least my husband still has time to think of his poor wife in these circumstances. Your presence is most gratefully accepted," Isabella replied. She looked the reverend up and down and noticed he was fully armed. There were four pistols, two holsters by his waist and two more across his chest. His sword was in its sheath, clipped tightly to his left thigh. He did not look like a man of God.

"How will they know you are our reverend, Mr Cunningham?" Isabella asked him.

"I have a book of prayer in my pocket and this cross around my neck, ma'am. If we are defeated and I am alive, I shall drop my weapons and show them the power of the Lord Almighty. Have no fear. You shall be protected, ladies," Reverend Cunningham assured them.

"Very well, but Molly and I have already discussed that if they intend to force themselves upon us, we will fight to the death before hands are laid upon us."

"I expect nothing less, ma'am. I salute both of you for your courage." The well-armed reverend slammed the door to the great cabin behind them before the long nines of the enemy's approaching ship fired again. This time, the cannonballs flew past them.

"Dammit, we're in range," Talbot muttered to himself. The pirate ship still had a few hundred yards to cross before the Dolphin's twenty-four-pounders could fire their first volley. They'd have to sit, wait and hope that the enemy gunnery was not at such a high standard as to hit them with too many accurate shots.

Minutes felt like hours as the crew of the Dolphin waited. Dawson had his marines crouch down in line formation, stretching from the foremast to the steps of the quarterdeck. Sharpshooters occupied the crow's nests way above them, and crew members with cutlasses and other blunter objects crouched behind the marines, waiting for their foe to arrive.

"Captain, I believe they can now receive their first volley." Fletcher approached Talbot. "I request permission to fire from the upper deck's battery."

"Try a ranging shot first, Francis," Talbot ordered.

"As you wish, sir," Fletcher answered, displaying his willingness to respect rank while a battle was looming.

The professionalism was not lost on Talbot, who had noticed how differently Fletcher behaved regarding real seamanship. Fletcher approached the first cannon, took hold of the lanyard and stood back, safely beyond the range of the gun's recoil. He waited until the ship rolled upwards to prevent from firing directly into the sea, saw that he was in line with his enemy's bow and yanked aggressively on the lanyard cord. The flintlock mechanism ignited the gunpowder inside the barrel and the cannon boomed. Fire and smoke came out of the barrel like a dragon's breath. The bar shot missed the target but displayed where it landed in the water that the ship was now within range. Fletcher looked towards Talbot, who nodded, showing Fletcher that he could now give the order to fire a full broadside.

"Full battery, fire!" Fletcher shouted along the deck. The remaining five battery guns on the starboard side of the upper deck let loose the iron venom within a few seconds. The ship shook and vibrated with the force of all the guns recoiling at once.

"Reload, bar shot!" Fletcher ordered.

Talbot extended his telescope towards the enemy and watched as at least two bars ripped through her sails. A second later, another struck the bow, sending splinters high into the air all around her.

Other shots hit the water and splashed harmlessly. The Dolphin violently rocked from side to side as the eleven starboard guns from the gun deck below received their firing orders from Lieutenant Jenkins. Again, Talbot watched the enemy ship receive a splattering of solid iron bars ripping through sails, cutting sheets and splintering her bow.

"One more volley, then it's ready about, Francis. We've less time than we first thought!" Talbot called down to him.

"Aye, aye, sir."

Both batteries were reloaded, and for a second time, the Dolphin was sent into a frenzy of vibrations even more violently than the first as all seventeen starboard-facing cannons blasted together.

The pirate ship received a full blow. Wood shattered and splintered, and the top of one of its three masts leaned to one side, creaked and collapsed, bringing down two of the ship's crew with it.

They were close enough to see detail of the ship without the telescope now, and everyone on board the Dolphin could hear the screams as the two men fell to their deaths. Fletcher was pleased with the firing, but now it was their turn to be on the receiving end.

From close range, the pirate ship's long nines fired straight into the Dolphin's hull. Two cannonballs punched directly into the gun deck, cutting one cannon loose from its carriage. The colossal barrel dropped to the floor, crushing the legs of three of its gun team. The powder monkey, a boy of just fourteen years old, ducked to avoid the splinters, but it was useless. Several pieces of sharp wood sliced into his neck, chest and face, along with hundreds of small parts that pierced his arms, legs and abdomen. There was no way for him to survive. Blood poured from his neck and teeth dropped out of his mouth as he spluttered hopelessly. The poor child attempted to raise his hand to his throat, but his arm hung loosely at the elbow by just a few strings of flesh. His other arm was gone from the shoulder and all his tibias and fibias had snapped. Another gun crew member's arm had flown across the deck, landing at Sholim's feet. Instinctively, he kicked it away, sending it hurtling back down towards the broken gun.

"That's us; let's go, Sholim!" Woodland called out. Broken wood needed repairing immediately before another shot could damage them further—Woodland set to work hammering in plugs to the fractured hull.

Half the crew had to grab hold of something, while the other half lost their footing as the Dolphin readied about as instructed by Captain Talbot. The wood creaked furiously, the sails flapped and the wheel turned, swinging the boat alongside the pirate ship.

The port side cannons were now loaded with grapeshot and the officers immediately ordered to fire. After the first volley had been fired Lieutenant Jenkins gave the order to fire at will. Gun captains yanked their lanyards and grapeshot mercilessly plastered into the pirates. From such close range, anyone caught in the line of fire stood little chance of survival. Men disintegrated and limbs dropped all around. A bearded head rolled from a newly created hole in the ship and plunged into the waves between the boats.

"Prepare for enemy boarding!" Talbot ordered from the quarterdeck. Heavy planks came from the pirate's ship, slamming into the side of the Dolphin as dark-skinned men in colourful clothing lobbed themselves onto it. They were bearded with long hair and screaming wildly. Fletcher and Talbot both realised they were fighting Barbary pirates. They carried giant sabres and many had cloth wrapped around their heads.

Captain Dawson ordered his marines into two ranks, one kneeling and one standing, to give them a volley of musket fire. Musket smoke ascended from the red line of men and metal balls cut down many enemy before they could cross onto the Dolphin. The sharpshooters above them had begun to fire at will, but the enemy also had their projectiles. Glass bottles filled with a flammable liquid were hurled across, setting the Dolphin's upper deck ablaze. Two of the marines were burning away. Their flesh could be smelt by all those who stood around.

"Fix bayonets!" Dawson ordered and he drew his own sword. "Charge!" The line of bayoneted musket-men charged through the fire on the deck and met their enemy, still jumping across. One man fell from a plank and tumbled into the water. The two ships collided, crushing the man. His skull caved in and his ribs crumbled. The battle between the decks ensued. Bitter hand-to-hand fighting raged. Talbot stood tall on the quarterdeck with his cutlass and pistol. He waited until one enemy fighter reached the steps of the quarterdeck. The fearsome-looking vagabond glanced up at Talbot and snarled before Talbot's pistol ball went straight through his forehead.

Francis Fletcher stood on the side of the Dolphin, holding onto the rigging with his left hand and lunging his rapier forwards with his right. He managed to pierce the stomach of one invader before chopping the hand from another. He continued to hack away at the relentless enemy, but there were too many. Dead marines began to pile up and the deck was swamped with pirates before long.

Fletcher only now began to worry. Their only hope might be that below them were still able-bodied men of the gun crews who could carry on the fight if they did not become trapped below. If they lost control of the upper deck, all the pirates would have to do was block the hatches and entrances to the gun decks and trap the men down there.

Fletcher swung from the rigging, hitting the deck and rolling away from a thrusting sabre whose owner had only one thing on his mind—to slice Fletcher in two. He had to crawl through smoke where the burning wood still simmered and onto the steps of the quarterdeck where he could see Talbot embroiled in a duel with a well-dressed enemy officer. Fletcher ran up the steps and plunged his sword into the enemy officer's neck. Talbot had not seen Fletcher approaching and was shocked to see him.

"He was mine, Francis. I almost had him!"

"You've never won a duel without me!" Fletcher smiled as he referenced his past duel with Talbot.

"No time for joking, Francis! We will be annihilated soon and we're too few!" Talbot said. He looked down to the main deck to see what few marines remained fighting for their lives.

"I'll be back shortly," Francis said.

"Where the hell are you going?" Talbot asked him.

"I'm following our old navigator, Master Laine."

Fletcher took a loose rope, tied it to a bollard and jumped off the stern. He swung down and flew straight through the broken window of the great cabin that Mr Laine's corpse had smashed. Molly turned to stab him with her dagger, and Isabella gasped in total shock as broken glass, a curtain and wood landed around her feet. Fletcher stood and brushed himself down. He quickly counted four pistols aimed straight at his head and Molly's dagger was now at his throat.

"Francis?" Isabella yelled. "Weapons down; it's Captain Fletcher."

"Excuse me, ladies, Reverend, but pirates blocked the entrance, so I had to find another way in." He brushed past them and opened the door to the great cabin, leaving the three non-combatants stunned at what they had just witnessed. He quickly entered the gun deck, taking Lieutenant Jenkins by the arm. The noise of the battle above them and the firing of cannons were so loud that he had to shout.

"Lieutenant, we must get above to the upper deck. We need more fighting men up top!"

The experienced lieutenant understood perfectly and ordered the gun crews from the starboard side to abandon their positions and make way for the upper deck. They ran past him, taking cutlasses and bludgeons, clubs, hammers, knives, and anything they could use for a weapon.

A small group of four pirates had already started to make their way below, and they had seen the door to the great cabin was open. They ran in to attack the captain's quarters, where Molly ignored Isabella's advice to let her kill the first two to enter and hurled her dagger straight into the first pirate's chest. Isabella put a pistol shot into him and he died instantly. The three remaining enemies clambered over their dead comrade's body. Reverend Cunningham fired both his pistols while killing the next pirate, and Isabella fired her last shot into the arm of the group leader, who drew his sword. Reverend Cunningham met him with his blade as they locked in a one-on-one clash of swords. The Reverand was skilful with a blade, but so was his opponent. The pirate pinned the reverend against the wall, knocking over the drinks cabinet and the globe, which rolled across the floor.

"Molly, use your knife; help Mr Cunningham!" Isabella pleaded. Molly drew her knife and jumped onto the pirate's back. She was clumsy and thrust her blade down, but instead of the knife going into the pirate's shoulder, it went straight into the Reverand's neck, slicing open his windpipe. The reverend dropped to his knees and died on the great cabin floor.

The pirate shrugged Molly off his back and slapped her with his hand.

Coming through the door were friendly crew members who wrestled the pirate to the floor and hacked him to death with swords and bludgeons.

"Molly, Molly, Molly! You've killed the Reverand!" Isabella was crying. She ran over to his body and held his head. Blood poured from his neck and Molly's blade remained firmly lodged. His eyes were still open and his skin was warm, but it was evident he was no longer alive.

"I'm sorry! I meant to kill the pirate! I'm sorry, ma'am, it was a mistake!"

"Come here, Molly!" Isabella hugged Molly, still shaking from the trauma of it all. "It's alright. He died protecting us. It's alright! No one will think ill of this act." The two women cried together as they embraced beside the dead Reverand on the floor. Shattered glass and broken pieces of wood were all around them.

On the upper deck, the arrival of the gun crews balanced the numbers against the pirates. Fierce fighting swelled the deck of the Dolphin, but discipline was better maintained among the well-trained British crew and remaining marines, who could still keep their line despite heavy losses. Captain Dawson regained control and ordered the marines back to allow the gun crews to club and batter their way into the clusters of pirates.

This action gave the marines precious time to regroup and, more importantly, reload. Even under the pressure of battle, they managed to draw their ramrods load in the musket ball, prime their pans and form two lines. Again, one was kneeling and one was standing behind them. Dawson could see that he was about to shoot his own gun crews in the back, so he quickly grabbed Lieutenant Jenkins and told him to wait for his command; then, all gun crews were to get down and hit the deck.

"On my command, both ranks are to fire. Wait for my command, lads!" Dawson cried out his order. "Jenkins, gun crews fall!" Jenkins ordered all fighting men to hit the deck upon hearing the command. Most of them did within a second or two, and as soon as Dawson could see that it was now or never, he ordered his marines to fire before the gun crews were maimed on the floor where they lay.

The volley of muskets ripped into the pirates, shattering bones and spilling blood from exit wounds the size of clenched fists. The volley was the turning point. The pirate ship captain could be seen in his green coat, with his broad cutlass waving and screaming frantically for his remaining fighters to return to his ship. Others from the enemy ship desperately pushed boarding planks into the water and cut ropes in a panic to break off the engagement they could no longer win.

On the quarter deck, Talbot seized his chance with his pistol. He took aim, straightened out his arm and fired a single shot in the direction of the pirate captain. The attempt missed its target but hit the ship's deck, sending more splinters into the frenzy.

As the two ships drifted apart, the last shot rang out. A musket ball fired from the enemy crow's nest plunged into Talbot's chest. At first, he felt nothing. He stumbled backwards with the force of the shot, but there was no pain. He looked down at the wound and unbuttoned his tunic to expose a fountain of blood oozing from his sternum. As he listened to the sound of cheering marines and gun crews replace the noise of battle, his eyes rolled back into his head and his legs gave way.

Chapter 15

The surgery was dark and smelled like rotten cheese. A groaning sound drifted between the creaking wooden hull as Captain Talbot opened his eyes and coughed, which caused immense agony through his entire upper body. He knew he was in a hammock, but he was unsure where. The ship's bell rang through the otherwise quiet morning, indicating the end of a standard four-hour watch.

Talbot tried to move some more, which caused so much pain that it was impossible. He could not feel his legs and lifting his head required more strength. His voice croaked.

"H-h-hello? Is anyone in here with me?" The only response was another groan, which resembled no words, just the moaning of a man seemingly in extreme discomfort. He closed his eyes and tried to send himself back to sleep, but he was too awake. So many questions were coming to his mind about where he was and how he'd got there. He could see over the side of his hammock that there were one or two other hammocks. A table was to his right and a partially open door swung with the ship's movement.

This is not my cabin, He thought. *It's also not the crew's sleeping quarters and it's almost certainly not the wardroom.* He continued to think through his confused and painful state. He welcomed the thought of someone bringing him some water to help his dry throat, but there did not appear to be anyone around. He took another glance at the table and then realised where he was. "I'm in the ship's surgery!"

Talbot did not remember taking himself to the surgery. He searched his mind as thoroughly as it would allow him. Something flashed in his mind that made him think there had been a battle. Although he could not remember any fighting, and therefore he could not figure out why he was in surgery and so much pain. He continued to think, doing his best to jog his memory. Gently whispering, he said, "I am Captain Percy Talbot, on board His Britannic Majesty's Ship Dolphin. I am on a secret mission to find and retain biblical gold." He was sure of himself thus far and searched his mind. "You have a wife, Isabella, and two children. They are safe at our home in Hampshire...No...no, that's not true. There is a danger. Isabella has abandoned the children! She is here with me!" His heart sped up the more he spoke to himself. "She left the children!" His voice broke from the whisper. "The Knights of the Golden Gift!" He almost shouted, "They must have tried to kill me!" He froze, swinging in his hammock, convinced there must have been some assassination attempt on his life.

After many minutes, a man entered the room with a limp. Afraid that the man might be a Knight of the Golden Gift coming to murder him, Captain Talbot instinctively attempted to reach for his sword. It was not there. Talbot cursed himself for being so foolish. "Obviously, it's not there," he whispered. He had, however, drawn the attention of the limping man over to him. A lantern appeared above his head, and as his eyes adjusted to the light, he could make out the face of Dr Brennan, the ship's surgeon.

"Captain! You're awake, thank the good Lord!" he said.

"Y-Y-Yes," the captain croaked back.

"Don't struggle, Sir. You've been badly wounded. Are you in pain?"

"Yes, Doctor," the captain could only whisper in reply.

"Would you like some rum, sir?"

"Rum would be fine, thank you."

The doctor picked up a glass bottle and pulled the cork out with his teeth before pouring a nice helping into a tin canister.

"Here you are, sir. It will help with the pain."

"Thank you, Doctor." Captain Talbot took a swig and instantly spluttered, dribbling some of the brown sticky liquid down his stubbly chin.

"That's it. Now have some water, and I'll fetch your wife," Dr Brennan said calmly.

"My wife?" Still angry at his wife for being on board, the captain was relieved to hear she was well.

"Yes, sir, your wife. She has often been here to give you water and lower your temperature with a wet cloth."

"I don't remember her giving me water, Doctor," Talbot admitted.

"You have been delirious for some time. I can tell you now, sir, she has been here very frequently beside you."

"Thank you, Doctor. I'd like to see her now."

"Very well, Captain. I shall go and fetch her. She may be sleeping, but she will be happy to know that you are finally awake and able to communicate," Doctor Brennan informed him.

Isabella appeared in the doorway. She was still wearing men's clothing, including his boots, and her hair was loose, dangling down her shoulders. She wore a red bandanna on her forehead, carried a pistol in a holster by her waist and had rolled up her white sleeves. She looked anything but the lady-like woman he'd been married to all these years, but she smiled, which warmed his heart.

"Thank the Lord, Percy. You have woken!" She clasped her hands in prayer and stepped towards him. "Does it hurt?" she asked.

"A little, yes. Though I have no movement in my legs," he told her. He'd noticed that she had placed her hand on his knee, but he could not feel it.

"You were wounded in battle. Your wound has numbed your senses, but in time, they will return, Dr Brennan has assured me."

"My wits, maybe, but I cannot feel my legs, Isabella!" He began to show some panic in his voice.

"Hush now." She brought a finger to his lips. "You've been on your back for God knows how many days. Once we get you up and about, you'll be able to feel your legs again and then you'll be running the ship like always!"

"How many days have I been in here, Isabella?" Talbot asked her, confused.

"I think nine, maybe ten. Honestly, I have lost count of what day it is today."

"Nine days? I must get out of this place, the ship. She needs me." He tried to sit up, but the wound in his chest caused him too much pain and he began to seep blood onto the bandage that Doctor Brennan had wrapped around his abdomen. He cried out a whimper before lying back down.

"Relax, Percy. The ship is in good hands. Francis has ensured that," Isabella attempted to calm him but failed by using Fletcher's Christian name. Talbot noticed immediately that she had referred to him as Francis and not Fletcher or even Captain Fletcher.

"Fletcher is in command?" he asked Isabella.

"Yes, since he brought you down here. He took command of the ship. He and Lieutenant Jenkins have continued our journey."

"And what about…" He paused and brought his voice to an almost inaudible whisper. "…and what about the Knights of the Golden Gift? Surely, our mission is in jeopardy." He had begun to sweat.

"We do not know. Francis and I have discussed what we will do next—"

Talbot refused to allow his wife to continue. A downpour of jealousy flowed through his entire body. "How much time have you been spending with Fletcher, Isabella?" he asked implicitly.

Isabella took a step from her husband, who had aggravated her temper.

"Percy!" She put her hands on her hips as she always did whenever anyone provoked her. "Francis is the man who scraped your dying body from the quarterdeck and brought you here while a battle raged around him." In truth, the battle was well over. Still, she added the extra drama to make Fletcher's deed seem more heroic than it was. "Francis is the man who rescued myself and Molly from having our bodies ravaged and abused by those bloodthirsty ruffians who attacked us! Francis is the man who told me I had to visit you constantly, as he was desperate to see that you live!" She frowned heavily.

Talbot could see that he'd struck a nerve with her and felt a little guilty for doing so. He began his apology.

"Forgive me, my good wife. I am still delirious from the fever. Tell me, what happened? Was there a battle? Was it The French? Those bastards!"

"No, Percy, it was not the French. It was pirates. Francis thinks they were from the Barbary states and says they're everywhere these days. They attacked us, but you managed to fight them off," Isabella explained.

"Good heavens, the Lord must have blessed me. Nine days, you say I have been in here? Do we know our position? And again, I must ask you, have we had any run-ins with potential Knights of the Golden Gift?"

"We passed by Gibraltar shortly after the battle and then Malta some days ago. Maybe four or five, I cannot remember—so many days at sea clouds one's mind, or at least mine. We've been so busy with the wounded, with the funerals, we are somewhere in the Mediterranean, but you must press more sea-faring folk for accurate response, for I do not have the exact answer. As for the Knights of the Golden Gift, there have been no incidents. Perhaps you were right about those Jacobites, or whoever intended to stop us was killed in the battle."

"Perhaps." Percy nodded. "They must have had ample opportunities to finish me off and have not done so. Therefore, I hope we can safely assume we are rid of our foes for now. Please, Isabella, do you know our losses from the battle?"

She stroked his hair, offering him some comfort before delivering the bad news. "Many have died, Percy. I heard Francis and the lieutenant speaking over dinner the other evening that we will not be able to fend off another attack should we encounter more Barbary pirates and that we had best pray, we can make it across the Mediterranean unseen. We've had funerals every day. At first, maybe fifty-something were buried at sea from the battle. Then the wounded began to die off day by day." A tear appeared in Isabella's eye. "I'd no idea that battle would be so grim. I saw the surviving crew carrying limbs belonging to only God knows who and tossing them into the waves. Dead pirates received no funerals. They were just dragged from the blood-soaked floor and chucked overboard. I've passed surviving crew members trying to eat with no fingers and a man with only half a foot still climbing the rigging. It's a terrible existence, this, your life at sea. I beg of you that this is indeed your final voyage!" she pleaded with him, holding his hands.

"I promise you now. This is my last." He smiled.

"I've heard that before!" She raised her eyebrows at him.

"This time, I mean it. I want to watch Edward and Estelle grow up. I want to become old, wrinkly, safe and on dry land!" He laughed, which hurt his wound. Isabella also giggled. It made him glad to see her smile.

"Do you think?" he asked his wife. "Do you think that perhaps Dr Brennan would allow me to be carried to the upper decks?"

"I shall ask him. I am sure I can think of one man who would be honoured to carry you out of here, and I know the crew would be pleased to see you. I will fetch the surgeon for you."

Isabella left her wounded husband to fetch Dr Brennan. When he arrived, he permitted him to go from the surgery and spend some time on a ready-made bed upon the quarterdeck. Fletcher had already lifted several crates onto the quarterdeck and placed a mattress with clean sheets across them.

Carrying the wounded captain was not so easy for Fletcher. He moaned and groaned each time his old friend had to turn a corner, and he was not such a light person as he appeared. Finally, they reached the steps to the upper deck. Men lined along the deck and cheered when Fletcher brought their captain into the open air. His face was white and stubbly. His bandage now had a giant splurge of red from his half-opened wound. He was clearly in distress and pain, but he put on such a brave face that he inspired a few crew members to clap their hands for him.

Fletcher carried him up the steps to the quarter deck and firmly placed him on the makeshift bed.

"There you are, you great lump, Captain, sir." Fletcher puffed, out of breath from carrying the man so far. The heat and humidity of the Mediterranean were apparent to Talbot straight away. Down below in the stinking surgery, hidden away in the dark, he had not felt so hot, but now that he was in the sun's rays, his skin began to burn. There was not a cloud to be seen. He glanced out to sea, happy to witness the endless blue once again. To the starboard side, he could see land.

"Where are we, Francis?" he asked.

"Mr Campbell tells me we are rounding Crete. We've made good speed. There have been very few sails on recent horizons, and I prayed we would not be called upon to fight off another attack, and God appears to have answered my prayers. I have kept a log in your cabin should you wish to read it, sir," Fletcher said.

"Yes, that will help pass what time we have left now that I am awake. However, I do not feel myself. I feel ill, Francis and my legs are useless."

"Dr Brennan tells us your legs will return to normal. Save your energy, sir."

"Us? What is meant by *us*, Francis? You mean you and my wife?"

"No, sir, I mean me, your wife and the entire crew, or what's left of it. Have no fear, sir, for though I have enjoyed your wife's *company*, I have not enjoyed your wife!" He turned with a smile for Talbot. "I made you a promise. Our friendship means more, Captain, of that you can be assured."

"Very well, though the thought of you and her in the same room together makes me sicker than these wounds." Talbot attempted to sit up, but the pain was too much.

"Be still, sir. Lieutenant Jenkins and I have the ship under control."

"How many crew have we remaining, Francis?"

"Less than one hundred, sir. And that includes the marines, of which we number thirty," Fletcher told him in a dark tone.

"Oh my, it is worse than I thought. Thirty marines and seventy sailors. What about the officers?"

"That includes the officers, sir."

"What a dark day we suffered, Francis." Talbot began to pant.

"Yes, sir, but what matters now is that we fulfil our mission. We are close. A day's plain sailing at most."

"Yes, you're right. We must press on. We…we…must…" Talbot's eyes began to roll and sweat dripped from his head in the sweltering sun.

"Sir?" Fletcher spoke as he could see something was wrong. "Captain Talbot, sir. Percy?" Fletcher edged forward and bent down to see the captain, but he had lost consciousness. He could smell the wound and the blood-soaked bandage. It reminded him of rotten meat. He peeled back part of the black and crusty bandage to reveal the open wound. The skin surrounding the gaping hole where the musket ball had entered him was yellow and green. Black and blue veins could be seen flowing into the stinking infection. It could be amputated if it were an arm or a leg, but this required more skill.

"Jenkins!" Fletcher shouted from the quarter deck down to the mizzen mast where the lieutenant stood, exhausted.

"Yes, sir," he called back.

"Fetch me Dr Brennan, if you please, the captain is not well."

"Aye, sir," Jenkins replied before disappearing below.

Fletcher took another look at the wound. He raised his head to remove his nose from the stench and wafted his hand before his face.

Dr Brennan arrived and examined the captain, who seemingly could withstand the awful smell. He was used to it. He had been a ship's surgeon for many years, and this was not the worst scene he'd witnessed.

"He needs fresh water and dry land," Brennan told Fletcher. "He'll not recover while we are still at sea. We have only grog for drinking. It makes most of us ill as it is. He's dehydrated and lacks the strength to heal. How many days are we from this mysterious island, Captain Fletcher?"

"A day, two at the most, maybe less if the wind picks up."

"Maybe we can sail into the port at Hersonissos?" Dr Brennan suggested.

"Crete?"

"Yes, we are passing by Crete, are we not?" Dr Brennan put to Fletcher.

"That we are, but we have no time to rest there. We have a most important mission to accomplish!"

"He may well die if we do not give him fresh water, proper food and decent rest."

"We may well all die if we do not continue on our course, Doctor. You know who hunts us. You know those who wish to slaughter us before we get there. The island has fresh water. I have been there before. It has trees for shelter and fresh fruit growing in the forests. Once we are on the island, I do not intend to stay there for long, however long enough to heal our captain."

"You are, of course, in charge of this vessel, Captain Fletcher, but I fear it may be a death sentence for Captain Talbot."

Fletcher pondered for a moment. He cast his eyes across the mountains of Crete, visible on the horizon, rising out of the water like monstrous statues. He thought of the ancient Gods, Poseidon and all the other myths he'd learned as a child.

"How many days would we be ashore if we stopped at Crete?" Fletcher asked the surgeon.

"Days? I'd be asking how many weeks, sir. An infected wound like this will not heal quickly."

Fletcher slapped his knee in frustration at the news. He could not stop for weeks. It would not be possible, for the Knights of the Golden Gift may have still been on board, waiting, watching, seeking the moment to strike. Weeks in a harbour would give them plenty of opportunities.

"I cannot do it, Doctor. I am sorry, but the mission takes priority. We will do what we must. Do your best, good doctor."

"Then we must get him to more comfortable and shaded quarters. If we leave him on the quarterdeck, he will dry up like an old grape."

"Very well." Fletcher nodded and carried the sick captain back down into the surgery.

The day dragged on with an eery quietness. Isabella seldom left the great cabin, where she had chosen to sleep, unless she visited her sick husband and forced grog into his mouth. Fletcher and Jenkins took shifts on the quarterdeck, rarely speaking to anyone other than themselves unless they gave sailing orders to the remaining crew. Captain of Marines Dawson kept a constant guard around the ship, something which Fletcher wished to commend him for his diligence.

Woodland and Sholim made their way around the wooden hull, patching up broken bits of wood or using other broken objects to hammer into different patterns to fill a gap or smooth an edge. They, too, decided to keep to themselves and did their best not to get in anybody's way unless it was each other. Molly had also started spending her time with them. Sholim had taken a liking to her, and she often followed him about the ship.

Everyone was on edge. A nervousness followed everyone on board like a cloud of ghostly fog, surrounding and hovering above them. As Crete's mountains eventually faded beyond sight, Francis Fletcher felt a mixture of awkwardness, guilt and shame. They were in almost the exact location where he'd lost his ship, *Blunderbuss*, and crew to the same guns of the vessel he was now commanding. It made him uneasy. It was possible that beneath the same waves he was now floating across were the graves of his old shipmates. Those who'd served with him at Quiberon Bay were loyal to him through seven years of war with France and Spain. They'd sailed the Atlantic, hunted and plundered many French ships, been branded pirates by their own country, been chased into this dark corner of the globe and eventually sunk. Fletcher only had himself to blame. He knew he'd been caught off guard and outwitted by the same man he was now trying to keep alive—the same man who had killed Fletcher's crew and tried to have Fletcher hanged.

Fletcher approached Jenkins on the quarterdeck at the changing of their watch.

"We're in the same location where this very same crew sunk my ship, Lieutenant."

"Where is the island?" Jenkins asked.

"It's what I want to know. It's not here," Fletcher answered.

"We must double-check our position. Perhaps we've made an error?"

"It's unlikely," Fletcher responded with a sigh. "But not impossible. I must check the captain's log for the last time he sailed. I am fairly certain where I lost my *Blunderbuss*, but as you can imagine, Lieutenant, I did not have too much time to complete my logbook as we were sinking and I was swimming for my life."

"That is fine with me, Captain, sir. I will remain on the quarterdeck until you relieve me," Jenkins replied.

Francis Fletcher knocked on the door to the great cabin and entered before waiting for an answer. Isabella was sitting in her husband's oak chair, holding her head in her hands.

"Excuse me, Isabella. I have business here. I do not wish to disturb you." He could see by the redness in her eyes that she was in distress.

"What if he dies, Francis?" She sobbed.

"He's had plenty of chances to die. He's a sailor. He's been to war before he will make it again this time, I am sure," Fletcher lied. He knew that Talbot's chances did not look favourable. Dr Brennan, the ship's surgeon, had stressed the need for fresh water and proper rest, but now, due to his insistence, Fletcher had sailed past the opportunity in search of an island he could no longer find.

"I must, of course, read Captain Talbot's logbook with your permission. The last time we sailed, we found this island. We need to know the coordinates of that island, for it should be here, and it is not. Both Jenkins and I agree that it could be a human error, so it will be recorded in Percy's logbook. May I?"

"Of course, if that's what you need to do, Francis," Isabella permitted with tiredness in her speech.

Fletcher nodded his gratitude to her, not that he needed her permission. He would have searched for the log anyway if she had denied him. It was not difficult to find. He found the book he was after in a chest of drawers under the big oak desk.

He flickered through the pages until he found a page that simply read *I have got him* at the heading:

4 February 1764

Today is the day for celebration. At dawn, with the 'Sealion' silhouetted by the sunrise and with the Dolphin hidden in the darkness, we captured the pirate Francis Fletcher. The Sealion was sunk in a matter of minutes, becoming nothing but a few pieces of broken wood by the time daylight had arrived. Our superior gunnery and masterly seamanship caught his majesty's enemy off guard and finished him off before they could fire a shot in response to our attack.

I ordered the captain of marines, Dawson, to take a shore party to a small uncharted island where some survivors had headed on a small raft. The island is located approximately fifty nautical miles east of Crete at a bearing of ninety degrees from the most eastern tip of the island.

Captain of Marines Dawson returned some hours later, and lo and behold, who should one of the survivors be, but Francis Fletcher himself, too cowardly to have gone down with his ship.

There are peculiar reports of strange happenings on the island, inexplicable to Captain Dawson, Sergeant Walton, Marine Lockwood and Francis Fletcher. I must ask the Admiralty for permission to return.

Without delay, we return to England to see Francis Fletcher hanged.

Fletcher smiled at the words he was reading and spent the next few minutes rereading the text several times. "Didn't get to see me hang, though, did you? You bastard," he muttered under his breath.

"What are you saying?" Isabella asked. Fletcher had forgotten she was in the room.

"I'm just reading how your husband wanted to see me hang," Fletcher answered, still smiling.

"Show me!" Isabella demanded. She stood up and walked across the room as assertively as she always did when angry or determined to know something. Fletcher did not try to stop her. He allowed the pages to slip easily from his fingers as she took the book from his hands. Isabella stood and read aloud the words that her husband had written. She repeated one particular line he had written, which caused her face to turn red with rage.

"I must ask the admiralty for permission to return…I must ask the admiralty for permission to return! That bastard!" She threw the book across the room, hitting the globe which had a few pieces missing from its damage during the battle. "He told me the admiralty had ordered him to return to sea! He promised me that his last mission would be his final voyage, but sadly, oh so sadly, he had been ordered to sea again. Now I discover that he *asked* to come to sea. You men are all the bloody same!" She growled at Fletcher, who felt she was scolding him and not her husband.

"Be calm, Isabella; you know he is a man of the sea. I believe this voyage will be his last," Fletcher tried to comfort her.

"Yes, because he's on his last legs. Indeed, he cannot feel his legs!" Isabella fired back angrily.

"You know it to be true. Percy Talbot will not sail again should he live. Try to take your mind off a misfortune that may not yet happen. You're alone in here. Where is Molly? Some company would do you good."

"Molly still dwells in shame. She sleeps with the Bohemian now." Isabella wiped a tear from her eye.

"She sleeps where? With Sholim? In the crew's quarters?" Fletcher asked, taken back somewhat by the unexpected comment.

"There are so many empty hammocks now, and she spends her time there. They seem to be able to communicate fairly well," Isabella explained.

"Does Molly speak his language? What is it, German or Czech, or something like that? I am certain his English is of a poor standard."

"I do not know. They use hand signals and words I do not know the meaning of. They pass notes to each other. I assume they're pictures to describe what they're trying to tell each other. Here's one Molly left the other day." Isabella reached into a drawer beneath the desk and pulled out a brown piece of paper. On it was a scribble of a leaf that looked like a child had done it. Fletcher assumed it must have been Sholim who drew the picture as he was confident the Bohemian had no skill with a quill.

"I wonder what that could mean. How odd that these two can communicate in such a way," Fletcher said. He turned the paper over to reveal the other side. Written were the three faded words *Repent the Verses.* "Why would she write this to him if he cannot read or understand English?" he queried.

"It was he that wrote it to her," Isabella corrected Fletcher.

"That's impossible. The man can barely speak a word of English. I doubt that the man has had proper schooling. I should think he is quite unable to read and write!"

"Then he has deceived you. He wrote it to Molly. I think they're fond of each other. It makes sense as they're both outcasts to the rest of us, what with him being a foreigner and her being a black woman," Isabella said.

"I find it very strange that these two should become so acquainted with one another and even more absurd that Sholim is able to write this note, whatever it means," Fletcher commented with a frown.

"I know not a lot of this man other than he stinks and he has written notes similar to this one and given them to comfort Molly. She's ashamed of killing the Reverand," Isabella told Fletcher.

"She killed the Reverand? Mr Cunningham?" That was news to Fletcher, who believed him to have been killed by the pirates.

"Yes…" Isabella paused, not realising that no one else knew about Molly's mishap.

"I thought he died protecting you from the pirates."

"Well, yes, he was doing just that, but at the spur of the moment, Molly jumped on the pirate's back and was clumsy with her knife, accidentally stabbing the reverend instead." Isabella suddenly turned white. A great feeling of realisation shuddered through her body. Her spine tingled and her lip trembled.

"What is it?" Fletcher asked.

"Molly…"

"What about her? Other than she sleeps elsewhere with someone pretending not to understand English this whole time!" Fletcher retorted, displaying his annoyance at being deceived.

"It's just that…well…before the battle, she told me she had great skill with a knife. She told me that her father taught her to throw a knife and where to stab a human in the neck. How could she have been so clumsy when stabbing the reverend?"

"Good God!" Fletcher also felt a dark awareness. "You don't think, no, it can't be. You don't mean to tell me that she intentionally killed the reverend and used the excuse of clumsiness in the battle to make it look accidental?"

Isabella Talbot and Francis Fletcher stared at each other with no words coming to them. They both thought the same thing at the same time.

"Your husband!" Fletcher broke the silence. They dashed out of the great cabin and down into the surgery. When they burst in, Dr Brennan was standing over Captain Talbot with a damp cloth on his forehead.

"Step away from the Captain, Doctor!" Fletcher ordered as he drew his pistol and aimed at the surgeon's head.

"Cease your madness, Captain Fletcher. Can't you see this is a surgery?" Dr Brennan yelled back, displaying commendable courage as a pistol was aimed at his face.

"Step away, or I shoot!" Fletcher ordered again. He hoped the doctor would agree, for Fletcher did not intend to pull the trigger. Fortunately, the bluff worked, and Dr Brennan shuffled to the side, dripping the wet cloth all over the floor.

Talbot was awake, but the weakness in his eyes was apparent. Isabella rushed towards him and held his head in her hands.

"Are you unhurt?" she asked him.

"I am weak, but the doctor takes care of me," Talbot answered in a whisper. "What is the meaning of all this?" he asked. Fletcher paced forwards.

"Captain, we were worried that you being down here alone might attract unwelcome visitors."

"You mean the Knights of the Golden Gift?"

"To speak plainly, Captain, that is what I mean. Now that you have shown the crew that you're still alive, we fear it might have been a mistake. Any assassin wishing you dead wouldn't need to risk revealing themselves if they thought you would die anyway. But now that they know you're alive, they might feel the need to come and finish you off."

"And who do you think might be suspect this time? Have we more Jacobites on board? Anyone else wishing to toast the king across the water?" Talbot asked as if he were exasperated.

"Well, there has been some suspicious activity from a most unlikely source, sir."

"Do tell." The captain suddenly felt more alert.

Isabella chose to interrupt the men and spoke, "Molly accidentally killed the Reverand in the battle. You sent him there to protect us, and when the time came, he did indeed attempt to protect us, but while trying to strike down a pirate, Molly missed and killed the reverend. I have doubts now that it was an accident at all."

"Heavens above, my dear, you cannot surely believe that poor Molly is at fault?" Talbot husked.

"Well, not just that, she has been communicating with the Bohemian, Sholim. They passed this note to each other," Fletcher said, handing the brown paper to Talbot. The captain beckoned Isabella to bring a lantern forward to see the paper better. He studied both sides intently. His face became serious and his eyebrows raised dramatically.

"Repent The Verses!" he whispered. "Sholim wrote this?" he asked Fletcher.

"Sholim and Molly pass notes to each other. This is one your wife found, sir."

"My God!" Talbot had also felt the realisation. "I am such a fool!" he said.

"What is it, Captain?" Fletcher asked as Isabella squeezed her husband's hand in fear.

"Repent The Verses! I have no idea what it means, but it is written on the painting in the solar of Lord Perceval's castle at Enmore. Molly's parents had commissioned the painting for him to say thank you after he rescued them from the plantations! And this leaf is on the frame of the painting, I am sure of it. The last time I was there, I looked at the painting. Lord Perceval asked me if I liked it and told me of its origin! I am such a fool. Molly found Mr Gale, and Molly was skulking the night Master Laine was slain!"

"And if I may, sir," Fletcher interrupted, "Molly had told your wife that she was extremely skilled in handling a knife. She even mentioned where to cut a man's throat. Wasn't Mr Ingham slain by his throat being sliced open? As well as the reverend now of all people. What a great way to make a death look like an accident in the heat of battle surrounded by panic. She stuck the knife into poor Mr Cunningham's neck with what can only be described as expert precision!"

"This seems to add up, Francis, but what about the Bohemian?" Talbot asked, still unable to make his voice more than a whisper.

"Holy Mother of God!" Fletcher burst out before turning round to make sure no one had entered the room to stab him in the back. "Sholim! He's immune to the snake's eyes!" Fletcher turned again to Talbot and looked at Isabella. "When we were last on this island, which we can no longer find, we were all of us, Woodland, Kilpatrick, Sergeant Walton and Lockwood entranced. We were caught in the gaze of the snake's eyes on the rocks. But Sholim was not stirred by the trap. Oh my, he is a servant of the Devil!" Fletcher felt his spine tingle.

"Then why, in the name of our good Lord Jesus, did he help you leave the island?" Isabella asked.

"Maybe because he knew more people were looking for us, Captain Dawson's search party. He wanted us to leave the island. If we had all been killed, more would have come to find their missing crews. And then there's the burning cross!"

"What burning cross?" Isabella asked. Her forehead had begun to sweat.

"That's right," Talbot said, lifting his head. "I remember being called up on deck to witness a fire on the island, apparently one of your crew," he said, looking towards Fletcher. "Kilpatrick, he died on the island, and when you made a cross for his headstone, it began to burn as we departed with no explanation. It is the Devil's island. No cross of Jesus shall be welcome there!"

Fletcher brought his palm over his face and pressed his eyes with his thumb and middle finger. The more he thought about it, the more obvious it became. He summed up in his head once again before speaking out loud.

"Sholim is immune to the snake. He can communicate with Molly in English. She killed Mr Gale after discovering he was spreading the story of the Knights of the Golden Gift to Lord Percival. She stole his books containing the fifth gospel. She killed Mr Ingham by opening his throat, and I will assume it was Sholim who was strong enough to hurl Master Laine over the side of the ship with a rope around his neck. Molly then stabbed the reverend, an obvious target. She cannot have allowed a servant of God on the island. We do not know who might be next, but Captain, sir, you are not safe at all. We must remain with you. We must not let Sholim or Molly know that we have discovered their little secret."

"I'd have them arrested and tossed into the sea with a cannonball around their necks!" Isabella commented.

"We cannot do that. Now that we know that somehow they're both descendants of Jagur, we need at least one of them to guide us to the gold. With hands tied and every musket available concentrated on them, we will use them to show us the way. We do not know how deep the caves behind the waterfall are. Molly may have never been to the island, but Sholim has, so we must use him."

"I agree with that, Francis," Captain Talbot said to Fletcher.

"I will select some marines to capture Sholim. We will take him ashore as if nothing is suspect, and then I will signal them to train their muskets on him. We will bind his hands and he will take us to the gold. Molly should remain here and she should have a guard, but neither Molly nor Sholim must suspect anything until they have been well and truly separated."

"Make sure Captain Dawson is well informed. We cannot let this go wrong lest they escape."

"Aye, Captain." Fletcher saluted Talbot, who was now going green in the face and the appalling smell from his chest becoming unbearable.

"Leave us now, Francis. I wish to speak with my wife privately."

"As you wish, I must find Captain Dawson and inform him of our plans."

Fletcher left the room, looking both ways along the dark corridor in case anyone had heard them talking.

Talbot attempted to raise his head but was so weak that he could only move his lips to speak. Even that drained him of more energy.

"Isabella," he whispered.

"I am here," she said, holding his hands. She noticed the vacant glare in his eyes as if they could not focus. The colour had faded from his usual bright green into a damp grey.

"Isabella. I fear I shall not live to see our children again," he said.

"No, Percy, you must not think like that. You are going to live. You need to rest; do not cast doubt on your survival!" She began to cry once more. Neither of them said anything, but instead, they just sat. Eventually, after seeing that he was asleep but still breathing, she decided to rest. Despite the smell, she sat beside him, placed her head next to his and closed her eyes.

Chapter 16

Fletcher closed the door to the officer's wardroom, checking for the third time that no soul could hear what he was discussing with Jenkins and Dawson and no one was lurking in the shadows.

"So let's go over the plan once more, Captain Dawson. Explain it to me if you would," Fletcher ordered.

"We go ashore in three rowing boats. We command one each. My boat with ten marines will beach first, and yours will be second, followed by Lieutenant Jenkins, whose boat will be behind yours. When your boat beaches, I will order my men, whose muskets will be preloaded, to turn and face Sholim, who will have unwittingly been placed in your boat. Your men will then disperse left and right to prevent him from running. Jenkins will then come up behind him to prevent him from trying to run into the sea. I thought he had issues swimming?"

Dawson asked after he had repeated the plan to Fletcher.

"And I believed him to be unable to speak English, but he has shown us, though he does not yet know it, not only that he *can* speak our language, but can read and write it too," Fletcher said, still irritated about Sholim's deception.

"We then have Sholim tied and gagged. We march into the jungle until we reach the waterfall, where Sholim will show us the way to the gold." Dawson completed his repetition of the plan they'd agreed upon.

"It is unlikely to go so smoothly, especially the last part. No doubt we shall have to improvise, but that is the plan. Lieutenant Jenkins, have you any more to add?" Fletcher asked the lieutenant.

"No, sir, the plan is clear," he answered.

"Good. Now, all we need to do is find this bloody island. It's that mysterious; it's completely disappeared. Let us return to our duties, and mum's the word about our plans."

"Aye, Captain." Dawson saluted.

"Yes, sir," Jenkins said before returning to the quarterdeck.

Fletcher kept a loaded pistol on him at all times. He paced the ship below the upper deck, ready to unsheathe his sword, and kept a dagger tucked into a small sheath hidden in his belt. After making a routine inspection of the gundeck where everything was as it should be, despite the smallness of the crew, he decided once more to pay a visit to Captain Talbot.

The atmosphere instantly changed as he opened the creaking door to the surgery. Isabella was there sobbing gently, and Dr Brennan was holding her hand. The surgeon looked up at Fletcher. No words were necessary. Fletcher could read what was written on the doctor's face. Dropping to one knee, Fletcher took hold of Isabella's other hand, but she immediately pulled it away.

"Don't come near me, Francis!" she said. "This is your doing."

"Isabella, I…"

"We could have gone to Crete! He could still be alive, but you and your bloody ego!" She turned to look him in the eye. Her face was soaked in tears. Lines appeared to have grown on her forehead, indicating an aging process had begun instantly from Talbot's passing.

"We are men of the sea, Isabella. We are men of war. Our decisions are not always based upon the wellness of a single being but the ship as a whole. You know as well as I and even Percy did that we could all be dead had we stopped at Crete. Failure in this mission is a death sentence for us all. For Edward and Estelle, for you, for me." Fletcher spoke softly yet convincingly. Isabella wrapped her arms around Fletcher's neck and began crying aloud. Tears poured onto Fletcher's neck, and for a second, seeing her in such painful emotion almost brought a tear to his own eyes. Holding onto the woman he had loved for many years but had lost out to his closest friend, he looked down at the corpse of Captain Talbot. His face was white as a sail and his chest was smothered red and black with patches of yellow and green where the infected wound had forced the captain to succumb to his death. When Isabella finally let go, she was breathing heavily and her hands were shaking.

"He would want to be buried at sea," she gently said.

"All sailors would," Fletcher agreed.

"Just like all you men, the sea was his real love. I am merely a mistress."

"No, it is not like that, Isabella."

"Yes, it is. It is exactly like that. He asked to come on this mission after promising me he would never sail again. I was just the woman in his house, the object that carried and raised his children while he carried on his affair with the waves." Isabella hung her head as she spoke the sad words.

"No, Isabella. Do not forget. He was willing to fight a duel for you. He was willing to risk his life for you, remember?"

"But he wouldn't *live* for me. He knew the risks of going to war and it didn't stop him the whole time he was away playing sailors against the French."

"And you knew too! You knew that being married to a sailor would bring the possibility of losing him, but you married him anyway," Fletcher reminded her.

"Because I loved him. I admit that in my younger days, I was more content for him to go and be the hero, but after the children were born, I begged him to come home to accept his role at the training academy, but he turned it all down to go back out to sea leaving our children and me at home without him. Now he's dead. How will I tell my children?"

"You tell them that he died on a mission to protect them! Now, more than ever, you must see, Isabella, that we must accomplish this quest for their sake and your own!"

As Isabella looked upwards from the blood-stained dark surgery floor to meet with Fletcher's, the whole ship shuddered and shook, sending them hurtling forward towards the bow. The gun deck roared above them, with cannons sliding and rolling over.

On the upper deck and quarterdeck, men fell forwards and backwards depending on which they were facing. Lieutenant Jenkins was flung down the steps into a heap on the floor, and one man fell from the mast, fortunately able to grab a rope. The lucky man dangled in a daze briefly until he could swing himself into the rigging.

After becoming lodged on a rock, the ship's bow had raised herself out of the water.

"Christ, we've hit a reef!" Jenkins called out from a kneeling position.

"What the devil is going on, Lieutenant?" Captain Dawson shouted.

"There's a bloody reef!"

Fletcher pulled himself together and hurried into the open air as quickly as possible. He first saw Jenkins kneeling, clearly unstable from his fall, and then looked about the ship to get a sense of the calamity.

"What's happened?" he said to Jenkins.

"We've struck a reef, Captain."

"A reef? Where the hell did that come from?" Fletcher asked.

"Exactly my thoughts, sir," Jenkins answered. Fletcher ran to the starboard side and held onto the rigging. To his utter disbelief and astonishment, not only had they hit a reef and become stuck on the top of a rock, but they had found the island.

"How the hell did you hit that?" Fletcher asked Jenkins.

"It…It wasn't there, sir!"

"What do you mean it wasn't there? It's bloody there now!"

"I swear to God, sir, we were just sailing in the open sea and then *smash*. When I came to my senses, I noticed the reef, and now it is as clear as day, sir, that there is an island here as well!"

"It is pure bloody daylight, Lieutenant. How can you miss something so big?"

"I promise you, sir, it was not here! It was not visible a few moments ago!" Jenkins insisted.

"Mr Campbell!" Fletcher called to the wheel, where Mr Campbell regained control of himself after taking his tumble.

"Sir?" he shouted back.

"Congratulations on finding the island, Mr Campbell, but you've run us aground!"

"As Lieutenant Jenkins says, sir, it was not here before! There was nothing, just the sea!"

"Bloody hell, we're in a situation and a half now! Where are the carpenters? They've got some work to do. Jenkins, find Mr Beatty and get me a damage report. I want the ship patching up as soon as possible!"

Below decks in the storage compartments, water was gushing through the hole put there by the ship's collision with the rock. Mr Beatty and Tom Woodland were hammering away, trying to fill the gap with wooden planks, but the water pressure was too much for them. Others came to join them, but it was to no avail. They were already waist-deep in seawater.

Fletcher took himself below to examine the damage. It was horrifying watching the water forcing itself through the heavy hull. Food stores and barrels had already begun to float. Fletcher waded towards the men working as hard as they could.

"What can we do, Mr Beatty?" he asked.

"Not a lot," Beatty offered an unwelcome reply. "We will have to wait until the water level rises to that of the sea, then possibly try to repair her from the outside, but we're lodged on the rock, sir. I fear this might be the end of the Dolphin. The hole is the size of a carriage, sir. If we weren't stuck on the rock, we'd probably be listing by now."

Fletcher was stunned. He'd found this island only twice; both times had now been with a sinking ship. He scratched at his head in thought, wondering what he could do. The mission was always at the front of his mind, taking priority even in dire situations. It is how he'd been trained and nearly always conducted himself whenever at sea or in action. As his mind gained clarity, his wet legs carried him back past the gun deck, where he could see many of the guns dislodged from the collision. He continued back up to the upper deck. He could see now that the Dolphin had begun to list to starboard. He had little choice now; he knew he would have to give the order to abandon ship, but that would scutter his plan to arrest Sholim and Molly.

"What are your orders, sir?" Jenkins demanded. "I suggest we get the boats into the water and start rowing for the island. We have little choice, Captain. I give it thirty minutes before we capsize. We can't sail her now; the mainmast is broken and we've taken on too much water. The rudder chain appears to be unanswering too! Shall I give the order, sir?"

Fletcher was desperate; a lump had grown in his throat, but he knew he had to do it. He looked across the ship from bow to stern and could see the panic-stricken faces of his crew, who were yet to be told that Captain Talbot had died.

"Give the order, Lieutenant!" Fletcher reluctantly answered Jenkins.

The discouraged crew began a scramble of graceless action, untying the rowing boats, cursing every other word as their beloved Dolphin began to sink. Fletcher knew there was no time to implement his plan. Dawson had not yet had the time to speak with his marines and go through the motions, so they would just have to get as many crew and marines to shore and arrest Sholim and Molly on dry land.

Isabella appeared on the deck just as the first rowing boats were loaded clumsily into the water.

"Isabella, stay close to me. We must leave the ship we're sinking and lowering the rowing boats. Do you understand me?" Fletcher shouted above the noise that was all around them. She still had tears in her red eyes. Fletcher hoped that she would understand without explaining that this would mean there could be no funeral for her husband. Captain Talbot would have to go down with his ship as he believed every captain should. Isabella said nothing. She nodded and made her way to the side. Fletcher helped her climb onto the dangling netting, which looked far too unsafe, and she made her way down past the gun ports into a rowing boat where several marines were already there to help her.

Upon turning around, Fletcher saw Sholim and Molly making their way to the ship's side and saw they were holding hands. As angry as he'd ever been, Fletcher approached them. He had not seen either of them for days, but his opinion of them had changed dramatically. In his free hand, Sholim held another brown note.

"What's this?" Fletcher asked, snatching the note from Sholim. Sholim stood and stared blankly. "Don't look at me like that, you bastard!" Fletcher said, unable to hold back his anger. "I know you can understand everything I'm saying! Repent The Verses, I assume?" Fletcher asked sarcastically to his former friend.

Sholim had a fearful look as he now knew he'd been discovered. The ship jolted once more violently as part of her began to break, but that did not bother Fletcher. Instead, he drew his sword and slashed at Sholim's face, cutting it with the point before swinging again. However, the Bohemian was too swift and ducked just before the blade could split his skull. Fletcher lunged again, aiming to stick the blade straight into his belly, but Sholim was quick to move. Seizing his moment, Sholim jumped onto the side, using the rigging to aid him as the ship shuddered and twisted to a heavy tilt. Sholim looked at Molly, smiled and dived into the water.

Fletcher ran to the side, looking overboard to see Sholim swimming towards the shore.

"That bastard can bloody swim as well!" Fletcher shrieked before realising Molly was still behind him. "Give up, Molly. We know who you are. You're under arrest." Molly looked petrified.

"Francis, I do not understand. What is happening?" she said, trying to sound convincing, but her acting was no longer good enough to fool Francis Fletcher.

"Don't play the half-wit with me, Molly!" he said as he aimed his sword at her throat. He saw Sergeant Walton aiding the last marines down the flimsy netting onto the boats by sheer good luck. "Sergeant Walton!" He called to him, "Before you disembark, bind this woman's hands. She is now a prisoner. There's no time to explain, tie her up and get her to the beach. Do not let her out of your sight. Do you understand me?"

Sergeant Walton carried out the order and rushed Molly to the side of the ship without question. Fletcher followed them down into the same rowing boat just in time before the Dolphin finally keeled over. It hit the bottom of the sea, leaving two of her three masts and the stern, where the great cabin was, poking out of the water.

The sound of men heaving on ores and the rushing of waves charging to the shoreline echoed vacantly and distantly in Fletcher's ears as he stood on his rowing boat, staring at the wreck of the Dolphin. He thought about Talbot and others who were in the surgery, unable to escape. He hadn't seen Woodland or Mr Beatty get out, but he hoped they were on one of the other boats, which had departed sooner than his. Once again, he was the last man on a ship, which had sunk, leaving him stranded on an island that held the gateway to Hell, only this time *he* would be conducting the manhunt.

Chapter 17

Fletcher sat around a fire on the beach, holding a blanket over Isabella's wet shoulders as the moon rose over the island's far side, casting long shadows from the tall palm trees. They chatted about their desperate situation with the other officers, Jenkins, Dawson and Dr Brennan. They had hung their soaking clothes on a makeshift line from some old rope salvaged from the wreckage of the Dolphin, which remained partially submerged. A party of marines had been sent back earlier in the day to the wreck to gather supplies, tools, weapons and anything they saw fit for use. The flooding in the hull had ruined most provisions save for a grog barrel and apples that floated. Nearly all the powder for their muskets was useless. Only some cutlasses, daggers and knives from the kitchen were worth carrying back as weaponry and a small pile of axes from the carpenters was brought out of the vessel to be used as tools.

Fletcher had ordered the surviving crew to build a camp immediately. They gathered dry wood and logs, lit fires and built crude shelters from sticks and giant leaves. They all knew they had to make the best of daylight hours. Tom Woodland was a busy man chopping logs and erecting wooden frames for the remaining men to sleep under roofs made from palm leaves. Some rowing boats were turned upside down and propped up with strong enough sticks to create a shelter.

Dawson prepared a guard of marines on the beach, the shoreline and the trees where the sand met the jungle. There were not enough of them to cover all possible entrances to their hastily built, rickety camp if they were attacked in force, but as far as they knew, the only enemy on the island that could cause them harm was Sholim. He was undoubtedly somewhere on the island, but his whereabouts could have been anyone's guess.

Next to the campfire, where the four officers and Isabella huddled in only their undergarments, was a wooden cage. It was the first thing Fletcher had ordered Woodland to build, and inside, it contained Molly. She had a glum look across her face, which glowed red as the fire lapped the air around her. Fletcher stared through the flames, never taking his eye away from her for more than a few seconds. He was still in disbelief that this young girl, whom he had known for many years, could be the servant of the Devil himself. She had played the part of innocence so well for such a long time. Fletcher pondered that if he had never discovered the island, how would it be possible that anyone could ever find her out? If she was a descendant of Jagur and a protector of the gold he had stolen from the baby Jesus many centuries ago, then her parents were too. He decided he would have to interrogate her.

The captain excused himself from the monotonous conversation the other officers were having about the weight of the burden their duties now carried. Apart from learning that they now numbered only seventy men after losing another thirty when the Dolphin had sunk, he had no interest in what they were saying.

Placing himself between the fire and Molly, he sat down. He picked up a twig and twizzled it between his fingers as he thought about what to say.

"Are you comfortable?" he asked, deciding to show Molly some sensitivity before giving her what he intended to be a vigorous round of questioning. He soon realised that it was a grossly unintelligent question.

"No!" she replied. "I'm in a cage. A place my father told me he'd never allow me to be."

"Well, there are some things I need to know, Molly, and it would be in your best interest to answer me truthfully. Can you do that, or are you bound by your service to protect the Devil?"

"I will tell you what you want to know unless you intend to kill me, in which case you can just get on with it, for I'll not move my lips so much as to breathe if I am to die here anyway," she answered him.

Fletcher had no choice but to trust her words, but he also knew it was nigh on impossible to rely on this woman who had managed to misguide so many people for so many years as to who she truly was.

"Well, I know not where to begin. I've known you for many years. When Percy and I were children, we knew you. Were you serving the Devil then, too?" he asked.

"My mother and father used to tell me who I am every night, usually after we were back in our sleeping quarters. They told me I was special. It is easy to believe. One can perfectly see that my skin colour differs from everyone else's.

We used to be enslaved until Lord Perceval took my parents away from Jamaica to be treated as equals."

"But you continued to pray secretly to Satan and turned your back on Jesus?"

"I turned my back on no one. I was born at Enmore and was only ever told to worship Lucifer, the fallen angel. We with dark skin were not permitted into the church to speak with *your* God anyhow. It suited us well."

"And when Percy Talbot visited and spoke to Lord Perceval of the island we'd discovered, you overheard them and murdered Perceval's friend? Tell me what happened!" Fletcher demanded.

"Percy came to beg Lord Perceval to reverse the decision to give you your freedom."

"Yes, I know that."

"He saw the painting on Perceval's wall. The painting was a gift from my parents, who also intended it as a shrine for us. Whenever we saw the painting, we could speak to our Lord whenever we went into the solar where the painting still hangs. The painting was our church. Perceval never knew. It is unlikely he ever will. Even now, other Knights of the Golden Gift will search for him. He might already be dead."

"So your parents deceived Perceval, not only because they're Satanists but also because what he thought was a rather delightful gift was, in fact, a way for you to communicate with the Devil? What happened after Percy talked about the island."

"Lord Perceval left Captain Talbot at the castle and returned some days later with his friend, Mr Gale. This old man unwittingly brought the final copies of what is known as the fifth gospel of Christ into my own possession. It is the only gospel that speaks of Jagur and the gold he stole from our enemy's son."

"And where is the gospel now?"

"I burned it as soon as I slit Mr Gale's throat," Molly whispered, sending a shiver through Fletcher's spine as she placed her hands on the wooden cage bars and edged closer. "Then I sent a letter to the head of my division explaining what I had found. Now, the knights are everywhere. They're looking for you." Fletcher was made uneasy by the way Molly was smiling.

"Good God!" He was dismayed.

"Good?" Molly asked. "Tell me why, why is the creator good? Has he not had a long history of brutality and murder? I have read your book, your bible. He is nothing but a murderer. An evildoer. Why does he create only to destroy?

His son, whom he sent only to suffer and die, did not deserve the riches of the Earth. That is why we protect it. The war between good and evil continues in the shadows of the world even to this day, but you must question who is evil and who is not. All my lord did was question your God and ask him to prove himself. Your God created floods and rained fire on cities."

"No, Molly, your God seduces us to sin."

"And who is the judge of sin?"

"Only God, our creator, will judge us."

"Exactly, it is only a sin if God says it is a sin. But is it a sin for him to kill? Was it not his sin to send the angel of death to kill the firstborns at Passover? Was it not a sin for him to create the plagues of Egypt and allow the world to commit slavery? No, it is only a sin if he says it is. Your God is corrupt. Mine is just an angel who questions the authority of your God, who deemed even that a sin."

"I did not come for lectures on morality; you can redeem yourself, and God will forgive you, help us."

"Help you do what?" Molly asked. "I am but a black woman in a white man's world. As you can see, I am in a cage."

"Where is the gold? Behind the waterfall?" Fletcher asked, but Molly only began to laugh.

"I have never been here in my life, Francis!" she said. "I was only brought up to protect the *secret* of the gold. I know not where it truly lies."

"Then help us find Sholim, he may know. He trusts you! How is it that he, too, is a descendant of Jagur?"

"We are many. Jagur came from Israel more than one thousand seven hundred years ago. The colours of his descendant's skin have long been diluted. Jagur sent children all over the world to populate. Some went to Africa, some to Europe, some to Asia, and they are now in lands yet to be discovered by colonial white men. You are showing your naivety, Captain Fletcher!"

"And how did you know *him*?"

"How did I know Sholim, you mean? That was easy. We have our signs and symbols known only to us. Were you blind to the tattoo which circles his wrist?"

"I have seen it but questioned it not, for it is a language I do not speak. He is Bohemian."

"Oh, Francis, the tattoo is in Latin!" She looked at him almost pitifully for his lack of intelligence.

"What does it say?"

"Paeniteat Versiculos."

"And what does it mean?" Fletcher showed his frustration.

"You already know what it means, Francis. Think about it for just a moment." Fletcher began to think. He remembered the note that Isabella had shown him. "Repent the Verses. Why is that in English?"

"Because last century, your King James rewrote the bible in English and the descendants of Jagur who dwelt in Britain had to adapt as Latin faded from your language. You will find it written in many tongues all over the world," Molly answered him.

"And what does it mean to repent the verses?" Fletcher asked.

"That I cannot tell you."

"Because you are too stubborn or because you do not know?"

Molly smiled. She knew now that Fletcher could not kill her if she held onto the information he wanted, and she had already given him enough.

"Damn you, Molly!" Fletcher shouted, prompting Isabella to place herself between Fletcher and Molly and put a finger on his lips. Fletcher had not noticed that she had joined them. Isabella led him away from the crooked cage and they returned to the fire.

"Captain Dawson, we must have a full guard on her through the night," Fletcher said to the captain of the marines.

"We'll guard her through the night, but how many nights do we intend to stay, sir?" Dawson asked.

"Not more than two. Tomorrow, you and I will take some marines inland to find the gold, and if necessary, we shall find Sholim, too. I do not care much for leaving him stranded here, but he threatens us. He may well be moving the gold somewhere else as we speak. He has been here at least once but may have been here more times. I want to get the gold and leave. The island itself is a land of true evil." The cogs in Fletcher's mind began to turn. He was always quick to think, and experience in battle had taught him how to make decisions on the spot. "Dr Brennan, Lieutenant Jenkins."

"Yes, sir?"

"Yes, sir?"

"I will take Captain Dawson and the marines inland. Meanwhile, I want you two and the crew to prepare the rowing boats. Provide fresh water on each boat, enough for several days at sea. I want you to collect fruit, catch fish and maybe return to the Dolphin and see if we can use any more barrels floating around with provisions that we could use. After returning from the jungle, we will row to Crete with or without the gold. I believe we are about fifty miles away. It will take a day or two to row there if we take shifts on the oars, including officers and women." Fletcher turned to Isabella, who nodded in agreement to her role behind an oar. "Any questions?" he asked his officers.

"What happens when we reach Crete, sir?" Jenkins asked.

"I do not know. We will probably have to explain that we are the remnants of a British ship that hit a rock, and we are seeking safe passage to England and then promise them payment for a vessel upon reaching the shores of our great island. In essence, we will tell them the truth, but they cannot know we are carrying the gold."

"How much gold was the baby Jesus given, sir? Is it a single bar? Is it old Roman coins?" Jenkins asked.

"That is a good question, Lieutenant, but the truth is that I do not know. If we re-tell the story of Jagur, it seems that one man was sufficient in carrying it," Fletcher added.

"One more question, Captain," Dawson said. "What do we tell the men? My marines know not what they're walking into. Should they know about the gold?"

"Let us keep it amongst us officers for now. I believe marines Lockwood, Bairstow and Sergeant Walton have been there before but were sworn to secrecy and can be trusted?" Fletcher looked at Dawson, hoping that he would confirm the stated question. Dawson nodded, much to Fletcher's relief. "My carpenter, Tom Woodland, also knows where we're headed. So, when we reach the waterfall, you and I, Dawson with Sergeant Walton, Bairstow, Lockwood and Woodland, will go up the rocks, but do not forget to cover your eyes and try not to look at the snake-shaped rock. Remember, this is a military operation. It will likely not go according to plan, so you must be ready to use your initiatives. Do you all understand?"

Everyone either nodded or muttered, "Yes, sir," before Isabella had a question to ask.

"Francis?"

"Yes, Isabella?"

"Where should I go?"

"I would prefer you to stay here with Dr Brennan and Lieutenant Jenkins and help out as best you can. Perhaps you can talk to Molly and get some more information from her. She's not the simple servant girl we all took her for. Now, if there's nothing else, we should get some sleep."

Sleep did not come quickly to any who attempted it on the island that night. The exhaustion and the hunger gnawed away at their bodies while flies landed on their faces or any other part of them that displayed flesh—covering up meant sweltering but sleeping in the open meant to be eaten alive. The sounds of the jungle coming to life during the night battled the waves rushing to dominate the eardrums of those who wished to drift into a slumber.

Isabella had given up fighting with herself to sleep. Her eyes refused to close and her ears could not shut out the inescapable noises. She walked along the beach, past the fire, which was now just a pile of smouldering charcoal, and then onto Molly, who lay in the wooden cage. Molly was sound asleep, breathing gently. *Of course,* Isabella thought to herself. *We're in the land of her fallen angel. She can sleep soundly. This is her heaven.*

The crack of a twig coming from behind startled her. She turned around and gasped before letting out an enormous sigh of relief.

"You do not sleep?" Fletcher asked.

"Neither do you," she came back at him.

"I cannot. I think only of tomorrow and what the day will bring. Will we live to see it through? And will we accomplish what we set out to do? It's difficult to lead men whom I know will possibly die. I did not sleep before Quiberon Bay, either. We knew the French ships were going to face us the next day. Some swung in their hammocks or rolled in their bunks with the waves, but not I. It was too difficult," Fletcher told her.

"I think now only of my husband," Isabella sighed. "Part of me wishes to join him, but his legacy is our children and I must survive for them. I cannot fail what he leaves me behind." Isabella could not bring herself to cry any more tears, but the sadness stretched across her face gave Fletcher enough cause to develop a lump in his throat.

"You will receive compensation from the admiralty when we get back home. He was a good captain. The Navy will not abandon you," Fletcher tried to comfort her.

"I know. He has savings that he told me to use if ever he should not return. It's our children I fear I have to face. That's if they're even still alive. These murderers. These butchers. They protect true evil by slitting throats. I feel ashamed to have placed Edward and Estelle in such danger."

"You're not alone in your shame, Isabella. Perhaps I should have gone to Crete, and your husband would still be alive. I do not know. My decision was purely military, but I did not listen to sounder advice."

"No, Francis, you made the same decision my husband would have made. You're men of war, and death is a part of everyday life for all of you," Isabella conceded after earlier blaming Fletcher for her husband's death on his ego and his military mind taking precedence over the lives of humans who stood a chance at life if they were appropriately treated. Fletcher was glad that she had accepted his decision.

They walked further along the beach, stepping over sleeping crew members and marines who had been allowed an hour or two to rest between their shifts guarding the beach. Fletcher warmly noticed that Isabella was holding his hand. He had not realised at first as his mind had been paying attention to the swaying trees and listening intently to the leaves rustling in the breeze and the waves which continued to lap away at the shore. The warm feeling comforted him. However, it came with a guilty burden. His old friend turned enemy turned friend again was dead only a few hundred feet away, trapped on the sunken Dolphin's surgery, deep beneath the waves, and here was Francis Fletcher, still alive and still in love with his old friend's wife.

Fletcher did not often think about the future beyond a few days. Years in military service had taught him that it was dangerous to think much further ahead. He'd lost count of how many men he'd known to die during his years at sea and war. Many of them had high ambitions. Some officers intended to further their careers in the Navy, crew members who had saved money for years and never had the chance to spend it. Men with skills such as Tom Woodland could easily have employment waiting for them back home if they chose civilian life, and many men dreamed of the days they could rest easy on dry land, but it was not to be for far too many of them. Run through with a cutlass, torn to pieces from splinters or shrapnel, musket balls, cannonballs, drowning, disease, starvation. There were a million and one ways to die at sea; therefore, Fletcher had never thought beyond the next few days. Tonight, however, he realised that maybe with the death of Percy Talbot, there might be a future for him with Isabella. The thought troubled him somewhat as now Fletcher felt that there was something to lose. He felt like a new world; a blanket of responsibility had landed on his shoulders, placed there by a higher power he could not control.

Well, why should I not be the one to be with her? He thought to himself. *After all, it should have been me anyway? If Percy is dead, someone needs to look after his wife and children? It's the kind thing to do and the right thing to do.* He tried to justify his thoughts to himself.

"Stop!" Isabella pulled her hand away from his, much to his displeasure.

"What is it?" Fletcher whispered. Isabella turned around, glanced across the dark beach towards the glowing fires and gasped. "Molly! There, quick!" A bright flame circled Molly's cage at the opposite end of the beach and suddenly dashed into the jungle. Fletcher instinctively drew his sword and ran across the beach, shouting for everyone to wake up as he passed them. Men murmured at first but quickly realised that something was afoot and soon the whole camp was awake. A scramble for weapons, clothing and lanterns occurred as the peaceful night became a rabble-roused hive of disorientation.

Panting from his sprint, Fletcher grabbed the wooden bars of Molly's cage. "Who was here?" he asked her. He sensed fear coming from her otherwise expressionless face. In her hands, she held a crumpled note. "Give it to me!" Fletcher demanded, which she did without hesitation, giving Fletcher reason to believe she was as startled as he was. He unfolded the scrunched-up brown paper. It was in the same childlike handwriting as the note Isabella had found, except it had been written in charcoal from a burnt twig. Fletcher knew that Sholim had written this, but he had no idea what it meant. He read aloud, "Kittlitz, Bohemia, find me." He looked at Molly. "What does this mean? Another riddle? Another secret?"

Captain of Marines Dawson appeared next to Fletcher. "Sir, I will head inland with a small party if I may. We will not go far."

"Yes, of course, find that Bohemian vagabond!" Fletcher agreed without turning to look at Dawson. Once again, he looked down at the paper and read aloud, "Kittlitz, Bohemia, find me!" Perhaps it was tiredness that was causing his mind to lose its ability to think, maybe the stress of their desperate situation, he could not tell. All he knew was that he had no idea what it meant.

Dawson returned thirty minutes later.

"We found only this and, apart from that, nothing, sir. We need to wait until daylight," Dawson informed Fletcher, who assembled Jenkins and Dr Brennan around their pitiful fire.

"What is it?" he asked, exhaustion in his tone.

"Just a burnt stick, sir. Your Bohemian used it to give him light before he scarpered."

"Who the bloody hell was guarding Molly, Captain Dawson?" Jenkins questioned him.

"Marine Bairstow, Lieutenant."

"And where is Bairstow now? Did he go with you into the jungle?" Jenkins fired a second question.

"I…I don't know, Lieutenant. I gathered what marines I could and headed immediately inland."

Fletcher was disturbed by Dawson's answer. "An officer of his majesty's armed forces must always know where his men are, Captain Dawson!" Fletcher interrupted angrily. "You ought to be reprimanded!" Fletcher demanded that Dawson and Jenkins both carry out a headcount immediately. The numbers added up, and there was Marine Bairstow.

"Where the hell is Private Bairstow?"

"Here, sir," Bairstow answered.

"Where did you go, Bairstow?"

"Just for a piss, sir."

Dawson stared at all the men who stood with blank faces against the dim glow of what was left of the camp's fires. Provoked by the silence that followed, Fletcher threw himself into a rage. "Not one man is to sleep! Do you hear me? All of you! That includes officers." He looked towards his officers. "No ship crew, no marines, no women," he said, thrusting his eyes on Isabella. "and no prisoners!" he shouted, pointing his finger towards Molly. He was infuriated, so Isabella left him to pace up and down the beach for the remainder of the night while the other men did whatever they could to keep themselves awake. Some tried in vain to get fires going, others just talked and some splashed water from the sea onto their faces to prevent tiredness from grasping their weakened souls.

When the sun finally appeared on the eastern horizon, Fletcher looked frightful. His eyes displayed dark rings, stubble and dirt smothered his face and his clothing was tattered and torn. Isabella feared she did not appear much better as she eyed the other men within the camp, who all had shabby appearances.

"Are you alright, Francis?" she asked as she caught with him at the water's edge. White foam drifted onto their feet and slid away again as the water receded. She could see that he was not right, but she wanted to speak to him, so she began her conversation with a question that had an obvious answer.

"Yes, thank you, Isabella," he lied. His voice was husky and weak. "We will be off soon, so you know your duty. Help load the boats with as much fresh water as possible and see if you can get anything from Molly."

"No Francis…" She grabbed both his hands with hers and swung him so they were face to face. "I'm not one of your sailors. I don't have to follow orders. I am coming with you."

Fletcher was elevated by her insistence to go with him. He secretly wanted it, but he pretended it was not. "You must stay here, Isabella. The jungle is no place for a lady."

"This is no place for anyone who worships God, and I fear that Sholim would want to capture me, knowing that you will come searching if he takes me captive. Easy bait were he to set you a trap. I am safer by your side." As Fletcher had already decided, her persuasive words were superfluous to their cause.

"Very well, but I insist you carry my pistol and stay as close to me as possible. Our party will be small, and we do not know what else, if anything at all, waits for us further into the island. I have been here before and it is not of this world. Are you sure you want to come?" he asked, immediately regretting allowing her the choice to remain on the beach.

"I am coming with you!" she said.

Fletcher smiled and returned to the fire, which was nothing but charcoal and a few glowing embers. He looked to Molly's cage, where she sat staring at the floor. He summoned his officers and the party who would go with them into the jungle and to the waterfall.

"Lieutenant Jenkins, I trust you know your duty?" he asked.

"Aye, sir. We will have the boats ready and loaded with as much fresh water and fruit as possible," he answered.

"Good. Dr Brennan, you are to stay by Jenkins as his second, and I am putting you in personal charge of Molly," Fletcher instructed. Molly looked up with a deep frown at the officers, who had all turned to gawp at her. Dr Brennan struggled to hide his fear, and as his eyes met with hers, a cold shudder climbed his bones as she softly smiled. In other circumstances, Molly had such an innocent face, but they knew she was dangerous. Behind the charade of sweetness and a dark-skinned servant girl's life was a killer.

"Aye, Captain," Brennan muttered.

"I have decided to take Mrs Talbot with us." Fletcher continued. "I fear that the Bohemian might see a woman as an easy target for a hostage, were she to be left in our camp," he explained. Although his statement was partially true, he still felt uneasy about lying to his men.

"So, we will go into the jungle, Captain of Marines Dawson. Are you ready, Captain?" Fletcher asked as he turned to Dawson.

"Aye, sir."

"Excellent, Sergeant Walton and the two privates Lockwood and Bairstow and carpenter Woodland. We remain silent in the jungle, keep our eyes open and be vigilant always. Any questions?"

There were no questions following the simple briefing, so Fletcher added one more thing. "Arm yourselves to the teeth. Including you, Mrs Talbot. Now, let's get going."

Fletcher went first into the jungle, typically leading his men from the front. Isabella frequently stumbled behind him, occasionally grabbing his clothing to steady herself. Behind her, Sergeant Walton stepped carefully, aware of the thorns and spikes that lay all around them. Woodland was the next in line, holding his musket and staying as close to the sergeant, fearing the backlash of sharp branches whipping him in the face. The two privates, Bairstow and Lockwood, dressed in red tunics, followed on, and lastly, Captain Dawson, also in red with a yellow sash around his waist and knee-high boots, was at the rear of the line. It was incredible that even though they were trekking through thick jungle, after being shipwrecked, the captain of marines still managed to make himself presentable.

Every few metres, Dawson turned to check behind them. He walked backwards for a few steps before returning to face his front. It was a strange way to walk, but he left nothing to chance. The sounds of this jungle could confuse just about anybody. When a bird chirped, one could not tell where it was, if it was to their flanks, ahead, or behind. The sharp noises bounced from tree to tree, flew over their heads and pounced from the bushes. The main sound was the hacking of undergrowth, accompanied by groans that came with the slash of a human using too much energy. The heat bore down as it had done the last time they set foot here. An uncomfortable humidity soaked their skin. Sweat began to sting the inevitable cuts on their open arms, legs and faces.

Isabella managed to hold her nerve well enough, but this had not been what she expected. Her clothing became torn, revealing far too much flesh for a lady, even one in men's clothing, and suddenly, a thin branch swung backwards and split open her cheek just below her eye.

"Yeow!" Isabella screamed. Instinctively, the other men in their party crouched down and readied their weapons. Fletcher turned and put his hand over Isabella's mouth to prevent another yelp from escaping. She panted heavily but managed to remain still until Fletcher let her go. Blood dripped down her face until she could taste it. She wiped her cheek with her white sleeve, staining the shirt and giving her an incredibly fearsome appearance.

Fletcher thought that if Blackbeard himself were to cast his eyes upon her now, she would strike him down with fear. Blood smeared across her tired face, matted wet hair mixed with sweat, more blood over her clothing and two pistols holstered into a belt that ran from her shoulder to her waist. With a cutlass, she certainly displayed terror if one were her enemy.

"Let's keep going. Are you alright?" Fletcher whispered to her. She wiped more blood onto her fingers and brought them before her eyes to see it. "It is just a scratch, nothing more," Fletcher told her. She nodded, and they continued.

Lieutenant Jenkins and Dr Brennan paced the camp. Due to its hasty construction, the camp was shoddy, but it had sheltered the men for the night. Now, it was offering them protection from the blazing sun.

The two officers had organised the remaining men into parties to work shifts. Small groups worked in sevens or eights, going into the jungle to collect fruit and water. Another party had been sent to row to the broken Dolphin to scavenge for more valuable things. Everything seemed to be working smoothly and before the sun had reached its zenith, indicating the coming of noon, there was a substantial amount of fruit gathered and a sizeable pile of full water containers. The scavengers sent to the Dolphin had used great initiative and had brought back many glass bottles, including one of Captain Talbot's whisky bottles. They appeared to have drunk the last of the whisky and carried the bottle back to the beach to fill it with water. Jenkins had paid no heed to the drunk men and instead of handing out punishment, he had praised them for their resourcefulness.

The two officers continued to amble in the sand.

"Well, what do you make of him, Lieutenant?" the doctor asked.

"Make of who?"

"The scallywag. That blaggard, our captain! Francis Fletcher!"

"Pirate he may well be, but he is a darn good sailor," Jenkins replied.

"Yes, I must admit he's doing a good job now. He certainly knows how to show assertiveness, but I believe he's still a pirate."

"Yet you obey him as you should, Doctor."

"Yes. I obey. Fletcher is a good leader. I find it hard to forgive a man who once turned his back on the king. I don't care much for his actions at Quiberon Bay; for all his heroics, he has still betrayed. Yet, if the crown forgives, then I must take its example. He is the captain now of this expedition. Voyage. Whatever you want to call it. I don't understand why we're here, digging up gold that belonged to Jesus Christ. We should darn well leave it there," Dr Brennan advised.

"Our duty is to follow our orders," Jenkins said condescendingly.

"I've obeyed my entire life. But what are our orders if Fletcher, or indeed any of them, don't return? Must we perish here, too? I think it prudent for you and me to agree on a timeframe for which we shall wait and what action we shall take if they do not return."

"What timeframe were you thinking? Two days? Three days?" Jenkins asked.

"No, Lieutenant, I am thinking much shorter. If they do not return by daybreak tomorrow, I believe that they will have failed and are probably dead. We should be ready to leave with or without them."

"My goodness, Dr Brennan," Jenkins puffed his cheeks, "we cannot just leave them here. What of the Knights of the Golden Gift? We know their secret."

"Do you think these knights know about you and me? If we escape this island, all we need to do is never speak of it again," Dr Brennan suggested.

"Perhaps you're right, Doctor. The memory would soon fade if we returned to England sooner rather than later and never mentioned it again. We'd be quite safe to continue our lives in peace. So long as there are no more wars, for we are military men, Doctor, peace is not our business."

"So it is agreed?" Dr Brennan asked. "If Fletcher, Dawson, or any of them have not returned by daybreak on the morrow, we shall depart and row for Crete as intended anyway."

"Very well, Doctor, tomorrow at daybreak, we row for Crete with or without them. But, we leave them a boat just in case," Jenkins added.

"Yes, we can leave them a boat. With any luck, Dawson, Mrs Talbot and the marines will make it unharmed and manage a boat to Crete. As for Fletcher, I do not care much for him or his pirate carpenter."

Fletcher inched forward, crouching towards the pool of water. He'd found it. It was the same as last time. On the other side was the same troop of monkeys as before. He did not want to startle the monkeys, remembering their behaviour from the previous time, as it would give away their position. Sholim must be on the island; protecting the gold would mean he was somewhere close. Inside the waterfall was the obvious place Fletcher could think of, therefore he intended to get up the jagged rocks and behind it without being seen. That would mean not arousing the monkeys into their usual wild frenzy and hoping none of his small group would look into the snake's eyes.

He could feel Isabella's warm breath on his neck. She was shaking too, and he felt glad she had turned to him for protection. Her arm lay across his back, trembling.

"Steady now, Isabella," he whispered to her. "Do you see the waterfall?" Isabella knelt up and looked across to the water falling over the rocks.

"I see it," she replied.

"From the centre of this water, those rocks appear like a serpent's face. If you stare into its eyes, it will immobilise you. You must not look at it. Hold my hand until we reach the rocks, cover your eyes if needed and look only at the ground." Fletcher looked beyond Isabella to give the men behind her the same instructions.

"Are you ready, Captain Dawson?" Fletcher asked.

"As ready as I'll ever be, sir," he replied. Dawson looked to Sergeant Walton, Lockwood and Bairstow, sweating profusely in their heavy clothing. They each nodded that they were ready.

"Are you ready for this, Mr Woodland?" Fletcher asked.

"Aye, sir," he replied.

Muskets and pistols were loaded and primed and daggers and other blades were gripped in tight fists, ready to be thrust towards any potential enemy in half a heartbeat.

As he thought they would, the monkeys began their inevitable howling the second the water was disturbed. The slightest ripple triggered them off, but Fletcher was not afraid. The monkeys started to retreat as the group slowly walked through the water, crouching, ducking and keeping their eyes peeled. For all the noise they had made, they certainly were not as aggressive as they appeared. The noise had done its job, though. Had anybody been near, they would surely have been alerted. Fletcher guessed that this was what the monkeys' real purpose was. They were an intruder alert squad. They were not suitable for fighting, only for scaring off anyone who had explored the land or informing other guardians of their presence.

Fletcher held his hand over his eyebrows as if to block the sun but instead prevented himself from catching a glimpse of the snake's eyes. He'd instructed Isabella to do the same, and she had. They stepped closer and closer towards the rocks until Fletcher knew they were close enough to lower their hands. He'd made it to the foot of the waterfall, where the stones lay conveniently placed so that one could ascend them almost like a giant staircase. They were safe from the hypnosis from this point on. Fletcher looked back to see that Isabella was with him, still covering her eyes. He took her arm, which had a pistol gripped tightly in her hand and guided her towards him.

"You're safe here. You can look up now. Well done," he told her. A gust of wind made her face turn white as she heard her name called through the rustling branches and treetops in a whisper.

"What was that?" she asked Fletcher. She looked around to discover the rest were still behind her but making their way steadily.

"Did you hear your name in the wind?" Fletcher asked.

"Yes, you heard it too?"

"No, I heard my name. I'll wager Woodland heard his name. It seems everyone only hears *their* name calling to them," Fletcher said.

"What is this place? Francis, I wish I had not come." She began to sob.

"Have no fear, Isabella. Fear is the enemy."

"I am not a sailor or a soldier, Francis! I am not used to needing such courage!" Fletcher ignored her last comment as the rest of the group arrived through the ankle-deep water. As he took one last look towards the pool, he saw what he had feared. Bairstow was standing in the middle, eyes fixated above them.

"Blast you, Bairstow!" Fletcher whined. The marine had glanced just for an instant upwards to see where he was going, and in less than a second, the snake's eyes had caught him.

"What the hell is he doing, Captain?" Dawson asked.

"He's been caught in the snake's gaze. I warned you not to look at the rocks from that angle!"

"He'll be alright, sir," Woodland commented. "Somebody come with me; we can drag him here and he'll come around in a minute or two." Woodland leaned his musket against a rock and started to walk towards the dumbstricken marine.

"Go on then, Mr Woodland, Lockwood, go with him. Everyone else, let's get scaling these rocks," Fletcher ordered. Before Woodland was halfway back to Bairstow, there was a crack, a flash and a small puff of smoke from above them. A musket ball plunged straight into Bairstow's heart, killing Him instantly. His lifeless body dropped into the water, face-down. Blood began to run out from underneath him, flowing gently down the stream.

Woodland ducked, but there was no cover in the middle of the pool. He ran half-crouched, covering his eyes from the glare of the snake. Fletcher looked towards the mouth of the cave above them. A figure appeared with an outstretched arm holding a pistol. The sound of the falling water dampened the flash and the bang, but it was clear enough. The pistol shot missed but kicked up a splash that sent a plume of water that was even taller than Woodland behind him. The figure looked down at Fletcher, half snarling, half grinning. It was Sholim. Fletcher cried, "You bastard!" But he receded into the cave, disappearing like a ghost.

"Upwards, let's go!" Fletcher shouted. He ascended the first rock before turning to give Isabella a helping hand. She could climb unaided, so Fletcher continued until he reached the waterfall and saw the red glow as the water fell like fire from behind. Fletcher stood with his pistol and sword at the ready, expecting Sholim to appear at any moment. Nothing came except his name, which whispered in the wind behind him.

As Isabella caught up with him, her eyes turned red with fire as the falling flame reflected in her eyes. After a short time, the others had made it, forcing each of them to inch further into the cave to give them space to stand. Isabella stared into the falling fire, fighting for breath, her mouth wide open. Fletcher looked at her.

"What do you see?" he asked, almost forcing a shout as the noise of the flames and falling water became louder the further they went. At first, she did not answer, but a solitary tear appeared. "Isabella, what is there?" he called to her again.

"I see you!" she cried back. "I see you and me!"

Suddenly, a yellowish glow grew from the cave behind them, a gust of wind and a voice growling, "THOU SHALL'T NOT COMMIT ADULTERY!" Isabella stood in horror. "Oh, Francis, what have we done? We have sinned!" She fell towards him, her face smothered with tears. He held her shoulders only to receive a slap in the face from her free hand.

"We have sinned, Francis! We're going to hell! We broke the commandment!"

The others stood behind them, also staring into the flame, seeing the sins of their past played out before them like miniature versions of themselves on a stage.

"We look no more into the fire! We must not be distracted!" Fletcher commanded, aware that Sholim was somewhere in the cave and could have a pistol or musket aimed at any of them as they stood. They could still hear their names and the more they stared into the flame and the further they went along the waterfall and into the cave, the more the voice turned from a whisper to more of a shriek, a deathly cry, or a howling scream. It pierced their ears, delivering a skull-splitting pain.

"We look no more into the fire!" Dawson echoed the orders of Fletcher to Sergeant Walton, Lockwood and Woodland, who stood behind him. Fletcher was grateful for the cooperation from the captain of the marines but was even more pleased that this man dared to continue.

"Isabella, take my hand. I know not what lies in the darkness," Fletcher said, igniting a fear that made her heart pound against the inside of her chest. "Have we those lanterns, Captain Dawson?" Fletcher asked.

"We have two, sir," Dawson replied. "Bairstow had the third. I dare not go back for it now," he informed.

"Very well, let's make some light with what we have."

With the lanterns lit, Fletcher went first, stepping away from the falling fire and into the cave. The air became slightly cooler but noticeably dryer. Slimy green moss lined the walls of the cave. Above them, dark, dripping stalactites each the size of a man, hung like shards of death, ready to drop and impale the flesh of the sinners beneath them. The cave was tall enough for them to stand up without crouching, but they naturally hung their heads low. They huddled as they stepped, eager to keep up with Fletcher and Dawson, who held the lanterns above their heads.

Eventually, the open cave became a narrow tunnel with a passage leading to their right and a large wooden door to their left.

"Lord, have mercy!" Fletcher whispered. Isabella clung to his arm desperately for the terror she was feeling. They stood, squinting to make out what was above the door. There was a panel carved of stone, three feet wide. There were squares the size of a hand in a neat row along the length of the stone panel. Inside some of the squares was a single letter. It was meant to spell something but was hard to fathom, with some letters missing. Fletcher and Dawson scoured the walls around the doorway, seeing a snake carved into the frame. A carved woman was holding an apple, passing it to a man.

"The forbidden fruit!" Isabella said. "Original sin."

Eventually, they illuminated the floor. Surrounding their feet were several stone squares. They each had letters on them. Fletcher and Dawson deduced that these square stones should fit the square holes above the doorway. Isabella guessed it, too, and they each began to pick them up.

"This one has *S* carved on it," Isabella announced. "And this one, *R*."

Fletcher looked at the men behind him. "What do you think it means?" he asked. They all shrugged their shoulders, not knowing what they had discovered.

"What does it say up there?" Isabella asked Fletcher. "Shine the light above the door."

Fletcher held the light to show what letters remained in their places.

"It looks like three words. The middle word has a *T,* an *H* and a blank space. It must be an *E*. It says *THE*," Fletcher said confidently of himself. He crouched and found a stone square with *E* written on it and stood to place it in the space to create the word *THE*.

"What else is there?" Isabella asked. "What could the first word be?"

"It has a *V* and an *E*," Dawson put in.

They looked at each other, confused and clueless. *VE THE*, Fletcher puffed out his cheeks as he thought about what it could mean. "What about the third word? Let's see what we have." He raised the lantern. "There is a *P,* an *E*, an *N* and a *T*. What other letters do we have down here on the floor?"

"I have an *R*. Would that fit into any likely word? *R* something *PENT*...*REPENT*!" Isabella declared. Fletcher went cold as he suddenly remembered the note Sholim had given Molly, which Captain Talbot had recollected, also written on Enmore Castle's painting. "Repent The Verses!" he said. They quickly scrambled the letters to make out the words "Repent the Verses" above the door, but it did not fit. The first word had only five places for letters.

"Take out all the letters," Fletcher said. They placed all the letters on the floor and spelled 'Repent the Verses'. "See, it must spell *Repent the Verses*. We have all the exact letters," Fletcher said, although frustrated. He lifted his lantern to the other men behind him, checking that they were still there. "Sergeant Walton, please be on your guard, Lockwood, Woodland, you too," he ordered.

"What do you think, Isabella?" he asked as he brought the lantern back over the letters on the floor.

She pondered for a moment. "I think it must spell something else. It's an anagram. Look here," she said, moving some of the letters around. "The first word has only five letters; taking the word *VERSES* is an anagram of *SERVES*. But only five letters, let us remove the *S* from the end of the word." She stood up and placed the letters *S E R V E* into the five spaces of the first word above the stone door frame. "Now, let us assume that the second word is *T H E*," she said as Fletcher handed her the flat square stones. "That leaves us with *R E P E N T* and an extra *S*." She swung her body towards the light and stared Fletcher in the eye. "Don't you see it, Francis?" she asked. Fletcher was a little embarrassed by his delay in not seeing what Isabella had, but he was brave enough to admit that she had solved the puzzle before he had.

"What is it?" he questioned her impatiently.

"*R E P E N T* plus an extra *S*. It is an anagram of *S E R P E N T*!" Isabella placed the letters in the spaces, and above the door frame, it read *SERVE THE SERPENT* in carved stone letters.

"Serve The Serpent, of course!" Fletcher said, putting his hand over his mouth. Those who worship the Devil protect the secret to Satan's lair, the gold. They indeed serve the serpent.

A shudder like a mild earthquake forced them to lose their footing temporarily. Dust fell from the cave walls. They used each other to balance themselves until the shudder stopped after a few seconds and the heavy wooden door in its stone frame creaked open, swinging away from them as if to invite them in.

Each of their hearts was beating faster than ever in their lives. They had all faced battle before, which brought out a huge mixture of fear and adrenaline, but that did not come close to how they felt now. Fletcher held up his lantern, took Isabella's hand and took the first step into the dark entrance. Isabella squeezed his hand tightly and checked behind her to see that Captain Dawson was following them. He was, and also Sergeant Walton, Lockwood and Woodland. They had worry written across their faces, which did not help steady Isabella's nerves. She gripped Fletcher's hand ever tighter.

The room they had entered was perfectly square. At Fletcher's reckoning, it was about twenty feet in all dimensions. At the far end of the room, illuminated by the lights of the lanterns showing its slimy green walls, was a stone table about knee height. Upon the table was a brown chest made from wet rotting wood, and next to it was what appeared to be a leather pouch.

Fletcher approached the stone table as the others entered the room. "Holy Mother Mary, could this be the gold that belonged to Christ, our saviour?" he muttered. He placed his lantern on the table and dared not touch the chest but instead took hold of the pouch and opened it. Captain Dawson stood beside him, holding his lantern, enabling Fletcher to see inside the small leather bag. There was a rusty key inside. It was clearly for the chest, so Fletcher took the key and dropped the pouch to the floor.

"I do not know if I should do this," he said, dripping sweat from his forehead and almost beginning to pant. No one spoke. Fletcher decided to conquer the fear that had gripped them all. He placed the key into the hole in the front of the chest and turned. It was stiff and it took him both hands to turn until the lock moved. He lifted the rotten lid, and the rest of the group gathered around him to witness the most significant discovery known to the human race. In front of the six mortal souls lay three nuggets of solid gold. They were small and shaped like fingers, but this gold had once belonged to the baby Jesus Christ in a stable in Bethlehem upon his birth one thousand six hundred and sixty-four years before them.

"Look what we have discovered!" Dawson spoke in awe.

"We must make haste," Fletcher shivered and his spine tingled. Everyone nodded and said "Aye" in agreement.

"Let us waste no more time in this Godforsaken place," Isabella hastened. She placed her pistol into its holster across her chest and took the three pieces of gold, instantly surprised by their weight. "What are we waiting for? Let's go!" she demanded. She stuffed the golden nuggets into her thin but tight chemise, making sure she had securely strapped them to her body using her holsters. She quickly paced towards the exit. "Come on!" she hurriedly said beckoning the others to follow her.

Sholim appeared out of the darkness as she approached the door to leave. He held one hand over her mouth, spun her around and pointed a pistol to her head. Fletcher and the others immediately drew their weapons. Woodland aimed his musket at the Bohemian's face but couldn't take a shot with the darkness and the impossible angle with which Sholim held Isabella. Lockwood had a musket aimed from a different angle but faced the same problem.

"Let her go, Sholim, you bastard! I know you can understand me!" Fletcher shouted with a cutlass pointing towards him.

"Shoot him, for God's sake!" Isabella cried.

"No more movement from any of you, or the lady dies!" Sholim spoke in English but with a strong accent. He held the pistol to her head and slowly stepped backwards until he was out of the door. He brought his bearded face cheek to cheek with hers, reeking of foul breath, and whispered, "Give the gold to me; be a good girl now. You need not die today."

She stayed still, hoping that someone, Fletcher preferably, would have thought up some quick-thinking plan, but their situation was dismal. The men inside the room could not see them clearly in the cave's shadows. They paced slowly towards the entrance, fearful of Sholim killing Isabella before their very eyes.

"Give him the gold, Isabella," Fletcher's voice echoed through the cave. "You need not die for this black-hearted snake of a man."

"You see, your man is right. Give me the gold," Sholim ordered again.

"Go to hell!" Isabella spat back at him. He reached into her clothing, creepily fondling her breasts as he did so, but eventually found what he was looking for. He took the gold from her undergarment, tearing it in the process.

"Hell? We are already here," Sholim laughed. He pushed her through the door into the room. Isabella stumbled forward into the arms of Fletcher as the door behind her slammed shut. They listened to the door locking from the outside. A scraping noise accompanied by stones smashing on the floor caused more panic. They knew Sholim was removing the stones with letters above the door and breaking them. Any hope of rescue was now out of the question.

"Darn, blast that man!" Dawson Yelled hysterically. "What are we to do now, Captain Fletcher? We are trapped!"

"Steady yourself, Captain Dawson. We must not lose our ability to think! Trapped we are, but a way out there must surely be."

"Even if we do get out, that bastard has the gold! What shame have we brought upon the king?" Dawson paced around the room aimlessly.

"How long will these lanterns last, Sergeant Walton? Have we more fuel or a candle?" Fletcher asked.

"Umm, no, sir. These will burn for a few hours but nothing more. I suggest we blow one out and only light it when the other one nears its end, sir."

"Good thinking, Sergeant," Fletcher complimented Walton's quick wits. "You see, Captain Dawson? Let us use our minds and we will think of a way. 'Tis only a wooden door, thick as it may be, we know it is our escape."

"Goddam, that man!" Dawson yelled again.

Chapter 18

The second night that Lieutenant Jenkins and Dr Brennan spent on the beach was darker than the previous. A heavy, thick cloud that could have broken into a downpour at any second but refrained hung over them like a pair of evil eyes. It was at least warm, so most of the men got a few hours of sleep each. They had tried to work in shifts, but the night's stillness and the monotonous repetition of the waves lapping the beach left some of those on sentry duty with eyelids too heavy to lift. A few murmurs amongst the first to awaken had begun as the sun's light crept eagerly over the eastern horizon.

"Are you awake, Lieutenant?" Dr Brennan asked from underneath his tunic, which he used to protect himself from the flies. "Yes, Doctor," Jenkins sighed in reply.

"The first light comes," Dr Brennan informed him.

"Does it so?" Jenkins asked, pretending to show interest.

"Fletcher and Dawson have not returned." Dr Brennan was keen to hint that they should start preparing to leave. With no response from Jenkins, Dr Brennan pressed his point further. "Sir, May I remind you of our agreement. We will depart without them if they do not return at first light." Jenkins still did not stir. Instead, he tactfully changed the subject and rolled over. "What information did you get from the servant girl, Doctor?" he asked, referring to Molly.

"Nothing, Lieutenant Jenkins. Only what we already know. She's a freed slave who worships the Devil."

"Has she eaten?" Jenkins queried.

"Yes, sir, she had milk from a coconut and I shared some of the strange fruits with her. But it did not sway her mind in keeping her tongue from spilling information."

"That's a pity." Jenkins yawned and sat up. He had to shake his long, brown, straggly hair to remove sand stuck to his head through sweat. Half of his unshaven face where he had lain was also sand smothered and he felt a few grains in his mouth, crunching them in his teeth.

"Do we depart, Lieutenant?" Dr Brennan asked again.

"What do we do with the girl?" Jenkins again brought the topic back to her.

"She is a servant of the Devil, sir," Dr Brennan hinted.

"I shall not shed the blood of a woman Dr Brennan!" Jenkins answered at the preposterous suggestion.

"Then we may leave her here. It will not be long before she can break out of that flimsy wooden cage. She will most likely be picked up by the next ship to come this way. She'll end up back in slavery, no doubt. If not one of ours, then the Ottomans will take her. We could leave her here with a pistol and a single shot. She can end it for herself, the gentleman's way." Dr Brennan had agitated Jenkins with his lack of care for the woman they were dealing with.

"Doctor, she is no ordinary girl! I will not escape to England only to tell Lord Perceval that I executed his servant, nor will I take the Devil for my example! I cannot kill her and do not wish to leave her here to die."

"You cannot be serious in thinking we take her with us, sir?"

"I believe you leave me with little option, Doctor. She is a Knight of the Golden Gift!"

"Women are not knights, sir."

"Well, whatever her position in society, female or not, she serves the Devil, and what if she escapes this place and locates more like her? Then, she could unleash a tidal wave of assassins against an unknown number of folks back home. We must imprison her and she may share information with us."

"I am warning you, sir, it is a bad idea," the doctor persisted.

"I am the acting commander of what remains of this expedition, and you, Doctor, will warn me nothing! The girl comes with us!"

"If that is your order, Lieutenant, then I obey as you command, but l hold fast my belief that she will try to kill us both."

"If she attempts to take the life of any of us, then you may kill her. That will be justified, but I cannot and will not execute a prisoner of value who has not yet seen fair trial." Lieutenant Jenkins stood and brushed the sand from his clothing.

The sun had risen and many of the ship's crew wandered the beach or sat eating fruit. Jenkins paced from different groups that had encamped with each other, informing them that they should begin their preparations to depart. They were relieved to hear they were soon leaving the island, but many had asked about Fletchers' party. Jenkins felt troubled by the decision. As he neared the far end of the curved beach, deep in thought about the morality of leaving so soon before Fletcher could return, Carpenter Beatty approached.

"Good morning, sir." He saluted.

"Good morning, Beatty. Has your boat made the necessary preparations for departure? Have you enough food and water?"

"No, sir, we have a bigger problem."

"Do tell." Jenkins poised himself, ready to receive the bad news.

"We appear to be missing one of our rowing boats, sir," Beatty informed him. Jenkins blinked in quick repetition, subdued by what he'd just heard.

"Say that again, please, Mr Beatty."

"We are missing a rowing boat, sir."

"Yes, that is what I feared you had said." Jenkins thought for a moment. He had no idea what to say other than to send out a series of questions to which poor Mr Beatty had no answers. He was only the messenger; the boat had not been his responsibility after all.

"Who the bloody hell was guarding the boat, Beatty?" Jenkins asked through gritted teeth.

"We had sentries, sir, but it was a dark night and some fell asleep. Just briefly, sir, but when the sun rose, we noticed umm…"

"You noticed your boat was gone?" Jenkins finished the stuttering carpenter's sentence for him.

"Yes, sir."

"Are any of our men missing too? Have we deserters who fled in the night? Bloody cowards, they'll hang for this."

"No, sir, all are accounted for. No one is missing, just the boat."

"Just the boat?"

"And some of the provisions that were with it, sir."

"Show me where the boat was, Beatty," Jenkins ordered.

They walked the beach to where Beatty had been camping with several others of the crew, who all stood up and said, "Morning, sir," not forgetting to salute their superior officer. Beatty pointed to where the boat had been. In front of him, as clear as day, were the tracks and footprints leading into the sea.

"Someone stole our boat, sir," A voice from the growing audience called out to Jenkins.

"Who the bloody hell was on sentry duty?"

"We all took turns, sir. But as I said, some of us drifted to sleep, and when the sun rose, the boat was gone," Beatty repeated.

"You stupid bloody bunch of fools!" Jenkins yelled, his face red with heat and anger. "And not a single soul is missing?"

"No, sir, we are all here to a man."

Dr Brennan approached after hearing the news from another source of crew members. He walked fast with a serious look and his face was still covered with sand.

"Who could have done such a thing?" Jenkins asked the doctor as he arrived.

"A few names spring to mind, Lieutenant."

"So tell me, Doctor."

"I am not a gambling man, Lieutenant, but this seems like a perfect escape for a man who has failed in his duty. I'll wager that this is the work of Francis Fletcher?"

"No, that is preposterous. Why would Fletcher want to escape without us? Seven of them went into the jungle and only one set of footprints is here."

"Exactly. The others are dead and Fletcher does not want to admit it. He has fled without us!" Brennan insisted.

"Could be that Bohemian, sir," Beatty put in.

"That is what I am thinking, Mr Beatty. It was Sholim. He has been watching us. He has seen Fletcher and Dawson head inland, and he has struck at the right time. Knowing that you delinquents would not be able to stay awake through the night, he has stolen your boat!"

"I disagree, Lieutenant. This was Fletcher. That turncoat has done it again. He has shied away from his duty and fled," Brennan said.

"I know you dislike the captain, and so do I, but I honestly believe this is not in his character. This was Sholim. He has managed to outwit us and make good his escape from the island."

"All the more reason to put an end to the life of that servant girl and make haste our own escape," Brennan went on.

"I already told you, Doctor, I am not going to execute the servant of our Admiral and, more importantly, a prisoner who can be useful to us! Make haste, yes, we must leave this place at once." Jenkins stroked his chin and turned to the gathered crew. "All of you, get to your positions. I want all of your boats manned with full provisions on the sea before the sun is above the tree line. I also want one boat to be left behind for Fletcher and Dawson should any of them still be alive. Do I make myself clear?"

"Aye, sir," the crew chorused and sprung to work immediately.

Jenkins turned to the surgeon, who had a frown across a severe face. "Doctor, this means you, too!" Jenkins walked away, angry at the man who had countered him twice already this morning. He sincerely hoped he would not do it again because he needed Brennan to be with him on his side in the coming days, which were sure to be testing.

Before the sun had reached the top of the trees, the fleet of seven rowing boats raced into the waterline, smashing head-on into the coming waves. With one of the boats missing along with its provisions, they were forced to make room amongst the others. Still, both Lieutenant Jenkins and Doctor Brennan had calculated that there should be enough for everyone to survive for two days. They had also left a boat for their stranded comrades, just in case. It was not a good boat, for it had been damaged during the scramble to escape the Dolphin, and there were only two oars. If Fletcher or any of his party were alive and able to leave the island, at least it was something, but it would be a difficult time for them.

Lieutenant Jenkins had left a note in the boat's centre, weighted under a rock. He had asked some of the scrounging party searching the wreck of the Dolphin for some last-minute supplies to enter the great cabin, which was still rising out of the water, and see if they could not locate some undamaged paper, a quill and some ink. Against Jenkin's expectations, the last of the scrounging party had managed to find them in Captain Talbot's old wooden desk, which was toppled but still intact.

Jenkins cast his eyes to the clouds above him, hoping they would soon fade away, leaving them a perfect Mediterranean blue sky. It was only a fifty-mile row to Crete, where they were heading, and a strong crew could achieve that quickly provided the weather was favourable, which he feared it would not be. He looked back towards the island as it became smaller and smaller. Guilt riddled his mind. Had he made the right decision? What if he saw Dawson, Fletcher and the others arriving on the beach, desperate to get away, needing his help? He sat and thought about how he would explain this to the admiralty if they made it that far once he returned to England. They still had fifty miles to row and the clouds looked more ominous the farther they went to sea.

Molly was at the front of the boat where Jenkins had placed himself to lead their way to Crete. Her hands were tied, her mouth was gagged and she lay uncomfortably rolling with the boat's motion. Jenkins did not know what to do with her. He wanted her imprisoned and executed, but only after a trial. There was nothing about her that he could prove. It would be his word against hers. Perhaps he should throw her overboard, let her drown and be done with it. His conscience was already nagging at him just for thinking that, so he quickly returned to the idea that he would not kill her. He pitied her as she knocked into the sides, unable to prevent herself from being bruised every other second in the unsteady boat. A large wave came rolling them one way and quickly the other, and as she could not control her balance, her face smashed into the side of the boat, splattering blood from her nose.

Jenkins could take no more of watching another human suffer needlessly and so he made his way to the bow past the twelve men, of whom eight rowed while four rested. He lifted her bloodied face and removed her gag. She looked at him with black eyes darkened by the iniquity of sleep.

"Sit up, girl. You need not be hurt," he said as he held out his arms to steady her. She shuffled next to him, breathing deeply and wiggling her jaw. She had sores on her mouth already from the gag. Jenkins looked at her hands and saw blue fingertips where the ropes were so tight that blood had not reached them.

"There is no escape from here, Molly. If I untie you, you must promise me you'll try nothing foolish," he explained to her as he untied her gag.

"Where exactly do you think I am going to go?" she answered him.

"Very well," Jenkins said. He pushed her forward to reach her hands and he untied her. The rope was so tight that it took several minutes, long enough for Molly to think up a plan. She had no desire to return to England just to be hung in front of an angry crowd. As soon as one arm was free, she grabbed Jenkins by the throat, squeezing as hard as her arms would allow her. She screamed with rage, digging her nails into his skin. His windpipe closed up; he could not move even though he was bigger and stronger than her. The speed at which she reacted had taken him completely by surprise. He could only hold her arms and try to pull her away. She used her free hand to reach into the lieutenant's holster, took out the pistol and placed her head next to his.

The rowers had their backs to the bow and had not seen what was happening behind them, though they had heard it. The two closest to Molly and Lieutenant Jenkins immediately dropped their oars and clumsily attempted to help the

Lieutenant. Still, the boat was rocking so wildly on the sea and with their motion adding to it, making it worse, one of them fell out. The splash alerted men on the other boats, of which the closest was at least fifty feet behind them. Molly aimed the pistol at the second crew member and told him to stay still or lose his life. The man paused and raised his hands. A musket shot rang out, clearly aimed at Molly, but at that distance and the lack of decent aim, the man firing it would have needed a lot of luck to hit his target.

With his throat as good as closed, the lieutenant struggled for air. Molly held the pistol to her head once again and pulled the trigger. A flash, a puff of smoke and a bang sent the pistol ball through her head and into the lieutenant's. Molly's body fell backwards into the sea, holding tightly onto the pistol as Jenkins fell forward into the boat with his brains now floating in the water. Blood spilled from his head, soaking the feet of the man who had tried to help. The man still had his arms in the air. The remainder of the crew had stopped rowing and faced the bow in disbelief. They looked overboard to see Molly several feet beneath the surface, leaving a trail of red as she sunk slowly through the crystal clear water.

Dr Brennan was now the only officer left among the flotilla of boats. When they were all together as one, he had shouted his orders for the others to stop and allow all the boats to come together. It took longer than an hour in the choppy sea, but the doctor hopped from his boat to where the lieutenant lay dead.

"You, help me, will you?" he said to one of the crew. The two lifted Jenkins's body and unceremoniously flopped him into the water. At first, he just stayed there, floating face-down and bobbing with the waves. The doctor took an oar, rammed into the lieutenant's back and forced him under.

Silence surrounded them. Behind them, the island had disappeared. Doctor Brennan ordered the men to row their hearts out using only the sun to navigate. All day, they pulled their oars in shifts, ate fruit and drank the water rations until dangerously low. As nightfall came, they continued relentlessly. Arms ached, legs seized at the knees and shoulder muscles pulled and became torn. They sweated and lost the ability to shed tears, longing for more water.

As another day approached and the sun rose once more on the distant horizon, at Doctor Brennan's estimate of twenty miles, were the recognisable mountains of Crete. It seemed that at least some of the crew would survive this voyage.

Chapter 19

The light from the first lantern began to flicker as it gradually dimmed.

"Sir, we should light the second lantern before this one goes out," Sergeant Walton suggested to Captain Dawson, the only two still standing.

"Yes, Sergeant, if you think that best," Dawson replied solemnly.

Fletcher had placed himself in the corner of the perfectly square green room, his head between his knees and his hands pressing into his temples. Isabella had slumped against the door, rarely taking her eyes away from him. She stared at him unnoticed, waiting for a sign that he had thought of some way to escape. The hours passed, but nothing came to him, fuelling Isabella's disappointment.

Lockwood and Woodland sat on the stone table next to the chest. Woodland flicked the lock up and down, clicking it into place and out again, irritating the others until, eventually Dawson snapped, "Will you stop that?"

"Sorry," Woodland griped and looked down to the floor.

"Sorry, *sir!*" the captain of the marines corrected him.

"Sorry, sir," Woodland repeated.

"That's better!" Dawson said and paced up and down the room. He was becoming impatient. He could see no sign of any plans coming from Fletcher. No one else had spoken a word for hours.

"Maybe, Sergeant Walton, we could use the flame from the lantern to burn the door down?" All eyes flung towards Dawson after he made the suggestion, and within a few seconds, the same heads turned to Fletcher to seek his opinion. Fletcher did not speak. He'd seen the proposal as so grossly stupid that he did not justify an answer. Instead, Sergeant Walton spoke.

"Sir, that door is one of the thickest I've ever seen. The flame from this lantern is too small. What's more, sir, I think the door is wet and…"

"And what's more is that if the door did catch fire, it would fill this room with smoke and we would suffocate in minutes," Fletcher interrupted. "Mr Woodland," he continued, "you're the carpenter here; tell us, how can we remove such a heavy door? Can we burn it down? Shall I poke holes through it with my cutlass? Maybe we can chip away at it with our tiny daggers," Fletcher jested sarcastically.

"I see no ideas coming from you, Captain Fetcher!" Dawson raised his voice back at the captain. Fletcher stood up and walked to the door where Isabella was sitting, shivering and breathing heavily with fear. He slammed his fists on the heavy, damp wood, only adding a thudding noise to their ears. He turned around and saw everyone staring at him. "Up, all of you. Even you, Mrs Talbot!" he ordered. She did not particularly like Fletcher calling her by such a formal name, but she rose to her feet like everyone else. "Come on, everybody," Fletcher ordered again. "Search every corner. There must be something in here, some lever, some code for us to break. God knows, there must be something!" he said as he began to feel the walls. His desperation was evident to everyone. After a few minutes of feeling the walls and staring at the ceiling, he began to get on his hands and knees to touch the floor. There was nothing—only solid green, slimy rock.

"Aaaarrggghh!" he yelled. With only anger left in him, he paced towards the stone table and kicked the empty wooden chest onto the floor. After it had clattered around his feet, he stamped on it. The lid broke and Fletcher kicked it across the room. He turned back to the table, put his foot against the top and thrust it into it to release some pent-up fury. Fletcher had seemingly lost control and had now resorted to breaking things. As he pushed his leg against the table, the top slid. It moved less than an inch, but it had shifted for sure. Stone scraping against stone alerted everyone.

"Good God!" Dawson exclaimed. "The tabletop…It's a lid!" Fletcher gawped at the stone table. The top now sat at an angle, showing one dark triangle which displayed its hollowness in the corner.

"Come on, let's help the captain!" Dawson ordered. Lockwood and Woodland immediately came over to help. They both heaved alongside Fletcher and Dawson to move the giant slab. Sergeant Walton handed his lantern to Isabella and joined in the struggle. They pushed and shoved with all their might, each straining their muscles as it moved several more inches. The further they pushed, the heavier it became. After several minutes, Fletcher squeezed his fingers underneath and lifted the stone. Woodland did the same and the heavy top jerked upwards and fell to the floor. It sent a vibration through their feet, and a boom echoed down. Dust puffed out of the hole where the tabletop had been.

They wafted it away, some coughing as they breathed it in, leaving a disgusting bitter taste on their dry tongues.

Fletcher peered down the hole into the blackness. It was too dark and the hole too deep for him to see anything.

"Give me something to drop," he asked aimlessly. Woodland handed him a piece of stone from the broken tabletop. Fletcher dropped and listened. The tiny stone fell for many seconds before the sound of it hitting the floor below bounced back up the tunnel. "Isabella, the lantern, please," he asked. He leaned further over and hung the lantern as far as he could. The others gathered around, leaning over and inquisitively looking down. They saw only a long, dark hole with a bottom too far away to see. It appeared man-made as brickwork lined the walls. Bricks were sticking out large enough for hands or feet to hold onto or stand. They all knew they were going to have to climb down.

"Right then," Fletcher said as he removed his head from the hole. "Who is going first?" The silence that followed told him enough. It was apparent they expected him to go first. "Well, I guess that's me then?" Fletcher asked rhetorically. Isabella nodded with her arms folded while the others just looked at him.

Fletcher sat with his legs dangling over the hole, placing the lantern handle in his mouth. He lowered his legs until he could feel the first brick to step on, then turned around and used his hands to lower his body further until he could feel the first brick against his chest. After fumbling his feet, he found the second brick and grabbed hold of the first. It was a crude ladder, but it took his weight well enough, and its purpose was evident.

"These bricks were supposed to be climbed on," Fletcher told himself. However, he began questioning whether they should be climbed up or down.

Captain Dawson insisted that he would go last to protect their escape from the room in case Sholim or some other creature from Hell decided to attack them as they descended. After Fletcher came Sergeant Walton, followed by Isabella, Lockwood and Woodland. Most of the bricks were dry, but occasionally there was a wet one.

Fletcher informed Sergeant Walton of the wet bricks, who warned Isabella and Private Lockwood in turn. Sergeant Walton glanced upwards, and even though he could not see her, he asked Isabella if she was alright. She was comforted by the thought that someone other than Fletcher was looking out for her. It had played on her mind that she might be without protection if something happened to Fletcher.

Fletcher reached the bottom after several gruelling minutes. Like everyone's, his hands were sore and worn from the climbing. He'd knocked his knees against the wall so often that he was certain to be covered in bruises and cuts. He removed the lantern's handle from his mouth and raised it higher to aid the sight of Sergeant Walton, who was still a few metres above him. One after the other, they had made it.

They huddled underneath the dark hole with only the tiny lantern. Fletcher raised it, showing they were in a long corridor. Everything again was slimy and green. Fletcher swung the lantern in the opposite direction. It was the same both ways—a passageway with no end.

"Well?" asked Captain Dawson. "Which way do we go? Left or right?" Nobody knew the answer.

"Maybe we should split up?" Sergeant Walton suggested. "Three go left, three go right. We can meet back here in a few minutes and see which way is correct?"

"No, Sergeant," Fletcher immediately answered him. "If we split up, then it's certain that at least three of us will never see the light of day again. We go together, all of us, or none of us. That's my final decision. I don't see what difference it makes. I do not know what we will discover either way we go, but we go together. I want everyone with their weapons ready. We go this way," Fletcher said, pointing to the right. He did not know why he chose that way. Perhaps because it just happened to be the way he was facing, or maybe because he had tried to orientate himself and felt that the beach was this way. Fletcher did not know. They'd been in the dark so long it made no difference. None of them could tell north from south any more than they could point the direction of the beach. Fletcher just had a gut feeling and he would follow it.

They went step by step, following the pathetic dim lantern that Fletcher did his best to hold above his head. In places, the ceiling was so low that he scraped his knuckles. They walked with their left arms firmly grasping the next person's right shoulder. Dawson remained at the rear, ever vigilant from whatever might creep up on them from behind. He sometimes swung his sword into the darkness because he thought something might be there. With no light for him to see, it was challenging to determine if anything was there. The blackness tricked his mind and he thought he saw shadows moving. He lunged repeatedly before quickly stepping back to reach for Woodland's shoulder.

"Are you alright back there, sir?" Woodland asked.

"I do not think you want my honest answer, Mr Woodland. Do not move too quickly away from me. I do not want to lose you," Dawson answered like a frightened child.

"Is there something behind us, sir?" Woodland queried, hearing that something was not quite right in Dawson's voice.

"I don't know," Dawson began to whisper. "It's so dark. If something is there, I cannot see it, but I can feel the presence of something following us. It might just be my imagination. I don't th—"

The entire passageway lit up, as bright as day and then suddenly plunged back into darkness in less than a second. A scream echoed along. They huddled instinctively.

"What was that?" Isabella asked, but no one answered. "Did you see something, Francis?"

"I did," he said as he took hold of her hand and squeezed it tightly. "Stay close to me, Isabella. Is everyone alright? Mr Woodland, are you still with us?"

"Aye, sir."

"Captain Dawson?" Fletcher called out.

"I'm here."

"Good, Walton, are you here?"

"Yes, sir, I am here."

"Lockwood?"

"Yes, sir, I am here too."

"Good, we are all here. Did anybody else see anything?" Fletcher asked them the question, knowing they had all seen it. During the flash, the walls of the corridor had disappeared. They were in a large cavern and dead bodies had hung from vines around their necks in front of them. They couldn't be there as the cave walls were now as close as ever, but for a split second, that was what they had each seen.

"We must continue," Fletcher insisted. They went further into the darkness until they had to stop again.

"Fleeeetcheeerrr!" Came Isabella's voice. She was directly behind him, but instead, her voice sounded distant. He was sure he was still holding her hand.

"Isabella?" he whispered to her.

"Yes." She trembled.

"Why did you say my name?"

"I did not," she answered. "It was not me."

"It was your voice, though, Isabella."

"It was not. It was my husband!"

"You are mistaken; it was your voice, but you are here." He turned around and shone the lantern into her face. He gasped as he saw not Isabella, whose hand he was holding, but it was Captain Talbot.

"No, Francis, it was the voice of Percy Talbot!" Talbot said, smiling.

In sheer terror, Fletcher stumbled backwards, edging further along the passageway, feeling the walls until he tripped and fell. Fortunately, the lantern did not go out, but it landed behind him so that he could no longer see Isabella, Captain Talbot or whoever's hand he was just holding. Footsteps approached him in the dark. A figure bent down, lifted the lantern from behind him and swung it between them. It was Isabella. She looked at him, her jaw shaking.

"Are you alright?" she asked. He nodded. She raised the light so that Fletcher could see Sergeant Walton and Lockwood behind her.

"I don't know what just happened," he said.

"Neither do I. I heard Percy's voice and then Sergeant Walton's face turned into Molly's, just for a second."

"I heard your voice and then you turned into Percy!" Fletcher told her.

"We are in hell, Francis; it is playing with our minds," she cried.

"Then we must hasten our way out of here!" Fletcher stood up, took the lantern from her and continued along the passageway. Whispers and the occasional distant scream echoed along the tunnel.

After several dark minutes of feeling and fumbling, they came to an opening. The walls began turning crimson red and stalagmites rose from the cave floor before them. The group spread into a line with Fletcher and Isabella in the centre. None of them could see where the light was coming from as the room they had entered opened up. It glowed both orange and red, warmer here than in the passageway. It was not such a tall room. They could have just about touched the ceiling with their fingertips if they had jumped.

Fletcher stepped forward again, taking the lead. Isabella quickly grabbed hold of his hand and followed. They weaved between the stalagmites, which had created a maze in the cave. They turned left and right, snaking their way along slowly in single file, with their weapons ready.

"What's that, sir?" Woodland asked after they had again stopped.

"It looks like a bridge," Dawson answered. He paced forward for a better look. A cliff edge was as deep as two houses with running water flowing away to their right below them. A single rock shaped like an arch crossed the gap that was just about too far for them to jump. At the foot of the walkway were some words that appeared to have been chiselled into the floor.

"What does it say, Dawson?" Fletcher asked.

"Tantum et transire pura. I do not know what it means. It looks Latin to me. It has been many years since I studied this language," the captain of the marines replied.

"Isabella?" Fletcher turned to meet her eyes. "You understand some Latin, do you not?"

"Some. Although Percy was far more learned than I," she said.

"Well, at least try. Come and have a look. Tell us what this says." Fletcher spoke to her more like it was an order than a request. Isabella cautiously stepped towards the rocky bridge and spoke the words Captain Dawson had read. "Tantum et transire pura."

"Can you translate?" Fletcher asked impatiently. She waited a few more moments, whispering the words to herself, trying to think. "Pura," she eventually spoke, "it means pure, of that I am certain. I can only guess the rest, but I think it means that only one pure or free of sin can cross the bridge."

"What do you make of that, Captain Dawson?" Fletcher turned to the captain of marines. "Are we pure enough to cross?"

"I can speak for no man other than myself, Captain Fletcher. Only the men here and Mrs Talbot know if they have sinned, but I believe you are stranded," Dawson said, impressing Fletcher with his ability to find humour even down here. Something about Dawson reminded Fletcher of himself, and strangely, at that moment, Fletcher realised that he had a friend in Dawson.

"Well, sinners or not, we must cross the bridge. Those who agree say aye?" Fletcher said, turning to Lockwood, Woodland and Sergeant Walton, who had been quiet for a long time. It appeared to Fletcher that they had also experienced frightening scenes in the passageway when Isabella had inexplicably turned into her late husband for a split second. He pitied them, for their fear was evident. Still, he knew he had to keep them going and lead them out of this Godless dwelling.

A chorus of "Aye" gave Fletcher the answer he expected. He went first, stepping onto the rock. He felt it with his foot, testing its sturdiness. His weight didn't move or crack the stone in any place, and it seemed strong enough. Holding Fletcher's hand, Isabella followed. They walked slowly, carefully balancing. By the time they had reached the centre, it was less than two feet wide. Fletcher eagerly glanced upwards to see the other side, almost inviting him across. It looked safe there, with no stalagmites or strange red glow, and a cool breeze as welcome as ever drifted pleasantly across his sweat-stained forehead.

Perhaps this is the exit to the entire cave, Fletcher thought. Smiling, he turned to see Isabella. Her eyes were fixated on the drop below them.

"Don't look down," he told her calmly. "We're almost there."

"But what are those?" she whispered back. Fletcher looked down into the water below them, seeing thousands upon thousands of white balls under the water. They shone like bright marbles, perfectly round and not flowing with the stream. The longer he stared, the clearer they became. After some time, Fletcher saw what they were. An unknown number of eyes were looking up at him.

"Good God!" he exclaimed. "Let's get across quickly," he ordered, but as he quickened his pace, the air called out, "Tantum et transire pura!" in a deafening howl, like a wolf in the wind. The entire cavern began to shake, the bridge beneath them crumbled and all six of them suddenly found themselves tumbling towards the water.

Isabella screamed as she fell. Fletcher tried to reach for her, but they had become too separated. A falling rock collided with Fletcher's face, scarring his brow before he felt the plunge as he hit the water.

Underneath the surface, he instinctively opened his eyes and saw Captain Dawson thrashing away and Sergeant Walton pointlessly clinging to his pistol. Woodland and Lockwood kicked with their legs and writhed, struggling with the current, but it was useless. Fletcher thought they would all drown; this was the end. Darkness began to consume him. The last thing he saw was Isabella screaming underwater, reaching out to him before he sunk into a pit of eyes. Now that he was closer, he could see the white eyes trailing a red string of flesh and blood. They swallowed him up and he lost consciousness.

What felt like a lifetime was only a few seconds. Fletcher dreamed a thousand dreams and recalled even more memories. Every emotion ran through his body as his life played out inside his eyelids. Taunting boys of a lower class during his childhood filled him with guilt. They were hungry and he was not.

They had no parents or shelter as he did. He had bullied them. Then he saw his first time with a woman, bringing the feeling of excitement that was quickly replaced by his first gambling loss in a tavern in Lancashire, bringing him the dread of being in debt. His first duel, Isabella, his first time onboard a ship, meeting with Percy Talbot at Lord Perceval's castle as youths, Isabella, Molly, the officer's academy, Isabella, the first man he'd killed in battle, his heroic actions at Quiberon Bay, the duel for Isabella's affections, the *Blunderbuss* sinking, Isabella, hunted for piracy, Isabella, the trial for his life, Isabella, Sholim, Isabella, the island, Isabella, Isabella, the death of Kilpatrick, Isabella, Isabella, Isabella...

When he woke, he breathed the cool, damp air of the cave. He had been the last to be pulled from the water by a mysterious rowing man with no face, just blackness hidden beneath a grey cloak as he pulled on the crooked oars of the small boat they were now on.

"He's awake!" Captain Dawson whispered to Sergeant Walton. The rowing man put a bony finger to invisible lips. "Shhh!"

"What in the blazes happened?" Fletcher sat up, trying to get a grasp of his surroundings. He was soaking wet. Again, the rowing man put his long pale finger to lips they could not see. "Shhhh!"

Isabella was next to Fletcher, also drenched.

"I do not know who this man is, but he pulled each of us from the water," Isabella whispered to Fletcher as quietly as she could so the rowing man would not hear her. "He does not speak. He only insists that we are quiet."

The rowing man pointed his empty, faceless hood towards Isabella as if he'd heard something but was unsure. Again, he put his long finger with black nails towards where his face should be. "Shhh!"

They continued on the small rowing boat, gently following the stream between the cliffs. Fletcher shuffled enough to raise his head over the side and looked into the water. The infinite number of eyes stared back at him from beneath the surface. Eventually, the cliffs receded and the rowing man stopped, pulling alongside a pebble beach. They had entered another cavern much bigger than the maze of stalagmites they'd seen earlier. Rocks arched in many directions, with many tunnels and passageways branching around them. Some were many feet above them. One of them was only just big enough for a small child to squeeze through.

The rowing man pointed to the pebbles as the boat stopped. They clambered out and grouped around Fletcher. Woodland was shaking.

"Keep your nerve, Tom," Fletcher put his hands on the carpenter's shoulders. Woodland nodded but was unable to find any words. "Good man," Fletcher said. Turning back to the water, the rowing man sat back at the front of the boat, and without giving them another glance, he took the oars and rowed away silently disappearing into the cave.

"Who was that?" Isabella asked.

"A servant of the dark lord. I do not know," Fletcher answered. As he looked around the cavern, he again began to think of how to escape.

"Captain Dawson…"

"Yes, Captain Fletcher?"

"Where is the light coming from? We are many metres below ground, and we've lost our lantern, but there is light; how? Can you see an opening?"

"There is no escape from here, Captain Francis Fletcher!"

"What do you mean?" Fletcher turned to Dawson.

"I did not speak, sir."

"You did…"

"I did not," Dawson insisted.

"This place is playing with our minds again," Isabella said as she edged closer to Fletcher and held his arm.

"There is no escape, Captain Francis Fletcher," the voice came again. Fletcher could see that Captain Dawson had not spoken this time. It was not Sergeant Walton, Woodland, or Lockwood who spoke either.

"Who speaks?" Fletcher called out and spun around, fearful of someone being behind him. "I am Captain Francis Fletcher of His Britannic Majesty's Navy. I carry the authority of the king, ordained by God. I demand you tell me who speaks!" A few moments passed before the wind each began to call out their names in loud whispers as it had done when they first approached the waterfall. It became so noisy that they had to cover their ears.

After the wind had stopped, Fletcher stood tall and faced a man he could see standing at the entrance to a tunnel above them. A yellow glow was behind the figure, who was wearing a fluttered red cape. He had a silver breastplate, a red toga and sandal-like boots. Under his arm, he carried a golden-coloured helmet with a red plume. The figure struck quite an imposing stance with his other arm on his hip.

"It's a Roman centurion!" Isabella stated. "could it be…?" Isabella did not finish her sentence. Something about this man made her afraid to say his name. Instead, Fletcher was more courageous and showed he was not a coward.

"Tell me who speaks, in the name of the king, I demand it."

"Your king has no authority here, Captain Francis Fletcher!" the centurion spoke and smiled. His voice was deep but old. His hair was also grey and his face was full of wrinkles.

"Tell me how you know my name," Fletcher shouted to the man as if issuing orders to his crew.

"I have been waiting for your arrival for quite some time. I must say I am impressed."

"Impressed, how?"

"I thought you were going to hang after they found you here last time, yet somehow you escape the mercy of a mortal man's noose and come back here, where the pain is eternal. Are you brave? Or are you too unlearned to understand where you are?" the old man taunted.

"I know where I am. And I know who you are, and what is more, I know what you are. Murderer, thief, traitor!" Fletcher stood equally imposing and pointed at the centurion he believed must be Jagur.

"Murderer? Have you not also taken the lives of other men? Many battles you have fought and the life of this poor woman's husband. Sacrificed by you, too eager to come here other than save his life. Or did you think that with Percy Talbot dead, you could have Isabella, his devoted wife, all to yourself?"

Fletcher stood flabbergasted. He was embarrassed to look at Isabella and surprised at how much this man knew about their journey and Fletcher's past. The centurion spoke again. "You, captain of marines Stephen Dawson. The blood of a sailor, Oliver Kilpatrick, whose life you ended on the very ground above us." The centurion pointed at Sergeant Walton next. "And you, Paul Walton, have served and thrust your sword into another man, and you, Thomas Woodland, have also killed. As has this man Fraser Lockwood. I have seen it in the water that falls as fire that you have pulled the trigger of your musket to take a life."

Lockwood and Woodland stood with their mouths wide open, utterly shocked that this strange man knew so much about them.

He continued to speak, "And that leaves our dear Isabella Talbot. Daughter of Admiral Norris. So sought after and thus so vain that she allowed two men to fight to the death for her." The centurion looked at Isabella with burning eyes as he referred to Fletcher and Talbot's duel over her in their earlier years.

"So, yes, Francis Fletcher, I am a murderer, as are all who stand before me at the gates of the underworld, too eager to share your sins. You will all be welcome here, yet you will suffer. As for being a thief, did you not also take into your possession a ship that belonged to your king, apparently whose authority you carry? You are thieves, all of you!" the centurion spoke, getting angrier and angrier. "And you have all betrayed!" he hissed at them, waving his free arm violently. "Isabella Talbot, you betrayed your husband and committed adultery with this man Fletcher, who in turn betrayed his friend!"

Isabella went red in the face as Dawson and Walton turned to look at her, unaware that she had once had a love affair with Francis Fletcher behind the back of their late captain and friend.

"You are thieves and you are murderers. You are traitors. My name is Jagur and I welcome you to Hell!" He laughed. "There is, however, one small act you can do for my master to save yourselves!"

"Never!" Dawson shouted up at the figure of Jagur.

"Let us hear what gracious offer your master has for us!" Fletcher cried over the top of Dawson. The captain of the marines looked at Fletcher. "What? Let us at least hear what he has to say before we decline our way out of here," Fletcher whispered to him.

"No, Francis!" Isabella said. "I'll not bargain with the fallen angel!"

Jagur spoke next, "My most generous master offers you this; find and kill the man who has betrayed us both. You know of whom I speak!"

"Sholim?" Fletcher asked.

"His name is Milosh Novak. Sholim is his name, Milosh, if you pronounce it backwards. It seems he has deceived you as well as us. Instead of protecting the gold he stole it. We now have an enemy in common. Will you share your fate with my master, Captain Fletcher?"

"You want me to kill Sholim? That is all?" Fletcher turned to the group and whispered again, "I was going to do that anyway!"

"I thought he was one of the knights, a descendant of yourself, Jagur," Fletcher called up to Jagur.

"He is. But he turned to God and supported a protestant uprising in Prague. He is a Christian now. Protestants, Catholics, you followers of our enemy's son, Jesus Christ, bicker among yourselves. You are pathetic people. So my great-

great, many times over, grandson has betrayed my master and me. He is the reason you found this island in the first place. Were he not onboard your ship, Francis Fletcher, you would have sailed straight over us. But my master knew that Milosh Novak was on board your beloved *Blunderbuss*. We knew he was looking for the gold and wanted it to buy his pardon from the Catholics who rule the Habsburg empire. He will take it to Maria Theresa, Queen of Bohemia and that wretched husband of hers, the emperor of the so-called Holy Roman Empire."

"That blaggard! He came here to do what we came to do! He's stolen the gold and is claiming it for the Habsburgs! It will buy his pardon," Fletcher exclaimed.

"Do we have an accord?" Jagur asked.

"I speak only for myself. I will kill the Bohemian!" Fletcher answered.

"And return the gold!" Jagur added.

"I will drop it into the sea. I wish not to return to this island!" Fletcher bargained.

"Very well," Jagur accepted the counter-proposal. "And what about you, Stephen Dawson?" All eyes turned to Captain Dawson. He thought for several moments before responding. He did not intend to break his commitment to God and make a deal with the Devil.

"I will go in support of my friend Captain Fletcher. But should he fail, you cannot count on me to kill the Bohemian and return you the gold," Dawson told Jagur bluntly.

"Then the Knights of the Golden Gift will slay you eventually if Francis Fletcher fails," Jagur warned.

"So be it. My allegiance is to God, but I will help Francis Fletcher. After all, John 13:15 'No greater love hath a man than he who lay down his life for his friends.' Does that suit you?" Dawson asked.

"My master accepts," Jagur nodded. "Isabella Talbot?" he asked next. "Will you go with Francis Fletcher?"

"I think I can now speak for all of us," she said, looking around to Woodland, Lockwood and Sergeant Walton. "That what Captain Dawson has said rings true for us, too. We will support and follow Francis Fletcher until the bitter end. But, should he fail, then my allegiance lies with God. You cannot count on me to do the Devil's bidding."

Jagur began to laugh a repulsive cackle and a string of drool dripped between his bottom teeth, which were broken and jagged. "Then so be it. You will leave this cave." Jagur, from nowhere, manifested a sand timer almost the size of his arm. He turned it upside down and sand began to fall. "You have until the last grain of sand drops to get out, for when the time runs out, the cave will collapse and you will be here for eternity." Jagur grinned.

"But which way do we go?" Isabella called out.

"It's that one!" Jagur pointed to a tunnel as if it was a simple and obvious answer. Fletcher grabbed her hand before Isabella could speak again and dragged her towards the tunnel.

"Let us leave!" he said sternly.

The six mortal souls ran into the tunnel. It sloped gently upwards and had tree roots on the ceiling, indicating they were not as deep underground as they had first thought. The tunnel was long, the floor not particularly smooth, and with no lantern, they were finding it difficult to edge their way along, half running, half stumbling, feeling in front of themselves blindly with their arms. A few minutes had already passed; where was the end? The ground began to shake and some dust and small stones fell from the ceiling.

"We've got to move faster. Come on, all of you!" Fletcher ordered. He turned another corner, and finally, he could see the light. It was still far away, but he managed to see the blue sky and the outline of a palm tree as he got closer. The cave shook violently this time, causing Isabella to lose her footing and fall. She let out a little scream as Sergeant Walton ran into the back of her. Fletcher stopped to help them both to their feet.

"Come on, go go go!" He pushed them past him until he was at the back of the line.

They continued to run and run, the mouth of the cave getting closer and closer. More stones fell from the ceiling and the tunnel shook them from side to side.

As Isabella approached the clean air, a wind behind her took hold of her body and swept her from the floor, hurling her out and calling her name in a deadly whisper. She rolled over and saw Sergeant Walton had landed in a heap next to her beneath a palm tree. Next came Woodland and Lockwood, collapsing on the ground and panting heavily. The cave began to collapse. Isabella rose to her feet and rushed back towards the entrance as a large boulder fell, blocking part of the exit. She screamed again as a blue and black striped snake hissed and flickered its tongue at her. The snake slithered over the rock out of sight, but not before it turned to look at her with evil eyes, displaying enormous venomous fangs.

"Ugh," Captain Dawson cried through gritted teeth and squeezed himself through the narrow gap. What remained of his already shredded red tunic ripped from his back as he struggled for his freedom. He was out; he had made it, but Francis Fletcher was still behind him. Dawson immediately spun around to help his friend. An arm was thrust out of the gap that was closing as the earth shook. Dawson took hold of the arm and began to pull. Isabella and the others tried desperately to pull away smaller rocks and stones that were easier to lift. Eventually, Fletcher was able to scramble his way out of the small exit, climbing up until he was free from his waist up.

One final quake knocked all those trying to help Fletcher to the ground. Dust clouded into the air. There was a terrific rumble like thunder had clapped at the treetops above them.

When the dust settled, Isabella brushed herself down and was alerted by the noise of small stones falling. It was Fletcher. He was wriggling his way out of the small avalanche that had blocked the cave's entrance.

"Everybody alright?" he asked as he stumbled down from the rocks.

"Aye, sir!" the men answered. Isabella did not speak, but she flung her arms around him and began to cry, thankful that he had managed to get them all out safely. Fletcher took Isabella's arms from his neck and looked into her eyes.

"We've got to get moving," he said. Isabella nodded. "Let's get back to the beach as fast as we can. I have no intention of staying any longer. Lieutenant Jenkins is waiting for us. Come on!"

Chapter 20

The run through the jungle was painful, though they cared not for the scratches and cuts they received from the thorns and sharp leaves that whipped and slashed them. The wind shrieked each of their names after them as it had done on their arrival, only louder and more desperate. Fletcher tried to hold Isabella's hand, but they had lost their grip in the turmoil. They had to use both hands to stop the branches from slapping their faces and pull away thorny stems from their clothing.

Nevertheless, they reached the beach together, Fletcher only a few seconds ahead. The others were not far behind, and when they arrived, they stopped and stared. The encampment was gone. A few pieces of broken bottles, some burnt patches where the fires had been and a few bits of rag, probably old clothing, were about all that greeted them. As they walked further into where the encampment had been, they saw that what was once Molly's cage was now just a pile of sticks, broken and brittle, next to the fire where Fletcher and Isabella had slept after they'd arrived on the island.

"Where is everybody?" Dawson asked. His eyes were wide, as was his mouth, hanging with incredulity that they had been abandoned.

"How long were we in that cave?" he asked, looking towards Fletcher. None of them knew the answer.

"The bastards!" Dawson cried.

"What will we do, sir?" Woodland asked Fletcher.

"Let me think, laddie, let me think." Even Fletcher was shocked at the abandoned posts, and possibly for the second time in his life, if not only his naval career, he could not think of a quick plan. Sergeant Walton kicked a coconut and cried out from the pain in his foot and the realisation that they had been left behind. Lockwood and Woodland both exchanged looks with one another.

"Come on, boys. We must not lose hope," Isabella said to them even though a tear had appeared in her eye.

"There's no hope here, ma'am," Woodland sobbed. "There's no hope left." Isabella approached the young carpenter and put an arm around him to comfort him, but he only pushed her away and dropped to his knees.

"I'm sorry, ma'am, but I have no hope. What did we see back there?" His sob had turned into a full cry, which he felt no shame about. "Did we really just escape from the very jaws of Hell only to find that our friends have left us behind? We're going to die here, all of us!"

"Enough of that!" Fletcher interrupted. "Look, there!" He pointed along the beach. He had spotted the boat which Jenkins had insisted on leaving behind for them.

They ran, half-hobbling in the soft white sand. Inside, there was the note that Jenkins had left them. Fletcher reached down into it and read the message aloud.

"Dear Captain Fletcher, Captain of Marines Dawson, Mrs Talbot, Sergeant Walton, Marines Lockwood and Bairstow, Ship's Carpenter Woodland,

If you have survived, you will be thankful that we have left you this boat. Last night, one of our boats was stolen. We believe the rogue Bohemian, known only as Sholim, is the culprit. We waited until it became clear you were not coming back soon. Therefore, we have decided to make our own escape by way of Crete. We have taken the captive servant girl with us.

May God, in all his might and glory, be with you.
Lieutenant Jenkins"

"That bloody coward!" Dawson roared as Fletcher scrunched the note angrily into his hand. "Thankful for a boat? They waited until it was clear we'd not come back. What a total coward! I'll see he never has a commission again!"

"As will I, Dawson, as will I!" Fletcher snarled like an angry canine. "God DAMN THIS PLACE!" Fletcher threw the paper to the floor. The others stood and stared aimlessly at the beach or into the sea.

"I guess we'll have to use the boat then, won't we, sir?" Lockwood commented. "I mean, I want to leave this island just as much as anyone, and from what I can see, we've got a boat! I reckon we can make good use of a boat, sir. There's six of us and we can take turns to row." He looked towards Isabella. "If you'll excuse me, ma'am, that's if I include you doing some time behind the oars as well." He felt awkward speaking to a much higher social class woman than himself. She was a captain's wife, after all.

"Yes, Lockwood." Fletcher straightened his stance to look more as if he were in command. "That's right, that is exactly what we have to do. We need a boat; by God, we've got one."

"And how long will it take us to row to Crete with just one set of oars?" Dawson asked in a sceptical tone.

"Crete? Have you lost your senses, man? We're not going to Crete. I'm going after that monster, that murderer, that bastard. I'm going to where he's going."

"Do you mean Sholim?" Dawson asked. "You mean you intend to keep your pact with the Devil?"

"Yes. That's right. I'm going after him," Fletcher suddenly adopted a very determined stance with clenched fists in the air and fire in his eyes. "I am going to Bohemia, and I know where. Kittlitz! He is going home. He'll go there after he has bought his pardon from the Habsburg Queen using the gold!"

"How can you be sure?" Dawson asked.

"Because that's where he told Molly to meet him if she can escape, and she might well have done for all we know. The night we arrived here, he slipped in while Bairstow was pissing and gave Molly the note saying, 'Kittlitz, Bohemia, find me.' Well, I'll bloody well find him. On my life, I'll find him! I don't want the Knights of the Golden Gift hunting me for the rest of my life. You can all stay here or make your way back to England if you wish, but I will find him. If you are to join me like you said you would then be ready to leave when I do, for I shan't wait one minute more."

"And when are you leaving, sir?" Woodland asked.

"I am leaving now, Mr Woodland," Fletcher said.

"Doesn't leave us much choice, does it, sir?" Woodland informed the captain. "You'll have the only boat!"

Isabella was the only one who thought they would need water and something to eat if they were to head back out to sea, so she had taken it upon herself to gather what they could. She'd briefly recruited Sergeant Walton and Lockwood to join her on a quick forage for fruit and coconuts. It was not a lot, but she knew it would last a few days if they rationed it. They made a pile at the front of the boat and covered it with leaves to prevent drying.

They had managed to push the boat out to sea relatively easily. The tide was out, and the waves were much calmer than they'd been since they had landed on the island. Fletcher decided to row first and set a steady pace and an example to whoever rowed after him. They decided to do only one hour each before changing. That would give sufficient rest to those who were not rowing.

"May I ask where we're heading, Fletcher?" Dawson asked from the stern, leaning on the loosely fitted rudder.

"Just point us northwest. We may hit some other islands. That will be useful; we can restock our supplies, but our main aim is the European mainland."

"And you know these waters well enough to find it?" Dawson asked another exhausting question.

Fletcher pulled on the oar using all his strength. "Yes, Mr Dawson, I have sailed these waters, fought in these waters and spent much of my time studying these waters. If we were fifty miles east of Crete, we can island hop all the way to mainland Greece. From there, we will continue to Trieste on foot or the water."

"On foot? You cannot be thinking we walk to Bohemia?"

"I won't travel on foot unless absolutely necessary, that's why I intend to commandeer myself a larger vessel than this and sail up the Adriatic to Trieste. Then we'll have little choice. We'll need to buy safe passage several hundred miles through Habsburg territory until we reach Bohemia. Once we reach Bohemia, we will have to look for a place called Kittlitz. I do not know where we shall find it, but as God is my witness, I will die trying if I have to."

"This is an absurdity, Captain Fletcher!" Dawson exclaimed. "Turn back to the island, I say. We can formulate a better plan than that!"

"We can't go back to the island," Fletcher remarked.

"And why not?"

"Because it isn't there."

Captain Dawson, Sergeant Walton, Private Lockwood, Carpenter Woodland and Isabella Talbot turned their heads around, and to their astonishment, the island had gone.